SIREN'S
LULLABY

SIREN'S LULLABY

WILLIAM P. KENNEDY

ST. MARTIN'S PRESS
NEW YORK

Design by Maureen Troy

Library of Congress Cataloging-in-Publication Data

Kennedy, William P.
    Siren's lullaby / William P. Kennedy. — 1st ed.
        p.   cm.
    ISBN 0-312-15658-8
    I. Title.
PS3561.E429S5   1997
813'.54—dc21   96-40469
                                                         CIP

First Edition: May 1997

10   9   8   7   6   5   4   3   2   1

With thanks to
Sam, Rachael, and Sarah
and
Zachary and Jack

PROLOGUE

SEAN PATTON HAD BEEN HERE BEFORE.

Fifteen years earlier he had placed a scale model of a twin-hulled aircraft carrier in the same test tanks and watched the performance numbers clatter out on the computer's printer. Bladesdale, then with a full head of hair and a cigarette fixed in the corner of his mouth, had run around frantically checking his equipment, unable to believe the numbers he was getting. Finally, satisfied that everything was in working order, he had smiled broadly, the glowing stub of the cigarette nearly searing his lip. "Fifty-two knots," he said. "That's the fastest hull we've ever timed in the tub."

Bladesdale was there now, thinning hair combed across a bald head, smaller shoulders and a larger paunch. The cigarette had been replaced by a pipe that was constantly spilling burning ashes down the front of his shirt. But the encouraging smile was still the same.

The computers were the same as well. When the Hoboken Institute of Marine Architecture had installed computerized test tanks in the cavernous cellars of the main building, faster computers were bigger computers. The deans had wanted the fastest, in terms of billions of calculations per second, so they had hocked the school's equipment budget to buy the biggest machines available. As much as the younger professors and most of the students would now prefer to work with microcomputers in a client-server environment, the giant supercomputers weren't yet close to being fully amortized. They had been updated with new graphics software, and with full-color workstations as parallel processors. But the machine that would do the calculations was the same massive box of logic circuits that Sean had used when he was an undergraduate.

Nor was Sean greatly changed. The jeans and T-shirt he was wearing were familiar garb during his undergraduate days. He still wore his dark hair shoulder length, but now pulled out of his face into a ponytail. His blue eyes were still blazing with the invisible flame of high-octane racing fuel, and his mouth was drawn into the thin, almost angry smile of an outsider. It all seemed to work on his big frame. The powerful arms and shoulders warned that he was affecting nothing. He was big enough to make his own way. But as an undergraduate, he had been long and lean to the point of being emaciated. There had been nothing obvious to back up the fire and the rebellion. His teachers had labeled him a pretender and a misfit.

Bladesdale had been his only supporter then, and it was Bladesdale who had now volunteered to sponsor Sean's experiment. He flitted around the edges of the main tank, checking the connections of all the sensors, and used the ancient but highly accurate gun sight to assure that Sean's hull was perfectly parallel to the direction that water would flow once the pump was turned on.

"We'll start it at five knots," Bladesdale said when he was satisfied with the alignment.

"Start at ten," Sean said. "I'm not interested in anything lower."

The professor smiled. It was the same Sean Patton he remembered: As a student, he had never been interested in going slow.

The tanks had been modified over the years to meet the needs of the institute's big-paying patrons. In the forties and fifties, when the United States was a shipbuilding nation, virtually every freighter, tanker, and military hull had been brought to the Hoboken test tanks for evaluation. A model of the hull would be anchored in the center, and water would be pumped past, simulating the ship moving through the sea. Then the model would be rocked by applying pressure at various angles and elevations, and photo sensors would provide time and motion graphs to evaluate its stability.

With a few famous exceptions, not much attention was paid to speed. The hull had been defined primarily by its carrying capacity, and speed could be added by simply increasing the power of the engines. Not too much speed, however. For virtually any hull design, the cost of moving the mass through the water rose out of all proportion to the speed gained.

But the United States no longer built ships. Instead, its naval architects had switched their talents to yachts. The country turned out more fiberglass runabouts, day sailers, and serious yachts than the rest of the world. Most of the powerboats were simple planing hulls with twice as much engine as they needed. The sailing yachts were built with commodious appointments, and the shallow-draft designs that would be comfortable tied to a dock. There was no need for testing those designs at Hoboken.

The exceptions were the high-performance sailing yachts that competed in the great offshore races and in highly publicized and lavishly sponsored match races. In this company, even a half-knot of speed could mean the difference between a world champion and a hull that would be auctioned to a salvage company. And even the most radical redesign of the hull, once allowance was made for the power of the sails that had to be carried, would probably not add a half-knot of speed.

As a result, the hull design for any serious yacht was subjected to hundreds of hours in the "tubs," as Bladesdale irreverently called the high-tech test tanks. And the yacht builders paid handsomely for every hour. As the water raced past the model of the hull, over two hundred sensors measured the increase in pressure caused by the yacht's mass. At some point, the pressure buildup in front of the hull equaled the hull's speed, which meant that increases in sail power wouldn't produce greater speed through the water.

The graphic displays produced color maps of the pressure surrounding the hull at every speed and every angle of heel. The pressure bars suggested points where the hull could be modified to yield a faster speed, and predicted new pressure points if the modification were to be made. The designers studied the printouts, altered their designs, and then returned to the test tubs for still more hours at the computer.

Bladesdale turned up the pumps, and he and Sean stared at the model. Her attitude remained fixed. "Steady as a rock," Bladesdale said.

"She should lift a bit at around twelve knots," Sean answered. As if on cue, the sleek model picked up her bow, planing over the surface. The professor noticed the speed—twelve point two knots—and shook his head. Patton hadn't lost his touch, he thought. He could still tell the characteristics of a hull just by looking at it. All the test tank could do was confirm what he already knew.

The pressure inputs should be rising to indicate that the design was beginning to push against the sea rather than slice through it. On the color monitors, the pressure lines should begin to bulge out, away from the lines of the hull. But that wasn't happening. The model was still leaving the rushing water undisturbed. Bladesdale turned up the pump. "Thirteen knots," he announced. Sean simply nodded, his eyes fixed on the model. The bow was high and steady.

"Fourteen," he intoned.

Sean took a quick glance at the monitor. The pressure ridges under the bow were sliding back. The boat was beginning to run past its own resistance, like a fighter plane cutting through the sound barrier.

Bladesdale checked the readouts. "According to your sail plan, she's got twenty-five knots of wind in the beam."

"And passing fifteen knots through flat seas," Sean said. His mouth curled into a victorious grin.

"Unbelievable," the professor agreed, shaking the last hot charge out of the bowl of his pipe. "Above the surface she looks like an ordinary sloop. But below the waterline, she's something else. I've never seen a sailboat with performance anything like her."

He now had the water moving through the tank at sixteen knots, and the resistance lines on the monitor were only beginning to build up. He turned on the disk drive and began recording the results. "When the deans see these figures, they're going to think they're imagining things."

Sean smiled.

"What do you call her?" Bladesdale asked.

"*Siren*," Sean answered.

FT. LAUDERDALE

1

SIREN SWUNG ACROSS THE WIND, HER BOW OPENING UP
the water like a surgeon's scalpel. Robert Cramm cranked furiously, and
the genoa hardened along the port side. She heeled, but only slightly.
The sizzle of the sea along her flanks never changed its musical tone.

"Whoopee!" Cheryl screamed from the helm.

Robert's set jaw slacked into a smile. "She's fast," he laughed to his
wife.

"Is she ever."

She let the bow slide up, close to the wind. "Look at this!"

He glanced up to the masthead, where the indicator showed that they
were steering well into the relative wind. "Careful," he warned her.

"She's not supposed to be able to do this. Not when she turns so fast."

"Give her air! Let her rip!"

She nodded and turned down a bit, across the wind. *Siren* leaned and
began to accelerate.

"How'd Sean do it?" Cheryl asked.

"It's magic," Robert answered with a grin.

He turned toward the chase boat and gave a thumbs-up signal. Sean

Patton responded with a casual salute, but his eyes stayed locked on the rigging. There was a flutter in the backstay. He'd have to anchor it to a small block and tackle so that they could add some tension when they were beating upwind. The mast had to be firmly anchored at every sailing angle.

"I want to take her around once more," Robert said. "You can swap with Beth and take the chase boat in."

Cheryl shook her head. "I'll stay with it. I need the practice."

"Like hell you do. You'll be the best helm in the race."

"Not as good as Beth," Cheryl said, checking the beam and quarter before she put the wheel over.

"Beth isn't sailing. You are."

"We still want to win," she answered, and then she commanded, "Ready about."

"Aye, aye," Robert said as he moved toward the jib winches.

"Hard alee!" She put the wheel over and instantly the bow began to swing. Robert eased the sheet around the winch head and let the big genoa fill. He glanced back to the helm and noticed Cheryl set her feet against the pitch of the deck. Her fingers were light on the wheel, letting her feel the sea against the rudder. Her long, black hair stretched out like a telltale from under her baseball cap. She was tall with a well-curved figure. But there was a spirit to her that made her more attractive when she was stretched into an athletic pose. Her body was right for her thirty years. And the brooding circles under her eyes that had made her seem much older during the past few years were almost faded.

Amazing, Robert thought as he watched her. The sea was in her genes even though she came from a line of land-locked Italian farmers who had never seen the Mediterranean, much less an ocean. She hadn't just learned all he had taught her; she had inhaled it and taken it into her blood.

"Nice," Beth Hardaway said in the bow of the chase boat. She turned to Sean, who was sitting at the stern, his hand on the outboard throttle. "Cheryl's good."

Sean sneered, showing white teeth against an oaken tan. "You'd get more out of her," he told her. "You and Robert should be crewing."

"What about you? You know the boat better than anyone," Beth reminded.

"I just design 'em," he answered. "I don't sail 'em. But all the yachties will have their stopwatches on *Siren*. I want her to blow their minds."

"Oh, she'll do that," Beth said as she watched the big sloop begin to pull away from them. "They're not going to believe it when she posts her time in Bermuda."

He wasn't reassured. "There's always a problem in a first race. He should go with all the experience he can get."

"Can't blame him because he'd rather go with his wife."

"He can take her cruising anytime. You should be aboard for the race."

He swung the chase boat around to follow *Siren* back out to sea. "Check the headstay," he ordered Beth. "See if there's any slack in it."

She lifted the binoculars and turned in the boat, kneeling on the bow thwart. She was wearing cut-off jeans and a man's long-sleeved shirt, her red hair stuffed into a floppy sailor hat. Beth dressed for the competitive man's world that she thrived in. But even in her salty garb, her well-formed figure was obvious.

She locked the glasses on *Siren*'s backstay. "Yeah, you're right. There is a little play in it." She turned to Sean. "We can fix it as soon as she gets back in."

He shook his head. "Nah, it's a one-man job. You go to the party."

"Aren't you coming?" she encouraged.

"Not if I can find an excuse."

2 THE YACHT CLUB WAS ON THE END OF A FINGER, DEAD center in the big marina. It was surrounded by the wooden decks and tall masts of the world's yachting fleet, and by the pure white hulls of oceangoing power cruisers that were bigger than the flagships of most navies. Painted on their sterns were their ports of registry, a listing of the world's great seaside watering holes. Many had traveled halfway around the world to partake in the pre-race festivities.

The race contenders were out of sight, scattered along the miles of floating docks, each group in a private corner where it could safeguard its design secrets. Large young men with blond hair guarded the ramps leading down to the boats to discourage visitors who might try to copy the angle of a transom or the set of a mast.

Robert led Cheryl out to the porch, where the breeze lifted the hem of her cocktail dress and pulled open his white dinner jacket. He nodded to the waiter who was circling with a tray of champagne flutes. The boy stole a glance down the top of Cheryl's dress as Robert lifted two glasses from the tray.

"You still turn 'em on," he told her as he toasted. "Good to have you back aboard."

She sipped. "How about you? Do I still turn you on?"

"More than ever."

But he was glancing over her shoulder toward the crowd inside at the bar. "There's George," he announced. "Let's go in and rescue him."

She turned away toward the water, which was beginning to reflect the red of the sunset. "You go. I'll join you." He had already left.

A lone pelican glided a few inches off the water, steering from the seawall toward the club. At the last instant, it pulled up into a stall and dropped on top of a piling. It made eye contact with Cheryl and then glanced toward the kitchen door, where they would soon be putting out the cuttings from the evening's seafood menu.

It *was* good to be back aboard, Cheryl thought. But she still wasn't completely at home. Certainly not in the cocktail party circle that was the social side of the yachting business. Not even in the Newport office that she had started visiting again with Rachael in tow. Whenever she was around people, she could feel their uneasiness, as if she were hideously scarred. They were falling over themselves, trying to act normal. The sailing had come back quickly. But that was because the sea left her some of the loneliness that she had embraced after Rachael's birth. It had no eyes to look away in embarrassment as she passed. It wasn't waiting for her to fall back into her staring silence.

Cheryl knew that her illness was behind her, but she wasn't sure that the others knew. Robert handled her like porcelain. George was overly solicitous, forcing compliments on her most routine achievements. The office staff suddenly got very busy when she stopped by, which was exactly the opposite from the yard crew. They stopped working and watched her when she jumped across the docks, ready to dive in after her if she should lose her footing.

It would take time. For her part, all she could do was take up her old responsibilities. And the time to start was right now. She set the half-filled champagne flute on the railing and turned back to the party.

Robert and George were at the bar, hunched so close together that their heads were nearly touching. "That's wonderful . . . and just in time. . . ." George was saying when Cheryl reached them.

"Just in time for what?" she interrupted.

George Williamson turned abruptly, and flushed as if he had been caught telling a dirty joke. But he quickly regained his composure. Williamson looked as if he had been born in a dinner jacket. He was in his early forties, the same age as Robert, but he seemed a half a generation older. Some of it was appearance. George had lost most of his hair, and he bulged a bit above his cummerbund. Robert, despite the fleck of gray, still had a tuned, youthful physique. But the generation gap was more a matter of attitude. George was cautious, where Robert was carefree. He clung to the black tie and accessories as opposed to Robert's more trendy pastels. George still had laces on his shoes.

"Cheryl! You look wonderful." He beamed.

"In time for what?" Cheryl repeated.

"I was telling George that you've never sailed any better," Robert said.

"And just in time for the race," George added in response to her question. "It's good to have you back onboard."

She was pleased by their enthusiasm. "I hope I'm ready. I know this is important."

"Just another new design," Robert said as he tried to get the attention of the bartender.

They carried their drinks to a round table that was marked with CRAMM YACHTS on a placard. Elliot Minor, their Ft. Lauderdale salesman, was waiting, a red-faced customer in his grasp.

"Robert Cramm, this is Peter Pawley." Elliot smiled through perfect teeth. "Peter owns one of our original Zephyrs." Robert completed the introductions and invited Pawley to join them.

"The Vector pirates have captured him for the evening," Elliot apologized. "But I invited him to join us in Bermuda. Peter likes to be aboard a winner."

"He's been telling me about your boat," Peter Pawley said with a nod toward the salesman. "Says it will be in Bermuda before the others clear the breakwater."

"Just before the others get to Bermuda," Robert corrected.

He waited until Pawley was well out of earshot. "Does he know his ladies won't be comfortable on a performance yacht?" He turned to Cheryl. "The guy orders his boats with circular beds and Jacuzzis."

"He'd better stick with his Zephyr," Cheryl laughed.

Elliot wasn't laughing as he leaned across the table. "You win this thing and he'll buy a brand-new Zephyr. With more electronics on it than the space shuttle. Peter Pawley's never going to race anywhere. But he's just like everyone else. He wants a barge designed by a champion. What the hell do you think he's doing eating with McKnight?"

Cheryl knew that Philip McKnight was the president of Vector Yachts. But she was still puzzled. She remembered Vector for their floating-hotel-rooms-with-brothel decor. Their boats were scarcely seaworthy, much less thoroughbred performers.

"Vector has been doing pretty well during the last few campaigns," Robert explained.

"Vector?" She couldn't hide her surprise, and then she couldn't hide her embarrassment. "I guess I have been away too long."

"They've been selling very well," George confirmed.

"While we've been slipping," Cheryl said, beginning to focus on the implications.

"We're doing fine," Robert corrected.

"I thought you said the market was dead."

"It is."

"Then why is Vector selling so well?" she persisted.

"Because they've been winning races," Elliot said.

Cheryl nodded. Now she understood the pressure they were all under. Cramm Yachts needed to reclaim its reputation for performance. *Siren* was racing for more than just a trophy.

The guests abandoned the bar for the tables as soon as the first course made its appearance. Each table displayed the name of one of the yachting companies, and its owners and sailors gathered around, with yachting editors, brokers, customers, and enough of the inevitable bow bunnies to create rivulets of bare, perfectly tanned shoulders throughout the gathering. For the guests, it promised to be a delightful evening at the expense of the builders who were launching their newest designs. For the builders, the whole evening was a business write-off.

Cheryl glanced over to the Vector table and caught a glimpse of Philip McKnight stealing a glimpse back at her. He covered with a smile and a tip of his wild white locks. McKnight was a newcomer to the sport who had switched from molding fiberglass swimming pools to casting boat hulls only a decade earlier. He had reasoned that most of the proctologists and slip-and-fall lawyers who had created the yacht industry would never leave harbor. So he had built spacious barges with plush accommodations and sold them for a fortune. Why worry about seakeeping qualities when his customers could care less? He was a bad joke to serious yachtsmen, but Philip McKnight was laughing all the way to the bank.

Now that he had his fortune, he was going for prestige, much like the Japanese car manufacturers who went after the Germans. When Vector yachts began to win races, the demand for his floating lounges increased.

"You really need this race," Cheryl whispered to Robert.

He shrugged his shoulders.

"You should go with your best crew."

Robert put his hand on top of hers. "I am going with my best crew."

Beth Hardaway appeared at the door, her face scanning the horizon until she spotted the Cramm table. She was wearing tailored jeans, a white blouse, and a slim-fitting blazer. The outfit earned appreciative glances as she worked her way across the room despite the competition from cocktail dresses and ball gowns. Robert was on his feet, and seated her to his other side, as a buffer between himself and Elliot Minor.

"Where's Sean?" he asked.

"Back at the dock. He's rerigging your backstay." Beth leaned across Robert toward Cheryl. "You were really kicking ass out there today."

"You should be racing," Cheryl answered. "You sailed all the trials. You know *Siren* better than I do."

"You're doing great," Beth assured her. "Besides, I still make yachting people nervous."

She turned to her left. "Like Elliot here. Bet you're wondering how many bucks it will cost you if people see you sitting with me."

Elliot pulled on his martini. "Don't be an ass!"

Sean arrived during the main course. The dinner jacket he had rented couldn't be buttoned across his chest, and the bow tie was holding together a dress shirt that was a couple of sizes too small. His physique was built from physical outdoor work. The suit had been cut for a musician.

"Look at you," Beth Hardaway said, smirking.

Sean lifted the lapels with his thumbs. "I guess you can tell it isn't mine," he said, allowing a rare smile as he enjoyed his own ridiculous appearance. He turned slowly, modeling the outfit. His dark ponytail hung like a stripe against the white dinner jacket.

Cheryl led the mock applause, and the others joined in. Except Elliot. "Jesus," he mumbled as he glanced around in hopes that none of his customers were watching.

"Changes?" Robert asked as soon as Sean was seated.

"You need to trim the backstay when you're upwind," he answered. He was glancing around for something to write on, and he finally pulled the CRAMM YACHTS placard out of its holder. Robert understood, and automatically handed him a pen.

Sean quickly sketched the backstay, connected to a chain plate on the transom. "I took off the chain plate and cut a pulley through the deck." He was illustrating as he spoke, a habit that both Robert and Beth had come to appreciate since he talked quickly and sometimes assumed knowledge that neither of them had. "Then I rigged a simple block and tackle under the transom. Helmsman can reach back with one hand and pull the whole rigging tight."

Robert smiled as he took back his pen. "Simple enough," he teased, admitting to himself that it was the kind of detail he never would have thought of.

Cheryl raised her glass. "You've given us a helluva boat, Sean. Fastest one I've ever been on." They all drank to Sean, who found the attention embarrassing.

"But I think Beth can get even more out of her," Cheryl continued. "I've been trying to persuade Robert that she ought to be crewing for the race."

Sean looked up hopefully, but Robert was already shaking his head.

"A mixed-couples crew is supposed to be just that. Cheryl and I are a couple."

"Every other builder has hired the best man and the best woman available," Elliot corrected. "They don't give a damn about family bonds." He dropped his nose back inside the rim of his glass. Elliot was getting on a miserable drunk.

"Beth knows her well," Sean said in Robert's direction.

Cheryl sided with Sean. "She was there from the beginning."

Robert stood as the band began to play. "I've picked my dancing partner," he said with a tone of finality. He put his hand down to his wife and led her to the dance floor.

3   THE MORNING SUN WAS STILL JUST A PENCIL-THIN line, but it had already set the gulls squawking and begun to scatter the clouds. The air moved gently, rattling the riggings against the masts. The weather looked promising.

Sean Patton was watching as the crane slowly lifted *Siren* out of the water. They had been working out around Ft. Lauderdale for the past week, and he wasn't surprised that there was already a whisker of marine growth along the bottom. He was ready with a high-pressure hose, and then he planned to spray on a final coat of wax. She'd be slick through the water.

As the boat rose, her radical lines became apparent. Above the waterline, she was a fairly standard offshore racing sloop. *Siren* was fifty-two feet from a gently curved prow to an abrupt stern, a touch beamy, with her mast set well aft. Half her length was given to an open cockpit, with plenty of room around the mechanical winches that would trim her massive sails. The forward cockpit housed the essentials for extended cruising: a small galley, a navigation table bristling with electronics, a head with hand shower, and pilot berths above the lounge benches. Adequate. Even comfortable. But certainly not commodious.

The shock came when she lifted higher. *Siren* seemed to be cut off at the waterline. There were hard chines at her bilges, forming sharp angles between her sides and bottom. The bottom was a gently tapered V, but at its deepest point it was no more than three feet below the surface. She had no more draft than many small day sailers or outboard runabouts.

At first, she seemed to have no keel. There was no gently tapered leader, nor a trailing skeg in front of the rudder. But when she was lifted high enough, a thin, vertical blade appeared. It was ridiculously abrupt, pointing straight down, and only five feet from its leading edge to its trailing edge. But it seemed to go on forever, still in the water when the boat was already ten feet in the air. Then the weight broke the surface, a bulbous shape of lead that reached ahead of the keel by five feet, and trailed it by seven.

To the sailor's eye, everything was wrong. *Siren* was grossly top-heavy. She should turn turtle at her mooring, much less than when running across a heavy wind. And she couldn't sail upwind at all. There was no underwater resistance to overcome the force of the air in her sails.

An engineer would laugh at the keel. It was like the pendulum on a grandfather clock, with all its weight at the end. As the boat heeled, the moment of the weight would snap the keel completely off the hull.

"What in God's name is it?" George Williamson had asked when Robert rolled the preliminary sketches before him.

"Sean Patton's first offshore design."

"Sean Patton," George had bellowed.

"Keep it down!" Robert had ordered. "He's right outside."

"Here? At Cramm? Why?"

"I thought we ought to talk to him. He's an interesting guy."

George had swiped his hand across the sketches. "He's an idiot. This joke won't even float."

"We need something fast," Robert had reminded.

"We need a yacht. Not a gimmick."

George had refused to open the door, or even listen secondhand to Sean's thinking. It didn't make sense to risk a whole company on the latest fantasy of a controversial designer. Cramm still had an excellent reputation. "Three generations," George kept pleading. "A Cramm Clipper still holds the sailing record to Perth. Cramm vessels landed Marines at Tarawa." The name had value. Its yards were modern. It was an ideal partner in a merger with another yacht builder. Or even for a takeover by a conglomerate whose board respected tradition and had a fondness for sailing. "Let me look for a deal," George had begged. "Don't throw away the value we have left on a boat with no bottom!"

Robert didn't want to discourage his college roommate. Williamson had proved to be an outstanding financial officer, and he was dead right about what Cramm Yachts needed. But George didn't care much for sailing. Yachting was his business; it wasn't his passion. Robert kept preaching that he had no intention of merging or selling. He would go down with the ship rather than hand her over to the enemy. He had kept secret conversations going with Sean until he had become convinced that Patton had a revolutionary boat.

George had taken the decision to bring Patton aboard gracefully. As he told the bankers, the project was something Robert needed. His wife had gone into a crippling depression after the birth of their first child. The yachting industry was in a slump. He needed a challenge. Sean Patton and Beth Hardaway were both racing professionals at the leading edge of racing design trends. Working with them helped keep Robert from joining his wife in her black despair. He had urged every possible sale out of Cramm dealers, cheerfully rolled over the notes that he knew he wouldn't be able to pay, and done his best to cover the bills that Robert was piling up as he threw himself into the new design.

He had been surprised at how accurate his cover story had proven to be. Robert, Sean, and Beth had become a team, replacing the team that he and Robert and Cheryl had formed when Cheryl came into the company. They were working together day and night, totally involved with squeezing extra seconds out of Sean's design. George was left with the business. Cheryl was left with round-the-clock nurses.

It was George who had named the boat the first time he saw the four-foot hull model that Sean was taking down to the test tanks at Hoboken. "She looks beautiful, but what's under the water can get you killed. You ought to call her *Siren's Song*." Sean had smiled and settled for *Siren*. He had come back from Hoboken with numbers that George couldn't believe. *Siren* was nearly a knot and a half faster than any sloop of her size that had ever been put into the tank. "The professors thought their computers were off," Sean had mocked. "Bladesdale didn't have the heart to tell them it wasn't their computers. It was their out-of-date thinking."

"Did they simulate heavy weather?" George had challenged. "Because that keel will tear itself off the minute she starts rolling." It had taken a winter of sea trials in the bitter waters off Block Island to convince him that the keel would probably stay on.

4 THE DOCKSIDE PARTY WAS REALLY FOR THE DEALERS. They traveled from yacht to yacht, toured all the candidate boats, and paused at each stop for a cocktail with the crew. Sean Patton was in hiding back in the hotel, which both Robert and George regarded as a blessing. Sean hated small talk, and he suffered fools badly, particularly dealers who pretended to great knowledge of seafaring. During trials, he had listened patiently to a dealer's ideas for retuning the rigging, and then had suggested that the man go back to selling used cars. Cramm Yachts had lost the account.

Beth Hardaway was wandering around the docks, looking over the competition. She wasn't particularly interested in the boats, but rather the professional racers who had been hired to sail the mixed-crew event. She had sailed with many of them—lived with two of the men—and could get straight answers about the yachts they were sailing. "You crewing with Cramm?" she was asked over and over again by friends who knew she had done the sea trials on *Siren*. Most were stunned when she told them that Cheryl Cramm was sailing with her husband. The common wisdom held that Cheryl was permanently ill, and there were rumors that Beth would eventually become much more than Robert's first mate. A few of the wags had her already sharing his bunk.

Cheryl was doing her part to entertain the visiting dealers. She saw to the drinks and snacks, and made small talk with the women, while Robert and Elliot gave guided tours to the serious customers. She had her head under the portable bar, looking for a fresh bottle of gin, when she heard Philip McKnight's voice.

"I understand she's very quick."

She popped up to see him fixing his own drink. "Damn quick," she said.

Philip was measuring dark rum into a glass of fruit punch. His smile was ivory white against the riding-saddle color of his permanent Florida tan. "And I understand that she has a beautiful first mate." He raised his rum-laced painkiller in toast. "I hope you'll finish a strong second."

"First, actually," Cheryl answered. "But we won't drink the champagne until you get there."

"I'm flying out tonight," McKnight said. He saw the surprise in Cheryl's eyes. "Well, you didn't think I'd *sail* to Bermuda, for God's sake." He gestured around the marina. "These things are too slow for me. It's only an hour by jet."

"Then you'll be the first one to see us dock in Hamilton."

"Probably," he said. "My spies have been clocking your practice runs. It seems that everything George says about *Siren* is true. She's a breakthrough design!"

She was puzzled. "George?"

"Oh, he was just boasting. I don't suppose George would know a breakthrough design any more than I would." He glanced quickly from the bow to the stern. "Seems straightforward . . . businesslike. Doesn't look like a revolution!"

"She'll surprise you."

He added a tad more rum to his drink. "I was surprised to hear that you're crewing. I thought you'd given this up for the joys of parenthood."

"I think I can handle both."

"Do you?"

His head was tipped skeptically, and there was mockery in his eye. He was reminding her that she hadn't been able to handle either, and Cheryl found herself looking away from the confrontation.

"I had heard that Beth Hardaway had taken your place," he added. "I'm glad you're still in the game."

The prick, she thought, struggling to control her anger as he retasted his drink and smiled with satisfaction. In ten seconds he had laid open all her wounds.

"Nobody has taken my place," she managed.

"Of course not." He set the nearly full glass on the bar. "Well, I'm afraid I have other ports of call. Nice to see you again, Cheryl. Perhaps we'll meet in Bermuda."

McKnight went down the gangway and joined the entourage that had waited on the dock. Cheryl took his glass and dropped it over the side.

"I tried to rescue you," Robert said, coming down from the bow to join her. "I was just being introduced to one of Elliot's guests when he came aboard."

"Bastard," she said. "He knows where to hit."

Robert looked suddenly angry, and she put a restraining hand on his arm.

"It's my fight. I have to prove I'm . . . okay. . . ."

He took her hand. "I want you at the wheel when we cross the line."

"Robert. Am I really back aboard?"

"Of course," he whispered, and looked around uneasily. "Don't be talking that way."

"If you'd have a better chance with Beth . . ."

"Then I'd sail with her. The boat has speed to burn."

"But she's better."

"You'll be fine.

He moved away from her to greet another of the dealers who was making the rounds. Cheryl forced a smile and stepped toward the young woman who was with him.

5 ROBERT WENT TO THE TELEPHONE AS SOON AS THEY returned to their suite and dialed their home in Newport. Cheryl left her clothes in a trail from the sitting room into the bathroom. She was exhausted from the day of entertaining, more from the emotional strain of reintroducing herself to customers and dealers than from the physical efforts, and had promised herself a relaxing soak in the tub. She heard Robert talking to the housekeeper as she turned on the water, and she took the robe from the back of the door, hoping that Rachael was still up and could be coaxed to the telephone.

"Gretchen," Robert said, when their young au pair came on the line. "How's everything going?" When she stepped back out of the bathroom, she could see the concern on her husband's face.

"What is it? What's wrong?" she demanded as she crossed the room.

Robert held up a hand, assuring her that she shouldn't be concerned. "Have you talked to her doctor?" he was asking.

Cheryl reached for the phone.

"Well, I'd call the doctor," Robert went on. "Just to be safe."

"What is it? Let me talk to her." She was practically wrestling the telephone away from him.

"It's probably nothing serious." Robert continued. "But let the doctor decide, even if you have to meet him at the hospital."

"Hospital? Let me talk to her." Cheryl was becoming frantic.

"Just a minute," he said into the phone and then put his hand over the mouthpiece. "Nothing at all. Rachael is running a fever. Probably just a childhood thing . . ." He handed her the phone and Cheryl snapped it to her ear.

Gretchen repeated what she had apparently told Robert. Their two-year-old daughter had a fever. Yes, it was high, but children often run fevers that would be dangerous in an adult. The au pair wasn't worried, but she would check it with the doctor.

"What did you say about the hospital?" Cheryl demanded.

Gretchen explained that the doctor might want her to take the child to the emergency room. She had the note authorizing treatment that Robert had left with her. Cheryl looked wide-eyed at her husband as she listened. By the time she hung up the telephone she had decided. She would begin to pack while Robert made arrangements with the charter service to fly her back to Rhode Island.

"Cheryl, it's probably not that serious," Robert argued as he followed her into the bedroom. "The doctor will know what to do."

She was already firing her things onto the bed. "I should be with her," she said, and then she pointed to the closet. "Could you hand me my suitcase?"

He kept repeating himself as she packed her bags. Gretchen didn't think it was an emergency. Kids get fevers all the time. She was probably overreacting. Cheryl kept nodding her agreement, but began gathering her toiletries into her night case. "I've got be with her," she said when Robert paused. "God knows I wasn't with her for the first two years of her life."

"Don't say that. You did what you could."

She began lifting the bag off the bed. "I couldn't do anything. Now I can."

He phoned for the charter outfit that had brought all of them down to Ft. Lauderdale, and found they could be ready to take off at midnight. That left them two hours to kill, so he fixed a drink and pulled Cheryl down beside him on the sofa, where she sat silently, her head resting on his shoulder. He remembered sitting like this night after night, staring across the room at the crib where Rachael was sleeping. Cheryl had lost touch with reality during the first months after their daughter was born, and Robert had spent the best part of a year waiting for her to come back. Then he had rallied himself and thrown all his energy into *Siren*. Cheryl hadn't held her daughter again until the tank model of the yacht was taking shape. She hadn't held Robert again until the yacht was ready for launching.

"I'm okay, Robert," she said, interrupting the dark silence of the suite. "I know what I'm doing."

He sipped at his drink. "Do you want me to go with you?"

Cheryl sat up abruptly. "No. You have a race to win."

"I have much more to lose."

"You're not going to lose anything. You're going to win. I'll make sure Rachael is okay, and then I'll be on the first plane for Bermuda. I'll be waiting at the finish line."

The next morning, only three hours before the starting cannon, Robert announced the change in plans. Beth would be sailing with him. He asked George Williamson to fly back to Newport before leaving for Bermuda just in case Cheryl needed help.

Robert took Sean and Beth up to the clubhouse, where he spread out the charts and tide tables. He went over the race strategy that he had worked out with Cheryl for Beth's benefit. She nodded her agreement to everything except his planned approach to Hamilton, where she explained her experience with the tricky tides north of the island. Sean smiled. Beth's savvy was paying off even before the race began.

"I'm sorry," Beth said as their meeting was wrapping up. "I know you wanted Cheryl to win this one."

"I just want to win it," Robert answered.

"I hope she didn't . . . step aside. Because she was really sailing well—"

"I was the one who called home," he interrupted. "I was the one who learned about Rachael."

Beth's head went down. "I shouldn't have said that."

Robert stood up and rolled the charts. "Why not?" he snapped. "That's what you're all thinking."

Sean and Beth headed down to the boat, where George handed Beth the final inventory of supplies that were aboard. Robert went to the committee desk to register his change of crew. An hour later, Sean took *Siren*'s bow line aboard the chase boat and towed her out to the starting area. The future of Cramm Yachts began hoisting her sails.

6 CHERYL AWOKE WHEN THE LATE-MORNING SUN FOUND the southeast side of the house and poured into her bedroom. She blinked for a few seconds, looking curiously at the high ceiling as if it were the chart of a strange harbor. She saw that she was still dressed in her traveling clothes, and then remembered the limo ride from the airport. She knew where she was when she remembered passing through the gates of the Cramm estate, which had been thrown open sometime before the turn of the century and kept open as a sign of welcome to anyone arriving from the sea.

She loved the house, a great New England Victorian with a wraparound porch at its base and a widow's walk at its top, its clapboard siding weatherworn to a nearly colorless gray. It was more homey than palatial, with dozens of small rooms fitted into each wing. Cheryl's room looked down the front hill and onto the harbor, with the Cramm yacht works on the water's edge to the north, and the open sea to the south. She smiled comfortably, and her eyes began to close. Then she remembered Rachael.

She felt her heart begin pounding in panic as she listened to the deathly silence, and then sprang from the unruffled covers toward the adjoining nursery. She raced to the small bed and pulled back the colorful comforter. The bed was empty.

"Rachael?" She was already calling before she reached the top of the stairs. "Rachael?" She ran down the steps that curved gracefully into the large entrance foyer. "Rachael!"

The little girl, still in pajamas, ran from the playroom and dove straight into Cheryl's waiting arms. Gretchen, in slacks and sweater, walked out behind her and smiled at the reunion. "She seems to be feeling much better," the au pair said. "In fact, she's wearing me out."

"You should have woken me," Cheryl answered. "I wanted to take care of her."

"Not much care required," Gretchen answered. "The fever went down and she woke up feeling like her old self. I'm not even sure that we should bother taking her to the doctor."

Rachael was chattering away, telling Cheryl the previous week's events in a single breath.

"I think we'll keep the appointment. Just to be sure," Cheryl sang as she swung her daughter in the air. "I was so worried about you." She showered the girl with kisses.

"I didn't really think there was any reason for you to come all the way back," Gretchen apologized. "I told Mr. Cramm that it didn't seem to be anything serious. . . ."

"There was every reason to come back," Cheryl reassured her. "You were thinking about the hospital."

"Just that the doctor would meet us there if I thought Rachael had to be seen. I meant it to be reassuring . . . not something to frighten you. I feel so badly that you're missing the race."

Cheryl was still hugging the little girl. "I'm not missing anything, believe me. And neither is the boat. Robert has a better crew without me." She carried Rachael back up the stairs, with Gretchen trailing behind. Then, while the au pair was getting the little girl dressed, Cheryl went back into the master suite to shower and change.

She would miss Gretchen, Cheryl thought as she peeled off the clothes she had slept in. Probably even more than Rachael would. It wasn't just that the young Danish woman had become part of their family. More precious was that she was a constant reminder of Cheryl's recovery. She was Cheryl's first conscious decision after more than a year in limbo. Gretchen had replaced the nurse who, while ostensibly caring for Rachael, had really been watching over her.

Rachael had been born during the third year of her relationship with Robert Cramm, and two years after their improbable marriage. She had brought the beautiful and perfectly healthy baby home to a household that was filled with the excitement of a new child for the first time since Robert himself had been born. The empty rooms, once filled with the children of Robert's father's generation, were furnished and brightened. The second parlor on the ground floor was turned into a playroom, with doors that swung to the outside. The bedroom next to the one she shared with Robert was enlarged and turned into a nursery. The cook modernized the kitchen as well as the menus, and a housekeeper was added to the staff. The first few months home were the happiest that Cheryl had ever known.

But then her joy had turned to fear. She had begun to worry about the child, sorting through a litany of all the horrors that might befall her. She had insisted on spending more and more time with the baby, until she was constantly at the side of the crib, listening carefully for Rachael's next breath. And then she refused to put the child down, holding her close so that she could feel the tiny tap of her heartbeat. Cheryl remembered the days of agony, filled with fear that Rachael would strangle, unable to draw air into her lungs, or choke trying to swallow. She remembered Robert unwrapping her fingers from around the baby, and remembered attacking him, screaming that her baby was dead. And then she remembered nothing.

There were flickers of reality. Cheryl recalled sitting on the porch in a rocking chair, looking down on the harbor with its heavy traffic of bulging sails and foamy wakes. She could see herself walking hand-in-hand with Robert through woods dappled with reds and oranges, the fallen leaves crumpling under her step. She remembered the pure white of her nurse's uniform, as white as the blanket of snow that rolled down the lawns from the house to its open gates. She remembered dead trees coming to life.

The memories were vivid. She could hear herself singing "Happy Birthday" to the child in her lap, and see the light flicker as she blew out the candle. She could feel Rachael's grasp release from her fingers as she took her first steps, and see Robert's smile as she stumbled toward him. She seemed to remember every detail, and yet was unable to remember why any were important. They were scenes played on a screen in an empty theater, unreal because no one was watching.

And then she woke up, and understood without being told that she had been mentally ill. Instinctively, she knew that she was in a process of recovery. She approached her daughter carefully, almost like an aunt coming to visit who wants desperately to be welcomed. She began speaking to Robert as if they had just been introduced. And she allowed herself to be managed by the polite woman who claimed to be Rachael's nurse, but whose eyes always lingered on her when she whispered her daily report to Robert.

"It's fairly common," her doctor told her with a forced smile. "After childbirth, the realities are easily confused. The abrupt physical changes. The sudden responsibility . . ."

"Am I mentally ill?" It was a straight question with no room for ambiguity.

"Heavens, no!" the doctor laughed.

"Don't think such a thing," Robert intoned from his place at her side.

Cheryl turned a clear eye on her husband. "For the past year I've been more a child than my daughter. You've tucked us both in every night. So we know I was mentally ill." And then to the doctor: "What I'm asking is whether this is something that I'll get over, like a cold or the flu. Or am I going to drop back into my coma? From time to time? Or permanently?"

The professional smile narrowed to a frown. "We don't know why this happened to you. Why you recovered. Whether it could ever happen again. I've seen it before with women after the birth of a child. A depression that lasts a few weeks or even a few months. They've all recovered, and none that I know of have ever had the problem again."

"But it wasn't a few months. It's been over a year."

The doctor nodded. "I don't even know whether that's at all significant. I'm told by the experts that you will, in all likelihood, be fine. But they can't tell me why they feel that way. What they advise is that you go slowly. Don't try to make everything normal at once. Take it one day at a time."

Cheryl had taken the advice, introducing herself back into her family and her life one day at a time. She had started caring for Rachael, cautiously spending more and more time with her as she watched for any symptoms of her crippling fear. She had begun driving again, taking short sight-seeing trips with the nurse as her passenger. Then she had ventured out alone, walking down to the boatyards where the yachts were being outfitted for delivery to customers. She had gone into the design shed, where Robert introduced her to Beth Hardaway and Sean Patton, and showed her the plans for the new racing sloop.

That had been her first setback. They stopped working whenever she came in. The frowns on their faces became idiotic smiles, and they stopped arguing so that they could bubble over with pleasantries. She was an interruption who had to be entertained, and then hopefully dismissed so they could get back to work. She felt like someone dying with a dread disease who has already been eased out of the company of the living.

"I'm okay!" she wanted to scream. "You can talk to me. You can involve me. I can understand what you're doing. I can be part of your project."

"How was your walk?" Robert would ask.

"Your hair looks terrific," Beth would say.

And Sean would drum his pencil, practically begging her to go back to her asylum so that he could build his yacht.

Cheryl understood that she would never be well until people accepted her as herself. She couldn't recover until they believed that she was recovered, until they forgot that she had ever been sick.

"Am I really better?" she had demanded of Robert one night when they were dining alone.

"Of course."

"Then why do I need a nurse?"

"A nurse? She's for Rachael."

"Why does Rachael need a nurse when she has a mother?"

"Just . . . to help you. To make it easier for you."

"An au pair can do that. And I wouldn't feel that she was watching me to report to you if I start barking at the moon."

"For God's sake, that's not why she's here. She'll just help you . . . for a few more months. Until you're . . ." His voice trailed off.

"Until you're sure I'm not a danger to anyone."

"Cheryl."

"Don't you see?" She got up from her place and went around the table to lean against his chair. "This won't be behind me until we all stop thinking about it. And we can't stop thinking about it while there's a paramedic following me around with her black bag in hand."

The next morning, Robert had called an agency and arranged for Gretchen to come and spend the summer with them. For Cheryl, it was a major step on her journey. She had made a decision that affected her life.

Robert had hesitated to commit for the full year that a foreign au pair's visa required. "A year is a terribly long time," he had explained to Cheryl. And now that year was nearly over. It wasn't a very long time at all.

SHE STOOD IN the shower, with the hot water running down her back. She hoped she was ready. Robert had wanted to bring another young college graduate over for a year to replace Gretchen, but Cheryl argued against it. It was time she began raising her own child. There was enough help around the house so that she could still do her part for the company. Rachael would have a difficult time separating from Gretchen. There was no point in giving her another substitute parent to love and then lose.

But even when Gretchen had arrived, Cheryl knew that things weren't back to normal. She still had to win back her husband. And that might prove to be the most difficult step in her recovery. He was still treating her like porcelain, handling her carefully as if she might break. The spontaneity, the casual acceptance, and even the momentary indifference that tests and proves the strength of a relationship were still missing.

For the longest time she had been outside his daily activity, almost like a religious icon that is visited only on Sunday. When she stopped in at the design shop he would be across the table from Beth Hardaway, arguing passionately and forcefully. At the ways, when the boat was being constructed, he might be ordering her up a ladder, or handing down heavy planking. Beth had become his friend and companion, while she had been relegated to the more formal role of wife.

He had not yet moved back into her bed. While she was sick, Robert had converted the small bedroom next to theirs to an office, fitted out with a desk, telephone, his books and files, and a sofa that was really a daybed. He was still living there, knocking on the door that connected the two rooms and entering as a visitor. He would help her on with her nightgown, tuck her in carefully, and sit on the edge of the bed chatting with her. If she suggested that he stay with her, he would lie down outside the covers, an arm around her, protecting her as he might a child who was afraid of the dark. He told her a hundred times that he loved her, but it seemed that what he meant was that he worshiped her. She wondered if his love had really gone elsewhere.

Then she had begun to feel jealousy. Robert had one woman who shared his child and another who shared his life. She had been put aside, like a broken toy mended with string and glue. She was there, a decoration, a reminder, but too fragile to be played with.

As Cheryl stepped into her bedroom, still wet and wrapped in a towel, she remembered the moment when she had begun to fight back. Like now, she had been stepping out of the shower just as Robert came into the room to ask after her. Instead of his solicitous "How are you feeling?" he had been stunned into shock to find a woman in his bedroom instead of a patient. She had seen a flicker of remembered desire in his eyes. She nearly laughed as he swallowed hard, searching for the polite word.

She had simply walked past him and pushed the door closed. When she saw that his eyes had followed her, she had made an elaborate show of turning the key in the lock. Then she had let the towel fall to the floor.

His eyes widened, and she heard him swallow again.

"I hope you still recognize me," she had said, walking toward him.

She could almost hear his mind whirring as he tried for a polite answer. His lips tried to form words.

She had begun unbuttoning his shirt.

"Let's see if I still recognize you."

They had made love physically, almost brutally, pouring out passions that seemed to burst through a dam.

Then, as they lay together panting, he had asked, "Are you all right?"

"Just fine," she answered as she squeezed his hand.

"I'm sorry. I should have been . . . gentle."

"Don't be. I didn't want to be gentle."

"It's so soon since you were . . ."

"It's been so long."

He had pushed up on an elbow. "I'm not rushing you, Cheryl. Maybe, until you're completely recovered—"

"Dammit! I'm fine. I feel fine. And I want my life back, Robert." She had sat up and snapped on the night-table lamp. "I want my daughter back. And my husband. And my work. I want people to stop treating me as if I have some sort of sad, lingering disease. And I don't ever want you to apologize for screwing the breath out of me. I'm your lover, not your patron saint."

Robert had returned to her bed and Cheryl had come back to life. But then *Siren* was launched, and the demanding work of rigging her and fitting her sails had cut into their time together. And when the sea trials began, he had disappeared. Robert and Sean and Beth literally moved aboard *Siren*, sailing her in the day and working all night to improve her performance for the next day's tests. On the few occasions when Cheryl had sailed with them, it had been strictly as a passenger. She had no part in the crew's business, her only function being to keep out of the way.

Then Beth had taken ill with a flu or virus that kept her feeling sick and made her weak. Cheryl had been thrilled when Robert had asked her to sail the last week of trials until Beth was back on her feet. She had been shocked when he asked her to crew for the mixed-couples race where *Siren* would make her debut.

Now she was back. Not as a sailor, but as a person. Robert counted on her and trusted her. Her daughter raced into her arms. Beth handed her the helm of the fastest sloop that Cramm had ever launched.

She glanced at her watch as she fastened it back around her wrist. Nearly noon. *Siren* should be just about at the starting line. She would enjoy the next few days with her daughter and Gretchen. And then she would fly out to Bermuda and be waiting when Robert brought his winner into the harbor.

7 THE STARTING CANNON WAS ONLY A SYMBOL. UNLIKE match racing, when the seconds around the cannon are critical, the boats could cross the line at any time. They were all handicapped according to their length and design. The clock started running on each yacht whenever it crossed, and stopped when it crossed the finish line in Bermuda. Then the appropriate handicap was added or subtracted from the elapsed time, and an event winner was declared. *Siren*, because all her dimensions were compromised for speed, carried a high handicap. She couldn't be satisfied just to beat her more commodious competitors into Hamilton Harbor. She had to beat them in by several hours. In particular, she had to take Vector Yachts' new sixty-foot ketch by almost nine hours in order to beat her in the event.

She was hauled in tight when she crossed the starting line, heading just off the brisk, southeasterly wind that was blowing onshore. As soon as she was away from land, Beth brought her slowly to a northeasterly heading, while Robert eased out the sails. It was a matter of feel to find the point where the relative wind was blowing squarely across the boat, putting her into a high-speed broad reach. But as they zeroed in on it, *Siren* began to fly. Heeling less than the other boats in the fleet, her sails captured and held more air. She began pulling away at an astonishing rate.

Robert was almost giddy when he settled beside Beth at the helm. "I wonder what they're thinking?" he mused, glancing over at the boats they were beginning to leave behind.

"The yacht clubbers can't believe their eyes," Beth said. "The designers see the speed and the straight stance, and they've figured out the design. They know we're shallow draft with a lot of weight down low."

"So they already know that they're beaten."

She nodded as she checked the heading. "They're beaten if the weather holds. The yacht clubbers might want to work on their suntans, but the designers would rather have a hurricane. They're figuring that we're a fair-weather boat."

The weather was important. *Siren* was optimized for flat seas and brisk winds, typical conditions for the spring mixed-couples race to Bermuda. That was exactly why this race had become the deadline for all their design and sea-trial efforts. This wasn't a boat they would want to take across the Atlantic and campaign around Fastnet. Nor one you would want to try to sail around Cape Horn. Sean's computer modeling and tank tests indicated she should perform very nicely in heavy weather and that, even with the tremendous weight at the bottom of the blade keel, she could ride out the worst storm. But her performance edge was in fair weather. The Bermuda race, run in the warm waters of the Gulf Stream, generally enjoyed flat seas and beam winds. At least until you broke out of the prevailing easterly winds and entered the less certain winds that blew across the island.

"Grand Bahama," Beth announced, pointing out over the starboard bow. Robert squinted and could just make out the trace of land. They would be coming up to West End, a long narrow bar that reached out northwesterly from Grand Bahama Island. They could shoot a visual fix and use that to test the satellite navigation system. Once they left Grand Bahama behind, they wouldn't see land until they reached Bermuda.

Their strategy called for them to swing to a more northerly heading, even though that wouldn't point them directly at the finish line. They were riding in the narrow branch of the Gulf Stream that raced through the Florida Strait, adding perhaps four knots an hour to their speed. They wanted to stay in the current until it joined with the major branch of the Stream that was coming up along the eastern side of the Bahamas. Then they would turn back toward their target.

Robert shot his bearings and then went below to plot the position. He then plotted the coordinates sent back by the satellite.

"Right on the mark," he told Beth when he returned topside. "Want to guess what our average speed is since we left Lauderdale?"

"Fast," she said, glancing back at her own wake. "Twelve knots?"

"Fifteen," he told her.

"Jesus!"

"If the weather holds, this race is already over."

"We'll be there in what? Eighty hours?"

He nodded. "That should turn some heads."

He stood behind her, glancing over her shoulder. "I'm glad you're aboard."

"I wanted to sail her," Beth said. "I feel like I've been part of her since she was nothing more than lines on paper."

"You understand why I had to pick Cheryl. . . ."

She nodded. "Yes . . . and she'd do just fine."

"Thanks," Robert said. He reached around her and put a hand on the wheel. "I'll take over."

She eased past him. "I'll bring up some coffee," she said. "Then you and I have to talk."

IT WAS DARK WHEN THE HEADLIGHTS OF GEORGE'S CAR appeared around the wide-open gates of the estate. He parked directly in front of the door, indicating that he wouldn't be staying long, and walked in without ringing the bell. He ignored the living room, which no one ever used, and walked straight into the playroom, where he found Cheryl picking up the debris of Rachael's things. Cheryl was startled to see him.

"Just stopped by to see how Rachael was feeling," he said by way of explanation. He gestured toward the toys. "Looks like she's up and about."

"I thought you were flying to Bermuda," she answered.

"In the morning. I had a few things to take care of at the office."

She tipped her face, looking at him skeptically. "Robert asked you to check up on me, didn't he?"

"No. Of course not. But I'll be calling him on the radio tomorrow, before I take off, and I thought he'd like to hear that everyone's fine."

She brightened immediately. "What time? I could come down to the office with Rachael, and she can tell him herself."

George was nodding before she finished her thought. "Great idea. How about ten-thirty? Then I'll book an afternoon flight."

He clapped his hands nervously. "Well, then. I'll see you in the morning." He almost ran to the front door. Cheryl raced to catch up.

"How are they doing? Did you get a fix on them?"

"No. Sorry. I was in the air when *Siren* would have signaled. But by ten-thirty we'll have the morning position."

She watched from the open door as George scampered into his car and pulled away.

It had taken her a long time to win George Williamson over. He and Robert had become close friends at Brown, and he probably would have resented any woman who barged into their relationship. But it was more than that. His real problem had been one of class. It was all right for Robert and him to date the blue-collar Italian and Portuguese girls who lived close to the water on all sides of Narragansett Bay. Even permissible to use the language of love to lead them over the sand dunes or past the desk at the seaside motel. But you wouldn't want to bring one of them home or, God help us, introduce her to polite society. The only caution was to make damn sure that her father was very old and her brothers were very young. Because nothing delighted the Italian or Portuguese men more than beating up on the blue bloods who came slumming down from the hill.

Robert had met Cheryl at a trendy waterfront bar in Newport, during the racing season. He was already chairman and president of Cramm Yachts, as well as the company's most publicized skipper, credentials that made him one of New England's most eligible bachelors. So when he brought a beautiful, dark-haired woman ten years his junior to an all-night drinking dive, it was easy for George to wink his approval. "Looks like you'll be sleeping aboard tonight," George had whispered to his friend. "No problem!" And then nodding toward a tall girl who was showing a good deal of cleavage, "I'm staying with her."

He had hardly noticed when Robert began seeing the girl regularly, his only comment a wink at Robert and an appreciative nod toward Cheryl. He had been civil when Cheryl joined them for their diving expeditions over ships that had run afoul of the rocky coastline. She had been new to scuba, and George had enjoyed her amazement as she discovered their underwater world. He wasn't even bothered when he was blatantly excluded. Robert began taking the girl sailing, sometimes putting in for the night at Buzzard Island, a small family-owned refuge at the west end of the Elizabeth chain. It was a rocky crag wrapped around a tiny harbor, with a small cottage set at its crest. As far as George knew, Cheryl was the only woman Robert had ever brought there.

"How was your outing?" he would ask Robert with a mischievous grin when he returned to the office. He hoped for whispered descriptions of sexual conquests on the floor in front of the stone fireplace, with explicit descriptions of the young girl's secret assets. He was always taken aback when Robert responded, "Very nice," or "Great sailing weather." Robert was keeping Cheryl all to himself.

But then he had begun bringing her into their circle of friends, introducing her to young women who had designs of their own on him, and to their acquisitive parents.

"What could he possibly see in her?" George was asked over and over. He was surprised at the density of the question. It was pretty obvious to him what Robert would see in Cheryl, and it should be obvious to anyone who opened their eyes. She was stunningly beautiful, physically spirited, and completely unimpressed with her own assets. Even from a distance, he could guess that a night in bed with Cheryl would be well worth a good beating by her father and brothers, and more memorable than a lifetime of evenings with any of the better-bred young women who were asking the question.

George was stunned by his own density when the truth finally dawned on him. Robert wasn't trifling with Cheryl, he was in love with her. She wasn't simply a good night in bed, but was the center of his life. Robert was spending every free minute with her, sailing, picnicking, skiing, and in dozens of other courting activities that weren't focused on the bedroom. George had suddenly realized that Cheryl was a serious rival to his position as Robert's closest confidant.

He had tried everything to undermine the relationship. Reminders of the risks to the business in bringing in a partner with no means of her own. Hints that some of their friends were aghast to find him in such an unexpected relationship. Then a memo that the banks had expressed some misgivings about his leadership. He had even neglected to pass on social invitations, leaving Robert to think that he and Cheryl had not been invited. But no matter how thoughtful the advice or obvious the slight, Robert had seemed totally unfazed. It was as if he and Cheryl shared some secret that made everything else irrelevant.

Failing with his friend, George had tried to discourage Cheryl. More than once he had arranged at the very last minute for Robert to take a sailing trip with a dealer, and booked other women aboard who were "knowledgeable about the business." At times, when her phone call was expected, he had left word that Robert couldn't be reached, even though he knew his friend would have welcomed the interruption.

Robert had never even hinted to her that anyone was cool to their relationship or hesitant about welcoming her into their company. But Cheryl had been well aware that Robert had two lives, and that only one of them involved her.

"You don't like me, do you, George?" she had said quite plainly during a casual luncheon when Robert was away from the table.

He had blown bubbles into his Chablis. "What makes you think . . . ? Why in hell would you ask . . . ?"

"You always have an agenda for Robert that doesn't include me. And you seem so disappointed when he chooses to stay with me."

"That's ridiculous!" He had tossed his napkin on the table. "Robert and I are business associates. I suppose I may seem 'unfriendly' when I have to remind him . . . that the business needs him."

"And what does he need?"

George had stood and pushed back his chair. "I don't know. I'll have to ask him." He had stormed out, and she hadn't seen him again for several weeks. He seemed to make a point of not joining his friend whenever Cheryl was involved.

Then Robert had announced their engagement, setting the wedding date at the same time. Local society was stunned and openly questioned the wisdom of his choice. The expected good wishes and social invitations were slow in coming, and Cheryl had wondered if perhaps Robert was paying too high a price. To her surprise, George had suddenly emerged as her staunchest supporter.

"Screw them!" he had told Cheryl and Robert. "They're like Great Danes. They've been intermarrying for so long that the brains have been bred right out of them." In private, he had advised Cheryl that she was exactly what the Cramm family needed. "You're a breath of fresh air," he told her. He had agreed enthusiastically when Robert asked him to be his best man.

They had been married at a small ceremony in her family's church, attended by her family and just a few of his friends. Robert had never reached out to the families who had disapproved of Cheryl, nor did he accept the invitations they offered almost as apologies. Instead, he had thrown himself into his work, gathering his wife and his friend close to him.

But Cheryl had never been certain whether Williamson had really grown fond of her, or if he had simply realized that Robert was cutting his ties with those who would not accept his wife. Was he really her friend? Or was he simply tolerating her in order to remain in the comfortable world of Cramm Yachts?

NORTH OF GRAND BAHAMA ISLAND, *SIREN* WAS beginning to kick up a salty spray. The winds, wrapping around an unexpected low, had moved to the northeast, putting the course of the race into the wind. The day's flat seas had swollen into four-foot waves with wisps of white water at their peaks. The yacht's bow, which had been carving effortlessly, was now plunging, digging into the base of each wave and then blasting out the top with an explosion of foam. She was still carrying very little heel, considering that she was beating into a strong breeze, and was still moving crisply. But her speed was down, and her crew was beginning to worry that some of the longer, deeper boats might be gaining on them.

Robert was at the helm, although his hands weren't on the wheel. He had set the steering mechanism, which used a wind vane to move the rudder. Whenever the boat began wandering off course, the change in the direction of the wind across the deck would move the vane. That, in turn, moved the rudder, bringing the boat back on course.

Sean's hastily rigged system for controlling the backstay had already proved its value. As soon as the wind had moved to the bow, the big genoa sail had lost its shape. By taking the slack out of the backstay, Robert had effectively moved the mast back and put the power back into the sail.

The night was crystal clear, with stars so bright that there was light in the sky and pinpoints of light on the water. But none of the other boats were in sight. Because of their early speed, *Siren* was far ahead of the fleet—too far for Robert to expect to see the running lights behind him. Besides, he was north of the course line that all the other yachts were probably following.

Beth suddenly appeared at the cabin hatch and came up into the cockpit, resting her hand on the boom vang.

"Trouble sleeping?" Robert asked.

She nodded. "This isn't the best foul-weather boat I've ever been on. We're doing a lot of pitching."

"It's not completely killing our speed," Robert allowed.

"Well, it's completely killing me. I'm sick as a dog."

He grinned. "Seasick? You?"

"Yeah. Especially in the closed cabin."

"Maybe it's morning sickness," he teased.

"I doubt it," Beth answered. "Not in the middle of the night."

"You said we had to talk."

She nodded. "It will have to wait," she answered, and then she darted to the downwind side and hung her head out under the lifeline.

10 CHERYL LIFTED RACHAEL OUT OF THE CAR SEAT IN front of the Cramm Yachts office, and held her hand as the child labored up the steps. George Williamson rushed across the lobby to greet them.

"Wait until you see his position. He's running away from the whole fleet." He led her into his office, where Robert's secretary was putting pins into a mounted chart.

"These are sunrise positions for all the boats," the secretary explained, backing away from the chart. Cheryl could see a cluster of colored pins north of Grand Bahama. There were two stragglers, just emerging from the Florida Strait, and then a white pin far to the north, a good thirty miles ahead of its nearest competitor.

George pushed around the desk and touched the white pin. "That's

Siren at six twenty-one this morning." He traced her course backwards, adjusting his glasses so that he could read the fine notations. "Here she was at sunset last night."

Cheryl studied the chart while she struggled to keep Rachael from stripping Williamson's desk. She knew that all the boats were navigating off the satellites and were rigged to signal their positions when they turned their navigation lights on at sunset and off at sunrise. Right now, the executives of each of the yacht companies were gathered around a chart that looked exactly like this. They already knew that Cramm Yachts was reclaiming its long-time reputation for performance.

"She seems to have slowed a bit," she observed. "She was faster the first twelve hours than over the last six. Winds die down?"

George shook his head. "No, but they've swung to the northeast. And the seas are up a foot or two."

Cheryl was suddenly concerned. The wind change wouldn't bother *Siren*. The boat could point high, as she'd seen for herself. But they were all worried about rough seas. Sean's design had cheated on stability and emphasized flat-water speed. If it got rough enough, some of the more traditional keel boats would start to catch up.

George noticed her expression. "It's no problem, really. There's a low moving past them. They should be back into southerlies by sunset."

He was right. There was no problem. In light swells, *Siren* was still probably the fastest boat in the race. Even if it were to get a bit rougher, the most she would give back would be half a knot an hour. And then, when the wind moved back to the south and flattened the Gulf Stream, she'd start pulling away again.

"Can we talk to him?" she asked.

"Of course." The secretary smiled. "We were just waiting for you to arrive. She led a procession out of Robert's office and into a room that housed their radio gear. There was high-frequency equipment for talking to boats that were running sea trials right out in the harbor. Then there was short-wave gear that would reach halfway around the world. George flipped on the short wave, which was pretuned to the company frequency. "*Siren . . . Siren*," he intoned. "Do you read me?"

Robert's voice answered immediately. "This is *Siren*," he said as casually as if he were answering a telephone.

"*Siren* indeed," Cheryl responded.

"Cheryl!" She could hear the laughter in his voice.

"I have someone here who caused us both a night of needless worry. She wants to say hello to you." She lifted Rachael onto the desk and sat her in front of the microphone.

"Hello, Daddy." She reached out for the lighted buttons and Cheryl had to pull her hand away.

"Hi, darling. Will you sing a song for me?"

The little girl looked blankly at her mother. Her fingers plunged into her mouth. Cheryl pulled her hand away. "You know Daddy's favorite song. Will you sing it for him?"

Rachael looked from George to the secretary and then back to her mother. She shook her head.

"A shy moment," Cheryl explained in the direction of the microphone.

Robert's voice suddenly sang into the room. "Oh, the buzzing of the bees . . . in the lollipop trees . . ."

Rachael smiled.

"You sing it for Daddy," her mother urged. Rachael looked suspiciously back at the radio.

"The soda water fountain . . ." Robert sang on, and then he paused to give the little girl an opening. "Oh, the lemonade springs where the bluebird sings . . ."

Rachael laughed, and then joined in, singing in a small voice, "In the Big Rock Candy Mountain."

The room burst into applause with Robert's laughter joining from the speaker.

"I guess she's not terribly sick," he said.

"Not at all," Cheryl answered. And then, as she lifted Rachael from the desk and handed her to the secretary, "And how's her daddy?"

"Okay. How are we doing?"

"Just great," George said. "We put your nearest competitor about thirty miles back. You keep going this way, you could be in twenty hours ahead of everyone else."

"I don't think so," Robert said. "We're plowing through the bigger swells. I figure we're down to about eight knots. We're probably giving back some time."

"You've got plenty to spend," Cheryl chimed in. "And George says you'll be back into southerlies sometime in the afternoon or early evening."

"That's good. The sooner the better. Because when this thing gets on a broad reach in flat seas, she's absolutely unbelievable."

"How's Beth doing?" Cheryl asked.

"Hanging in there. She's a real trooper." His tone sounded guarded.

"Is she okay?" Cheryl asked, her concern obvious.

"Embarrassed, I guess," Robert answered. "Got a bit seasick as soon as we started pitching. I guess she's been ashore too long. I'll be single-handing it for a while."

"She's below?" George was surprised.

"No, but she's stretched out in the cockpit, and looking kind of green. I don't think she'll be much help until she gets her sea legs. So I think I'll cut this chat short."

"We won't bother you," George promised. "But if you call after sunset, Sean will give you an update. He'll be here all day. I'm flying out tonight—"

"And I'll probably be coming tomorrow," Cheryl interrupted.

They said their good-byes and hung up.

"She must be damn sick," Cheryl said to George.

He nodded gravely. "An experienced sailor. She knows she has to keep herself going. I can't believe she'd be flat out."

"I'm sure she's standing by if she's needed."

George shook his head slowly. "We'll see how they're doing tonight," he said, sounding as if he expected the worst.

11 PHILIP MCKNIGHT LANDED IN BERMUDA A FEW minutes after noon, and a waiting car whisked him from St. George to his hotel in Hamilton. The day was bright, with cooling breezes from the northwest. The island's spring flowers were in glorious bloom.

He had taken off from the Ft. Lauderdale airport after he had seen the morning standings in the race, so he knew what everyone else in the yachting world knew. Cramm Yachts had come up with a lightning-fast sloop that would put its name in the headlines of all the industry publications. By the curious chemistry that makes a yacht builder's name a valid currency among the yacht club set, Cramm's sales were sure to take off. And that, of course, would greatly increase the value of the company.

It was no secret that McKnight was interested in buying Cramm. More than a year earlier, he had presented Robert with a leather-bound folder tooled with a new logo for Cramm Vector Yachts. Inside was a detailed proposal of a planned merger that was really a takeover. Vector would acquire enough of the Cramm family stock to have a controlling interest. Robert would become a vice president for product development, which meant he could put all his time into designing and sailing new yachts, a position he would certainly enjoy more than running a business. George Williamson would become McKnight's executive vice president and would run the day-to-day operations of the new company.

The scheme had been well thought through, with benefits to all the important players. Cramm would monetize his stock at far more than its present value, and would have a free hand not only to pursue his real interest in sailing, but also to devote more time to his sick wife. Williamson would have a free hand in running a much larger operation. He wouldn't be hemmed in by Robert's concerns for tradition, nor be forced to sacrifice the lucrative luxury yacht sector of the business in order to meet the Cramm imperative for seaworthiness. And McKnight would own one of the great names in shipbuilding, putting himself among the royalty of the yachting trade.

George had suggested opening discussions. He was very confident that McKnight could raise his price substantially. "Let's see just how far the bastard will go to satisfy his ego," he had teased Robert. Robert had rejected the idea out of hand. The Cramm name, he insisted, was not for sale, and never would be. Instead, he planned to rekindle its magic by campaigning a winner.

But George had not cut Philip McKnight off at the knees. Instead, he had held out the possibility that a deal similar to the proposal on the table might be better received at a later time. "We're all distracted by Cheryl's tragedy," he had explained at a secret meeting with Philip.

"Business is the last thing Robert is thinking about right now. Perhaps in six months, or a year . . ."

McKnight had been sympathetic with Robert's problems, but unyielding when it came to business. "Don't wait too long," he had cautioned. "Cramm hasn't had a winner for a couple of years, either at sea or in the market. In a year, I may be able to pick the company up from the banks for a lot less money and with far fewer headaches."

His eye had twinkled as if he were joking, and they had both joined in a friendly laugh. But if Philip's smile was genuine, George's was forced. McKnight was closer to the truth than even he could possibly know.

Philip took a tall gin and tonic out onto the balcony of the penthouse suite while the hotel maid was unpacking his things. In a few days, all the yachts he watched sail from Ft. Lauderdale would be moored in the magnificent harbor below. The owners and the crews would be gathered on the docks, toasting one another's success: "Congratulations! Well done!" and all the other niceties of a rich man's sport.

Of course, no one would mean it. Racing skippers had bigger egos than symphony conductors. They would all loathe one another's success and harbor suspicions that their victorious opponents must have cheated. Even while they were hoisting their drinks they probably would have divers checking out the bottoms of other boats for possible rule violations.

The owners, too, would go through all the niceties, smiling generously as they presented loving cups to one another. But they all would be on the line with their accountants trying to analyze what their finish in the race might mean to sales.

McKnight expected to do quite well. The two Vector boats would post very good times for their classes. On adjusted time they would probably be in the top ten overall and either first or second against their direct competitors. But a big victory for Cramm would greatly complicate McKnight's plans for taking over the company. It would certainly raise the price.

Even though Cramm's performance had continued to disappoint the industry, Philip had never lowered the per-share number of his original offer. It wasn't altruism, but simply the realization that holding his price for the company as it grew weaker was no different from raising his price if the company had held steady. And, as George had suspected, he had been ready from the very beginning to take his bid higher. But more important, he had no desire to publicize Cramm Yachts' failures. He fully intended to own the company, and he wanted to be seen as buying up rather than down. He wanted to capture a prize, not claim a financial derelict.

When his people had clocked *Siren* during her sea trials, and when his spies had reported on her design, Philip knew that Cramm was slipping out of his grasp. He had decided that he couldn't allow that to happen. And now that *Siren* was flaunting her speed, he knew he had to move quickly.

McKnight stepped back inside the suite and dialed the hotel desk. "Is George Williamson arriving today?"

He listened to the clicking sound of a computer keyboard. "Yes, he is," the clerk responded. "Our car is picking him up at the airport at six."

"When he arrives, would you ask him to be so kind as to give me a call?"

"I certainly will, Mr. McKnight."

Philip was about to hang up when he had another thought. "Connect me with room service," he asked. "I'd like to order up a supper for two."

12   GRETCHEN JOGGED EASILY DOWN THE HILL TOWARD the water, pulling back on the handle of the three-wheeled carriage in which Rachael was riding. The little girl was nearly immobile, wrapped in a light blanket and strapped in securely, but her eyes were dancing. She loved the fast rides that were part of Gretchen's daily run. Her face turned constantly to follow each of the passing sights, and her voice sang out the names of everything she saw. "The gates!" she yelled as they passed through the estate entrance and out onto the public road, and then "Boats!" as soon as the harbor came into view.

"What kind of boats?" Gretchen asked, her voice as effortless as her stride.

"Sailboats!" Rachael shouted in a happy response.

"That's right. Sailboats. And where are the boats going?"

"To the ocean."

The dialogue never stopped. For the past year, Gretchen had turned every waking minute into a learning experience, and her success was obvious. Rachael had been silently shy when Cheryl's nurse had turned her over to the new au pair. Now she was noisy and outgoing, fully aware of all that she could do and eager to show off. Gretchen's formula was simple: constant conversation no matter what they were doing, and endless praise for the little girl's achievements. Her reward was that she saw herself in Rachael's eyes.

Rachael's gestures were like Gretchen's. When she was angry, she folded her arms and put one foot out, exactly as the hired girl did. When she read, she tossed her head from time to time, throwing imaginary hair out of her eyes. Her voice had none of New England, neither the accents of her mother's immigrant heritage nor the nasal twang that typified her father's Narragansett inflections. Instead, there was the good bass timber of well-spoken Danish. Rachael knew the Danish words for half her toys.

But Gretchen also owned a debt to Rachael. She had been an outsider when she arrived from Denmark, and had suffered embarrassingly from homesickness. "I've traveled," she had explained to Robert, listing all the European and Middle Eastern countries that were part of every European education. "I'm used to being away."

"I'm not a child," she had confessed to Cheryl, implying not just that she was nearly Cheryl's contemporary, but that she had fully experienced both joy and disappointment and had handled them well. They had tried to make her comfortable, but she had remained a visitor in their lives until Rachael had accepted her. The little girl knew nothing of bloodlines and countries, but only the joy of companionship. She couldn't know that Robert and Cheryl loved her more, but could easily understand that Gretchen gave her more attention. When she woke up frightened in the middle of the night, it was Gretchen she looked for. It was the little girl's embrace that made Gretchen part of the family, and then she had become more than "part." She had moved to the center of the family because she spoke for the child who was the center of the family.

"Light!" Rachael called as they turned the point south of the harbor. "What kind of light?"

"Lighthouse."

"That's right, smarty, a lighthouse."

Gretchen was still running easily despite the dark line that was soaking through the back of her sweatshirt. Even though the sun was well down in the west, the spring air was still hot. "And what's the light doing?"

"Blinking," the little girl answered. Gretchen laughed out loud.

My little girl, she thought without any embarrassment because Rachael was even closer to her than to Cheryl. Cheryl had said it herself: "I think she'd rather that I went away than you. You'll have to come back to visit her. I don't mean 'visit.' Because it will really be a homecoming."

She thought of the estate as her home. She had left her parents' small apartment nearly ten years ago and had lived in a succession of dormitories and rooming houses while she went through schools. The Cramm home was the first house she had ever had the run of, and the only house that had its own lawns and gardens. She couldn't bear the thought of leaving it.

And then there was Robert. He had never thought of her as the "hired girl." At least he had never acted that way. She could remember how confused he had been trying to establish the proper relationship. He couldn't treat her as a daughter. His daughter was only a toddler. Nor was she a guest. He wasn't trying to make her comfortable, but was counting on her to make his family comfortable. And certainly not as a wife, even though she ran his household and took care of his child. His wife was there, right beside her. He had decided that she was Cheryl's closest friend and had tried to find just the right combination of familiarity and deference. But by the time he had decided, it was already too late. Gretchen had fallen in love with his strength and gentleness, and then with Robert himself. And by the time she realized that she was in love with him, it was no longer unthinkable that they would someday be together. She recognized the wall of doubt that he had thrown up between himself and his wife. She saw him beginning to lean on Beth as he built his boat. And to lean on her when he returned home. She wouldn't be taking him from Cheryl. She would be winning him from Beth.

Gretchen had no intention of leaving, nor did Robert want to let her go. They had already spoken about it. Her visa as an au pair was running out, but if he found another kind of work for her she could stay on. There were many jobs in his company that she could learn. And if she was working in the company, then she would be close to the house and available whenever she was needed.

Robert hadn't said yes, only that it would probably depend on Cheryl's needs. But Gretchen felt certain that it would depend more on Robert's needs. And she knew that he needed her as much as she needed him. She couldn't lose him to Beth. Nor could she let Cheryl come between them.

13 GEORGE WILLIAMSON CALLED PHILIP MCKNIGHT AS soon as the bellboy closed the door behind him. Casual, he reminded himself. Never appear anxious. Not even very interested. The phone was on its fifth ring before McKnight answered.

"Just got in," George said. "No problems with the race, I hope."

"No. Everything seems to be going splendidly. Particularly for you. My people tell me *Siren* is all by herself."

Keep it casual, George thought again. "Glad to hear it. She was doing nicely this morning. As were a couple of your boats. We both have reason to celebrate."

"Exactly what I was thinking," Philip laughed. "I have a well-stocked bar, and I'm ordering up dinner. Why don't you come up and join me?"

As he stepped into the shower, George tried to rehearse the meeting. A couple of drinks. Some casual chitchat while the waiter was setting the table. A few words of praise for the hotel's kitchen during their appetizers. Then McKnight would get down to business. He wanted Cramm Yachts. Based on the speed that *Siren* was posting, he would figure that the value of the company was on the upswing. If he was going to make a deal, it would have to be now. So he'd quote a price. A damn good price. Seventy million, George guessed as he toweled himself off. The Cramm account would clear nearly forty million. George would put twelve million in his own pocket. The rest would be scattered among George's useless cousins, and several private charities that the family supported.

Or was he dreaming? The original offer had been sixty million for a company that probably wasn't worth any more than fifty, and had fallen to half that since the original offer. Maybe it would be a more modest sweetener. Sixty-five million would be more than generous no matter what kind of time *Siren* was sailing. But he could probably argue for seventy-five, and then settle for seventy, with a few additional perks for himself. Seventy! Sixty! What in hell difference did it make? At any number, the problems of Cramm Yachts were over.

Philip turned the conversation to business exactly on cue, just as George was slipping the edge of his fork into the Dover sole.

"We should be working together," he said wishfully, completing his thoughts on how alike their tastes in wine and food were. "You know I'm still interested in Cramm Yachts."

George forced a smile. "I thought you might be interested in more than just a dinner companion."

Philip set down his fork. "The two companies are a perfect fit. I can see Cramm being the performance division, winning all the offshore races and building boats that sell at an obscene premium. And then Vector would clean up in the under market. Everyone would want to own a Cramm Vector, even people who have no intention of ever leaving the dock."

George signaled his seriousness by setting down his own fork. "I won't lie to you. The idea has tremendous appeal to me as well. But it's tough to get inside Robert's head. I really don't know whether he has any interest at all. I know that his pride would never let him sacrifice the company in a fire sale—"

"That's why this is the perfect moment," McKnight interrupted. "He's designed a winner and he's sailing her to victory. He's added value to the family name, and I'm willing to pay for that value. He gets the money, the acknowledgment of his peers, and has the rest of his life to take care of his beautiful wife and daughter. Plus, he can have carte blanche to design and build anything he wants for the new company. *Siren* has turned everything around. There will never be a better moment."

George swirled the wine in his glass. Casual, he reminded himself.

"You're probably right. I have no doubt that it would be in Robert's best interest. But he's my best friend. I couldn't force anything on him that he didn't believe in." He tasted the wine with a conspicuous inhale of air and let the two mix on his palate. "I suppose it would depend on you coming up with a number that he felt was clearly flattering to the Cramm tradition. The problem is, I have no idea of what that number would be."

McKnight blotted his lips as he pushed his chair back. "I'm not sure what the goddam number is either," he said while he crossed the room and retrieved an envelope from the desk. He set the envelope next to George's plate. "That's my best guess."

George tried not to look at the envelope. "Is that a revised offer?" he asked when Philip had pulled himself back up to the table.

McKnight nodded. "My financial people think I'm crazy. But that should be an adequate number unless Robert is even crazier."

"Should we be talking about this before the race is decided?" George wondered.

"We can talk about it whenever you're ready. There are just two points to keep in mind. One, this is a firm offer no matter how the race comes out. And two, I'll need an answer in a few weeks."

"A few weeks?" Crumbs of food fell from George's open mouth.

"It has to be that way," McKnight said. "As you've probably heard, I'm looking at buying a different company. Another one of the contenders whose boat is doing quite nicely in the race. I have to give my answer in thirty days. I'd prefer Cramm Yachts, and the figure in that envelope will indicate just how strong my preference is. But it's one or the other, so I'll have to press you for an answer. I don't want to lose both companies."

George nodded sagely, a serious expression covering his confusion. He hadn't heard a word about Vector talking with one of the other companies. Was this just a ploy, or was McKnight ready to abandon Cramm? And if he was going with another company, which one was it? He tried to remember the order of the boats that he had seen that morning. North Star's boat was right up with the leaders, but North Star was part of a conglomerate. Could they possibly be spinning it off? And at what price? Or maybe it was the Italian outfit, CGI. They had one of the biggest boats in the race. Maybe Philip was thinking of an international merger.

"I realize that a deadline is apt to make Robert angry, so I even put something in the offer to smooth his feathers," McKnight added. He seemed sincere when he said, "Sorry, but it just can't be helped."

George went back to his fish. He hoped that his host didn't notice that his fork was shaking. It took all his effort to keep his fingers from tearing open the envelope.

He slid it nonchalantly into his shirt pocket when he set down his brandy glass. "I'll bring this to Robert as soon he docks. One way or the other, I'll get an answer to you." He and McKnight were all smiles as they said good night at the elevator.

The envelope contained a copy of the original offer to establish a new company called Cramm Vector Yachts. All George had to read were the amendments that were written into the margins, each initialed in Philip's elaborate hand. He turned quickly to the financial transaction. The figure of sixty million dollars was crossed out. In the margin, McKnight had written a hundred million.

Williamson sagged into the sofa, his eyes locked onto a figure that represented an incredible windfall. It was an opportunity he couldn't afford to miss.

14 SEAN PATTON ARRIVED AT CRAMM YACHTS WHILE the morning sun was still dancing on the eastern horizon, and let himself into the empty offices. He threw his windbreaker across the back of a chair that was already buried in books, and walked straight to the communications room. He snatched up the computer printouts of the sunrise positions that had just been recorded, and scanned them on his way to George's office, where he would enter them on the chart. The pins recorded the previous evening's sunset positions and showed that *Siren* was once again opening her lead. The previous day's rough weather had slowed her down and kept her competitors in the race. But when the wind had moved back into the south, she had lifted her bow just as

his model had done in the tank. The morning position, Sean guessed, would show an insurmountable lead.

He stopped abruptly in the middle of the secretarial area and studied the printout. There was no report from *Siren*. Somehow, when she had turned her lights off at sunrise, the equipment had failed to signal her satellite position readings.

Sean smiled as he turned back toward the communications room. Whoever had the night watch had probably set the steering vane and dozed off. He guessed that the helmsman had slept through sunrise and forgotten to turn off the lights. Careless, he thought, but then with the kind of lead *Siren* had built up, it was probably natural to relax.

He glanced around in case he had dropped the report on the desk, and then keyed the computer, hoping that it might have come in while he was walking to George's office. When he couldn't find it, he picked up the radio and keyed the company frequency. "*Siren . . . Siren*," he called, "this is the sunrise. It's time to wake up!"

He expected to hear a groggy voice trying to cover up for the gaff. Instead, he heard only the air return on the open circuit.

"*Siren . . . Siren . . .* this is Home Base. . . . Over. . . ."

There was the crackling sound, but no response from the boat.

"*Siren . . . Siren . . .*" he tried again, his tone now more impatient than apprehensive. He released the transmit key and listened to the rush of static. "C'mon, you guys," he whispered to himself. "Get off your asses and answer the damn thing."

For the next fifteen minutes he alternated between the company frequency and the international emergency frequency, trying to hold down the bubble of panic that was pushing up from his gut. He was still in the communications room when the staff began to arrive.

"Problem?" George's secretary asked as she brought in a cup of coffee.

"Can't raise them," Sean said. "And they didn't send a sunrise position."

A look of fright crossed the woman's face.

"Probably just a power failure," he said in a reassuring voice. "Looks like they drained their batteries. Maybe a short in the running lights."

He followed her back out to her desk and tried to sound casual when he asked for a phone number where George could be reached. And he kept a calm voice when George came on the line.

"*Siren* didn't signal a position this morning," he told Williamson. "And I can't raise her on the radio. Have you heard from her?"

He heard George gasp. "What do you think?" he asked.

"I'm hoping it's just a power failure," Sean said. "But if there's a problem, we shouldn't be wasting time. I ought to contact the Coast Guard, and the Brits in Grand Bahama."

There was a long pause. Then George's voice answered, "Let's give it a few hours before we press the panic button."

"Okay," Sean agreed. "I'll keep calling."

THE BERMUDA TRIANGLE

15

"SIREN . . . SIREN . . . THIS IS HOME BASE. . . . DO YOU READ me?"

Sean listened carefully for any hint of a voice coming through the air noise. But by now he didn't expect one. He had been listening on the company channel for over four hours and had called on the international radio frequency every fifteen minutes. He had pretty much decided that the next time anyone would hear from *Siren* would be when Robert and Beth brought her into Hamilton Harbor.

He glanced at his watch. He had told Cheryl that the boat hadn't reported when she had called in the morning. "Probably some kind of short that drained the batteries," he had said, hiding all hint of concern. "I'll keep you posted." At the time, he had been pretty certain that he would be calling her back with good wishes from her husband, and with news of *Siren*'s widening lead. Now, as he lifted the telephone, he wondered if he could still sound nonchalant.

"Hi," he said when Cheryl came on the line. "Sorry to disappoint you, but their radios are still down. I can't raise them."

"Shouldn't take nearly this long to recharge the batteries," Cheryl fired back, putting words to his own fears.

"Unless they couldn't get the engine started," he tried, knowing full well that they had put the small diesel auxiliary through hundreds of cold starts during their sea trials using compressed air to turn her over. "Or maybe the short is in the generator. There's lots of possibilities."

"Some that I don't like to think about," she answered quickly.

"No reason to think they're in trouble. Christ, even if the boat sank, the radios would automatically have put out an SOS position. The only problem we know about is her electric power, and Robert sure as hell wouldn't break off a race for that."

"Can he navigate? I don't think Robert has shot a star fix in a couple of years."

"He won't have to do anything that drastic," Sean laughed. "There are handheld satellite receivers onboard that will give him his position. They have their own dry cells." Then he added, "There probably isn't a sailor out there who remembers how to shoot stars."

Cheryl forced herself into a light mood. "I never learned. Robert tried to teach me but I never got the hang of it."

"Me neither," he said. "For my kind of racing we never needed it. If you couldn't see the markers, they called off the race."

They both managed to laugh. Then Cheryl ended the conversation by asking Sean to call her the minute they made contact. He promised that he would, even though it was likely that she would see Robert in Bermuda before he heard from him on the radio.

He patched the company radio frequency out to the speaker at the receptionist's desk, where the young college intern could guard the channel. Then he set his watch to alert him in half an hour, and walked from the communications room back to his office. When he saw his windbreaker tossed across his chair, he realized that he had been on the radios the entire morning. He threw the jacket at the coat hook on the back of his door and swept the books off his chair. Within seconds, he had the bound stack of *Siren*'s plans on his desk.

He opened to the drawings of the hull, and the thin keel that stuck like a dagger through the bottom of the boat, connecting to the huge, torpedo-shaped weight. Even to a layman, the design seemed impossible. The boat's hull would be heeled on the water's surface, driven down by the force of the wind in her sails. Below the water, the ballast at the bottom of the keel would be pulling down, trying to bring the yacht back to upright. As *Siren* rolled through the seas, the opposing forces would constantly be bending the keel back and forth, like bending an old credit card over and over in order to tear it in half. It seemed inevitable that the keel would tear off the boat, and that *Siren*, suddenly without her counterweight, would turn turtle instantly.

That had been George Williamson's thought when he had first seen Sean's sketches. It had been laughingly obvious to the professors at Hoboken when they had first seen the scale model. And the yard crew at Cramm hadn't been able to believe their own work when the construction cradle was raised to make room for the oversized keel.

"What makes you think you can keep it together?" Robert had asked when Sean first proposed the idea. He was well aware of an offshore racer with a similar design that had been found floating upside down, its long, thin keel snapped off at the hull.

"This," Sean had answered, unfolding a photograph of Boeing's huge new 777 airliner. "The wing is five times longer, relative to the diameter of the body. And the engine hanging on the wing weighs about twice as much as the boat's keel weight." He had paused while Robert took in the picture of the airplane, then added, "Boeing figures that the wing won't break off."

"But it's an airfoil," Robert had reminded him. "It generates its own lifting force to support the weight of the engines."

"It flexes twelve feet under the stress of air turbulence," Sean had countered, "and it loses all its lift twenty feet before the plane touches down. Each time it lands it supports the weight and descent speed of the plane. And Boeing still has a billion computer runs to prove that it won't break off."

Robert had smiled. "A boat like that would be unbeatable . . . if you could find anyone crazy enough to take her to sea."

Sean had taken back his photo of the 777. "This thing carries four hundred passengers. A couple of them must be sane." He had stuffed the picture in his shirt pocket and begun rolling up his sketches.

"Not so fast," Robert had said. He had eased the sketches out of Sean's fingers and spread them back out on the table. "Let's say the keel doesn't break. What holds it to the bottom of the hull?"

"Think of it as one structure. The ribs of the hull turn down into the keel and run right down to the counterweight. The hull is just an expansion at the top of the keel."

Robert had continued studying the lines. "What would you use? Aluminum?"

"Probably synthetics with embedded fibers. At least for the ribs and the keel struts. But I'm not sure. Nothing like this has been tried before."

"What will it cost to prove it out with computer modeling?"

Sean had shrugged. "Like I said, nobody's done this before. Maybe a couple of hundred thousand. There's really no way to know until you get into it."

Robert had left him sitting outside of George Williamson's office, and Sean had heard Williamson bellowing his concerns. The issue had seemed to be decided when George pronounced himself "dead set against working with Sean Patton," so it had come as a startling surprise when Robert stepped out of the office and asked, "When can we get started?"

As he studied the plans, Sean had no doubts about the seaworthiness of *Siren*. The moderate winds that were blowing over the race course and the modest seas they were churning up posed no threat to the boat. And now, with the wind back out of the southeast, she was probably back up to speed, pulling away from the fleet on her way into Bermuda.

But then why had Robert gone silent? Sean's best guess of a power failure had become less and less likely with each passing hour. Robert would have no problem changing the generator if it had shorted out, and he would certainly be able to get the diesel started. If he had lost power before sunrise, he would have it back by now.

And it probably wasn't a promotional ploy. Sean had considered that a builder might go off the air in order to create suspense about his whereabouts. Get the whole world looking for him, and then miraculously appear at the finish line in record time. But Robert wasn't big on gimmicks. And he would be the last one to do anything that might cause Cheryl anguish.

Unless she's in on it, he suddenly thought. Maybe that was why she pulled out of the race. He knew that little Rachael had been singing over the radio the day after she was supposed to be deathly sick. Maybe that had been a stunt to get Cheryl off the boat so that she could play the worried wife when *Siren* disappeared. And if that were the case, then

George Williamson would be in on it. They certainly couldn't keep him in the dark if he had to play Cheryl's comforting companion when she got to Bermuda.

Sean reached for his telephone.

16 In Bermuda, there was little concern over *Siren*'s disappearance. George had been informed early in the morning that the yacht had not reported a sunrise position. He agreed with the other builders that she must have had a power failure, and then Cheryl had supported his assumption when he had called her midmorning. He had repeated Cheryl's confident assurances whenever he was questioned, and the advanced parties in Bermuda had taken it as fact. Cramm's boat had suffered an electrical short and drained her batteries. She would be back on the air shortly.

But by late morning, patience was wearing thin. Representatives of the other contenders were demanding to know *Siren*'s position. The race rules required that each boat signal its satellite position at sunrise and sunset. No matter how big Robert's lead, they grumbled, he had no right to assume that he was the only boat in the race.

George had been on his way to lunch with a major Caribbean yacht broker when the president of North Star had grabbed his sleeve. "Where the hell is she, George? This really isn't fair. The other boats have a right to know."

"She hasn't posted a position yet?" George had responded, looking completely flabbergasted.

"You know damn well she hasn't. Just what are you trying to pull off?"

George had turned back to the hotel elevators and pushed the button for his floor. He was opening the door to his suite when the telephone rang.

"George Williamson," he answered.

"This is Sean. What the fuck is going on?"

Williamson swallowed hard. "I was just about to call you. That's what people here are asking. Cheryl told me it was just a power failure."

"That's what *I* told *her*," Patton shot back. "But that excuse ran out an hour ago. I'm going to start worrying unless you know that Robert's up to something."

"What in hell would he be up to?" Williamson suddenly sounded angry.

"I don't know," Sean said. "Maybe a dash into Hamilton hours before anyone expects him to arrive. Or maybe he's going for a new record to England."

"Don't be an ass, Sean. Robert would never resort to that kind of nonsense. He's obviously having a problem."

"Then maybe we ought to be talking to the Coast Guard. Or to British Air-Sea Rescue."

George paused before he answered. "We better wait," he decided. "If we send the Coast Guard on a wild-goose chase, it will really look like a publicity stunt. We ought to give it a few more hours."

"A few hours is eternity," Sean responded, "if you're floating in a life jacket with a shark doing lazy eights around you."

"Jesus, you're not suggesting that the boat . . . is gone. . . ."

"No. But I can't believe that it's just a dead battery. Not for eight hours."

There was a long pause. "What's your best guess?" George finally asked.

"Well, she could have lost her mast. Robert would cut the rigging away before he thought about stringing a new antenna."

"And he would probably be motoring to the nearest land," George added eagerly. "So, whether it's just a power failure or something more serious, they're probably not in any real danger . . . unless . . ."

"Unless what?" There was an edge to Sean's voice.

George sighed. "Unless your keel failed. That would explain—"

"The keel wouldn't fail," Sean answered. "We've been through that every day for the past year."

"You're certain," Williamson demanded.

Now Sean sighed. "I'm certain."

"Okay," George agreed. "Then let's assume that whatever happened, they're in no great danger. And let's give them another couple of hours.

We'll look like fools if we stir up a panic and then *Siren* sends in a sunset position."

"It's your call," Sean concluded reluctantly. "But a couple of hours is really until tomorrow. If we don't start them looking now, it will be dark before they can get a plane over the area. They won't begin looking until sunrise."

"It shouldn't matter," George snapped back, "unless your synthetic hull came apart. And if you're so damn certain—"

"I'm certain," Sean said. But his voice was beginning to lose its confidence. "I'm certain. . . ."

17 CHERYL WAS ABOUT TO LEAVE FOR THE AIRPORT when Sean's call came. He sounded ridiculously casual as he suggested that she might want to wait until the next morning.

"What's wrong?" she demanded.

She listened patiently as he speculated about possible problems with a generator, and explored the unlikely situation that *Siren* might have lost her mast or her rigging. "It's probably best to wait for a sunset position," Sean concluded. "They might be heading back to Grand Bahama or making for the mainland. No sense in you leaving until you're sure where he's going to turn up."

"They might be in trouble. Serious trouble," Cheryl told him.

"Not very likely," he tried to assure her.

She didn't hesitate an instant. "I think we ought to contact the Coast Guard and start a search."

"George is afraid that it might look like we're trying to stir up some news coverage."

"The hell with what it might look like. It's been eighteen hours since we heard from them. What's it going to look like if they're floating in a raft and we're not bothering to look for them?"

Sean didn't answer.

"Sean, do you agree with me or not?"

"I suppose we can't rule out the possibility," he admitted. "I'll call George—"

"I'll call George," Cheryl interrupted. "You call the Coast Guard." There was more authority in her voice than he had ever heard before.

The sun blazed over the western shore, tinting Newport Harbor a crimson stain. Sean squinted out his office window and then glanced down at his watch. The sun had already set out over the Gulf Stream, where the yachts were riding a broad reach as they raced toward Bermuda. They had already signaled their exact positions back to the satellites, and then down to the race headquarters in Ft. Lauderdale. The race officials would be transmitting the positions of all the boats to the computers in all the contestants' offices.

But Sean wouldn't have to wait for the official report. The race officials were well aware that *Siren* hadn't been heard from since the previous night's sunset. He had already told them that he was requesting an air search, and had endured their initial skepticism until he was able to convince them that they might be facing an emergency. They had promised to phone him the instant they had the sunset position reports, and let him know whether *Siren*'s had been received.

He watched the blazing ball of the sun spill out on the horizon and then disappear. The water in the harbor held the pink reflection for several minutes before it began to darken to purple. He stared at the mute telephone. Its silence told him what he had been expecting. The race committee certainly had the reports by now. If they had heard from *Siren* they would have called. The delay told him that they were waiting as long as they decently could before they concluded that the Cramm yacht wasn't going to be posting a position.

When the phone rang, he lifted it with a weary hand. The soft, sympathetic voice explained what he already knew. "We've advised all the boats," the committee representative went on. "Based on her last position, the fleet would already be past *Siren*. But we don't know how far she might have gone before she . . . experienced difficulties. She might be still out ahead of them, and they'll all be keeping a sharp eye. If we still haven't heard by morning, the fleet will turn around and head back over the course."

"Thanks," Sean managed.

"The race doesn't seem all that important," the voice sympathized.

"No," Sean agreed as he cradled the phone. He was wondering if Robert's small radio telephone was picking up the low-powered transmissions among the boats around him. Even if he couldn't get up the power to send a message of his own, at least he would know that help was on the way. That would be reassuring, if *Siren* could hear anything.

He slipped on his windbreaker and walked down to the boatyard where *Siren* had been built and launched. Despite the warmth of the evening, he felt himself trembling with a chill. His gut was trying to tell him what his mind was unable to consider. Somewhere, in the boat design, in the engineering data, in the materials test results, there was an error. The keel didn't hold. The wing had come off his airplane.

Where? he wondered. Where did it break? That was important, the difference between life and death for Robert and Beth.

The huge weight might have torn off the bottom, leaving the inadequate keel intact. In that case, the boat would have rolled over onto her side and settled with her sails lying on the surface. For experienced hands, there would have been plenty of time to launch the life raft. And as the boat settled, the emergency buoy would have floated off her deck, activated itself, and signaled an SOS position to the satellites above. But there was no signal. Which meant that the buoy hadn't floated free.

Another possibility was that the keel snapped off at the bottom of the hull. If that had happened, *Siren* would have flipped over abruptly. The enormous strain could have torn the rigging and dragged the sails under the surface. She would have turned completely over in a matter of seconds. Certainly too quickly for Robert and Beth to launch a raft. Maybe too quickly for the emergency buoy to float free from the deck.

But still, they would have a chance. There would be a hull to cling to. They could dive down and recover the raft. There was every chance that they would be able to save themselves.

The third possibility was the most disastrous. The keel struts were also the ribs of the hull, fusing the entire boat into a single structure. The enormous forces generated in rolling seas might have ripped the boat in half, leaving the counterweight to drag the shattered wreckage down. She would have disappeared in an instant, taking her crew to the bottom of the sea.

Sean walked out to the end of the dock that reached from the launching ramp out into the channel. He leaned on a piling, looking out at the water that had now been drained of all its color. He had been here all his life, standing at the water's edge and dreaming of new ways to master its forces. Never before had he felt so completely defeated.

Boats were all that he knew. Navy ships, with their electronics-encrusted masts, were the skyscrapers of his youth as he moved up and down the Atlantic coast to each new base where his father was stationed. Living on the move made it difficult to hold friends. But there was always a dock thrusting out into the water, and there was always a boat to be sailed. Even when his father had been posted ashore, it had been at the water's edge, in Newport at the War College, and in Annapolis at the academy. It was simply assumed that Sean would become a midshipman and follow his father through the ranks of the navy. But the boy had little interest in the military, and even less in the stuffy etiquette of the seafaring tradition. It was the ship itself that fascinated him, and finding ways to make it master its environment.

Instead of the academy, he had gone to the Hoboken Institute to study naval architecture. By the end of the first year he had demonstrated that he had little ability and even less interest in most of the classroom curriculum. But he had also demonstrated an uncanny feeling for the forces of wind and tide, and an insatiable curiosity in the ways ships and boats could use these forces to their advantage.

In his second year, he caused a rift in the school's prestigious faculty. Many of the deans thought he had no respect for the time-honored rules of naval design. "I'd rather not hand a Hoboken diploma to someone who thinks that an airplane wing, standing on its end, would make a suitable sail," one of his teachers scoffed. But Bladesdale, who thought the idea workable, came to Sean's defense. "I'd hate to have been the first person to suggest the hydrofoil in this place," he told his colleagues. "We should be encouraging new thinking."

In a third-year project, he had designed a twin-hull aircraft carrier that used movable foils to pin itself into the sea. His faculty adviser had disqualified it, claiming that the design would tear itself to pieces. But Bladesdale had taken the model down to the school's test tanks, found it incredibly stable and half again as fast as a monohull of similar capacity. "It's a great concept," he had argued at a faculty review. "Promising enough so that we should let him explore the materials that could give it the strength it needs."

"It looks like something that should be racing in the Detroit River, with a beer company's name painted on its side," the adviser had countered. In the end, the administration had sided with the adviser and disqualified Sean's entry as "impractical." That left him short of the credits he needed to complete the semester. Instead of repeating the course, he had stormed out of the school.

He had headed straight for the yacht-racing circuit, where he had added physical strength to his uncanny intuition and made himself a valuable crew member. As he got to know the players, he had begun to suggest his design ideas. Ideas for everything. A superplaning sailboard that literally went airborne as it skimmed across the surface. It had hit fifty miles per hour in a twenty-knot wind. An open class racing catamaran with a clear plastic airfoil rising up in place of the sail. It lapped the same hull, equipped with conventional sails, in a match race. He had even proposed a powerboat driven by air fans instead of underwater propellers. Sean's boats performed, but the more speed he demonstrated, the more he was shunned by the traditional yachting fraternity. *Unconventional* and *freakish* were words the yacht builders used to describe his work. *Noncompliant* was the word they used to keep his boats off their race courses.

Then a French team had asked his thoughts about designing an America's Cup boat. The syndicate's financier, an eccentric French baron named Murot, who had made his fortune in the United States, was already something of a joke in serious racing circles. He had little to lose by his association with a designer who "shows little respect for tradition." Despite the handicap of the baron at the helm, the boat had made it to the challenge finals.

Suddenly, Sean began to receive invitations to the model shops and sail lofts, feeding ideas to the name designers. His work was always subordinated to someone else's overall design, but gradually the industry began to appreciate his value. "He's difficult . . . argumentative . . . even impossible," an internationally famous designer had told Robert Cramm. "Ninety percent of what he thinks is nonsense. But somewhere in that other ten percent is a gem. And that makes him worth keeping around."

He had vanished from the circuit for over a year, and then suddenly appeared at Cramm Yachts with a thick roll of sketches and plans under his arm. "They say you need a winner," he had announced to Robert. "I think I've got one." Robert had trusted Sean with the future of his company. He probably hadn't realized that he would also be trusting the controversial young designer with his life.

Sean turned away from the water and walked back up the finger dock toward the boatyard. There has to be another explanation, he told himself. *Siren* had been tested over and over again. Every stress had been simulated on the computers. He had watched graphic displays of the keel flexing under forces five times greater than those it could possibly encounter, and then returning to its lines. All the materials had been tested to destruction and had demonstrated strengths far in excess of what would be required. And they had taken *Siren* out in heavy seas for real-world testing. It wasn't her best environment. She lost most of her advantage in speed. But she was stiffer than any boat he had ever sailed, and she had never showed even the faintest hint of cracking.

Then where was she? If she hadn't broken up, why wasn't she reporting? What possible sequence could have deprived her of all power for a full day? A short that drained both batteries? Unlikely. Coupled with the failure of the compressed-air starter? Even more unlikely. Or of a faulty generator? Sean couldn't assemble a plausible sequence of events that would leave the boat unable to send out a radio signal for so long a time. And yet he couldn't believe in the failure of the structure that had been so carefully engineered. All logic dictated that *Siren* was still afloat and sailing her own course. But if that were true, then why had Robert decided to take her to silence?

18 THE HELICOPTERS TOOK OFF AT FIRST LIGHT, A Coast Guard Sea King from Brunswick, Georgia, and a British Puma from the Turks. The British helicopter searched south of *Siren*'s last reported position, on the theory that she might have turned back to

the Bahamas, the closest point of land. The Sea King looked to the west, in case she had turned inland toward the coast.

The race officials were not surprised when *Siren* failed to broadcast a sunrise position report. They knew the boat certainly would have called in the moment she restored power. And, like Sean, they knew that Robert would have been able to raise power long ago, except under extreme circumstances. The committee members were divided almost evenly. The optimists were betting on a total electrical failure, perhaps a fire that had destroyed the electrical busses. *Siren*, they reasoned, had simply kept sailing, and was now so far ahead of the fleet that her battery-powered handheld equipment was beyond anyone's range. They guessed that she would sail into Hamilton sometime the next afternoon. The pessimists saw the boat either ravaged by an electrical fire or broken in half by the choppy seas. Their scenario had *Siren* somewhere on the bottom, with its crew bobbing helplessly above. There was one other possibility, but none of the committee was rude enough to give it words. Harbored in the back of everyone's mind was the fact that Cramm needed to have a dramatic and well-publicized victory. Reporters were already calling for information on the missing boat, and the coverage would grow with each report from the searching choppers. What could be more dramatic than the ghost ship sailing across the finish line in record time?

The race was officially canceled, and the yachts on the scene were thrown into the search. Those in the van were directed to continue on to Bermuda. It was entirely possible that *Siren* had kept sailing long after it lost power, and that the yacht was still ahead of the fleet, somewhere between the lead boats and Bermuda. The trailing boats were turned around and sent back over the course they had just sailed, toward the Cramm boat's last position. The message had cautioned the crews to "keep a sharp eye for debris on the water." Rarely did any boat sink without a trace, and it was life preservers, deck boards, nautical gear, and even personal effects that generally confirmed the loss of a boat.

Cheryl had come to the Cramm offices to be with Sean in his vigil. It didn't make much sense. It would be hours before they were likely to receive any report. Even another day if, as Sean kept promising her, Robert were to turn up in Bermuda. But she couldn't simply wait at home. The house staff, well aware of her health problems, seemed sure that she couldn't cope with the uncertainty. She felt them watching her as if waiting for her to begin frothing at the mouth. Even her closest companion, Gretchen, had gone morosely quiet, dabbing at her eyes as if Robert were already being waked. She was at least doing something when she sat by the radios waiting for *Siren*'s call letters to come crackling across.

"I'll call you the instant I hear anything," Sean promised for the third time since her arrival. "You're not doing any good here."

She sipped the heavy black coffee that he had poured for her. "We've both got someone out there. We might as well be waiting together."

His eyes widened in surprise. "Beth?" he asked.

Cheryl nodded. "You were . . . close, weren't you?"

Sean paused, trying to remember for himself what he and Beth had been to one another. "We spent a lot of time together," he decided.

"I thought . . ." Cheryl began, perplexed by his answer. She remembered that Sean and Beth had arrived at Cramm on the same day, Beth traveling almost as if she were his baggage. She had never been hired by Robert, but he had begun to pay her when he realized that she was completely involved in the project and was always at Sean's side.

"That we were lovers?" he said, completing Cheryl's thought. "We tried that for a while, when I was working on *Siren*'s original design. I guess we figured that if we were living together, we should be sleeping together. But that wasn't what we really had going."

Cheryl's expression was empathetic, interested.

"We were both losers," he continued. "Serious sailors didn't want to spend a lot of time with either of us. I suppose we both needed someone to talk to."

"No one ever thought of you as losers."

"You didn't," he said. "You had problems of your own. And maybe your husband didn't. He wasn't doing so well himself. But you must have heard people talking. I was the wild man with no respect for tradition. What kind of yachtsman doesn't own a clean shirt? And Beth was the drunk who turned the wrong way and killed one of her crew. Neither of us was asked to join the better yacht clubs."

Her jaw went slack. "Killed one of her crew?"

"You didn't know?" He thought for a moment and then he nodded.

"It figures that Robert never told you. He likes Beth. He wouldn't put her down."

"I'm sorry," Cheryl said. "It must have been awful for her."

"Yeah. Because Beth didn't do much drinking before the accident. It was after the collision that she turned into a fish. But the yacht club admirals decided that the two things went together. They drove her right off the circuit."

"What happened?"

Sean took the two empty coffee cups and walked to the electric coffeemaker. "She fucked up," he said, with his back to Cheryl. His shoulders shrugged. "It happens." He turned back with the two steaming cups. "Two experienced captains coming to the same mark. They're both on starboard and they're nose to nose. Neither one is going to give an inch. Each is waiting for the other to give way."

"It was her fault?" Cheryl asked as Sean slid the cup in front of her.

"No, it wasn't anyone's fault. Maybe she had the faster boat and could have made up the distance if she'd given way. But at the last second she swung hard, going astern of the other boat and then between the other boat and the mark. The other guy turns, trying to cut her off and force her into the marker. The boats bump, and her foredeck man goes over. But he's wearing a safety line, so he doesn't go into the water. He's hanging along the side between the two boats when they crash together again. And then Beth comes around the marker with a dead man hanging off her bow, and blood streaking down the side of the hull. It's the kind of thing that no one in the sport can ever forget."

Cheryl's hands had gone up to her mouth. "My God," she whispered.

"She had just killed somebody, and I had been fired by the French. I'm not sure which the yachtsmen thought was the more shameful, but neither of us were hot properties."

"How did you get together?" she asked.

"I decided to design an open-water racer, and she was a great racing skipper. So I asked her to help me with the deck layout, where she had lots of experience. No one else was offering her anything, so she jumped at it. And then I found out that she was on the sauce."

"Bad?"

"It's never good"—he sneered—"but she was getting real bad. She was doing a great job on the design, but half the time I had to pick her up, wipe her off, and throw her into bed. Until one day, while I'm working in a sail loft to pick up a couple of bucks, she set our place on fire. Lit a cigarette and then tossed the match into a trash can. When I got home, half my drawings were ashes, and she's sitting in this puddle of soot wailing about how she's no good for anyone."

Cheryl was listening intently, the coffee getting cold in her hand. "What did you do?" she asked.

"I dumped her booze and flushed down all her cigarettes, and then I just sat there watching her day after day. It was a couple of months before we got back to work on the plans. But once we got working again, she was okay. She never went back to the stuff . . . at least as far as I know. And she never let up. *Siren* became her life. Not me. I was just sort of a partner."

"You saved her life," Cheryl said.

Sean stared down into his cup. "I hope to Christ I haven't taken it back from her."

The phone on the desk rang. Cheryl froze in her chair. Sean jumped up and then tried to slow to a relaxed pace as he crossed to the phone and picked it up.

"Sean Patton." He paused to listen, his eyes flicking up toward Cheryl. "Could you hold on for a second? I want to take this in the radio room." He reached for the hold button.

"No!" Cheryl's voice cracked like a whip. "If it's about *Siren* put it on the speaker."

"It's nothing definite," he tried to assure her.

"Please," she said. "Whatever it is, let's hear it together."

He pushed the speaker phone button and set the handset in the cradle. "Thomas, I have Mrs. Cramm here with me." He was still talking toward the phone when he said, "Cheryl, this is Thomas Greeley, of the race committee. I think you met him at the dinner."

"How are you, Thomas?" Cheryl called at the instrument.

The voice that came back was perfectly clear, almost as if Greeley were in the room with them. "I'd feel a lot better, Mrs. Cramm, if I had better news for you. One of the boats picked up some floating debris that they think came from *Siren*. Nothing definite, I hasten to add. Nothing with a name on it that they can identify positively. But there's a red sail cover like *Siren*'s that's the right length for her boom. And there are seat cushions that look familiar."

"Jesus," Sean whispered, his face falling into his hands.

"Now, there are a lot of red sail covers and seat cushions around, and lots of boats they could have come from. So none of this is conclusive."

"The sail cover was floating," Sean stated.

"True," Thomas Greeley admitted. They all knew that if it had been in the water a long time, it probably would have sunk. It had to have gone over the side within the past few days, and odds of two boats with identical covers and cushions being in the same place at the same time were not promising.

"The helicopters are refueling now," Thomas's voice continued. "When they get back in the air, they'll concentrate on the area where the debris was found. The boats are spreading out to do a vector search. And a Coast Guard cutter has arrived in the area. So if it's them, we're going to find them."

"Which is the nearest port?" Cheryl asked.

"Nothing is very close," Greeley told them. "They're about halfway between Grand Bahama island and Bermuda. I'm going to stay put here in Lauderdale until I hear something. What about you? Where can you be reached?"

"I'll be right here," Sean shot back. "Mrs. Cramm will be at home but I'll be in touch with her."

Greeley said his good-byes and offered Cheryl a few feeble words of encouragement. Then the line went dead.

"Can I drive you home?" Sean asked.

"I think I'll stay here a little longer," she answered weakly.

"Please don't," Sean said. "You need to be with your daughter."

Cheryl was about to protest when Patton added, "And I need to be alone."

19 REPORTS CAME QUICKLY.

One of the boats spotted what it thought might be a life raft, and pulled aboard a section of wooden foredeck. It had broken away cleanly from a fiberglass hull, but had pulled traces of boron fibers from its anchor mounts. Sean knew that *Siren*'s deck was connected directly to the hull's fiber-impregnated ribs. The deck could be part of his boat.

The Coast Guard Sea King spotted a field of floating debris and recovered saloon seat covers and bunk mattresses. The description matched the ones that Sean had installed aboard *Siren*.

Another boat, sailing toward the hovering Sea King helicopter, charged into a heavy oil slick. It was not the thick, tarry smear typical of ships flushing their bilges, but rather a spectrum-colored film of fresh, light oil.

Sean plotted the location of the findings. It was close to the track that *Siren* had been sailing, and was in the boat's approximated position at the hour when it had first missed filing its sunrise position. Whatever had struck *Siren* had come very suddenly in the pale, predawn light. It had hit without warning and completely dismembered the hull. The wreckage had sunk instantly, probably in a tangle of rigging and fittings that kept the emergency beacon from floating free. The evidence seemed to support Sean's worst fears. It appeared that some combination of wind and sea had put enormous strain on the hull structure. *Siren* had shattered like a piece of crystal.

"They'll keep searching?" he asked the race committee chairman after he had listened to the most recent report.

"Yes, of course. We're going on the theory that they were wearing life jackets and are floating near the scene. There's every reason to be hopeful. . . ."

Sean set the phone down gently. "Every reason," he whispered to himself, and then smirked at the irony. If Robert and Beth were floating, it was with their heads cracked open and their lungs full of seawater. If they were alive, they would be clinging to the decking or the mattresses.

They were experienced sailors. They knew that a head bobbing in the water was nearly invisible. They would hang on to a large piece of wreckage that would be easily seen.

Beth had been ill, Sean remembered. Chances were that Robert had taken the watch and sent her below to rest. He could easily envision the events.

The weather had probably been worse than the glib reports from the crews. Not dangerous, or frightening, but with gusty winds and large rollers. *Siren* had raced through the night, rolling to starboard as the wind swung around her port beam, and then snapping upright as a wave rolled against her side. At the fulcrum point between the force of the sails and the weight of the keel, the hull had been stressed over and over again, until cracks started through its ribs.

In the cockpit, Robert would have no idea that the yacht was breaking up under him. There was no reason to be apprehensive. Far greater stresses had been simulated by their computer model for thousands of accelerated hours without even approaching the test strength of the materials. Months and months of testing had proven conclusively that the boat could handle seas far more destructive than those he was experiencing. More than likely, he was enjoying the pink light on the eastern horizon, planning to turn the wheel over to Beth shortly after sunrise. He was exhausted from the long watch, Sean guessed, looking forward to a few hours of sleep.

He would have planned to switch off his running lights, automatically transmitting his position coordinates to the satellite. Perhaps he would brew a fresh pot of coffee and have a bite of breakfast. He certainly would have waited for the call from Cramm headquarters, giving him the position of the other boats in the race. He would have expected to have held, or perhaps increased, his lead from the night before. And, with the winds swinging back to his quarter and the seas flattening, he would have been looking forward to a record day's run, leaving the rest of the fleet hopelessly behind.

He would have been startled by the sound of the hull failing, an explosion like a rifle shot as the synthetic keel cracked in half. Before he could react, the boat would have heeled abruptly, firing him out of his seat and smashing him against . . . what? A stainless steel winch fitting that would have hit his head like a hammer? The wooden edge of the cockpit that would have struck like a giant club? He probably never had the time to understand the scope of the disaster and realize that *Siren* had no chance. Certainly he never had the time to launch a life raft, or even to disconnect the safety line that bound him to a track on the deck of the yacht. The line was intended to keep him from falling overboard, but now, as the wreckage was being pulled under by the weight of the keel, the safety line would keep Robert from floating free.

Belowdecks, Beth would have even less of a chance. The explosion of the hull might have alerted her, but she would be instantly submerged by the walls of water that would smash through the shattered shell. Every point of reference would be instantly reoriented, bulkheads becoming decks and decks becoming bulkheads. There would be no familiar path of escape as the tangle of broken hull and fallen rigging dragged downward into the sea.

"There's every reason to be hopeful." Right! Hopeful that they had been killed cleanly before they could struggle in their watery coffin. Or hopeful, at least, that drowning had been as painless as the living tended to predict. A brief struggle against the urge to breathe, and then a quickly enveloping darkness.

20   IN HIS BERMUDA HOTEL, GEORGE WILLIAMSON HAD already assumed the role of corporate mourner. He was secluded in his suite, the blinds lowered to block out the beauty of the setting, the slats tipped to admit a splash of daylight. The luncheon table, with most of the courses still hidden in warming dishes, waited in front of the straight-backed chair. Only the coffee cup had been used. There was an open bottle of Scotch on the bar, and a bucket of melting ice cubes.

Williamson had spent the afternoon at the desk in his bedroom, receiving reports from the search boats that were being relayed in sympathetic tones by the owners ashore. Several of the builders' advance parties were already on the island, and vice presidents had made formal sympathy calls. There were two-handed handshakes, or arms over his shoulder as words of encouragement were whispered. "Robert will make it. He's the best seaman in the business," one visitor had promised. The public relations director of a competing company had been particularly encouraging: "What they've found means nothing," he had reasoned. "Could be from any boat. Might have been floating around for months." Words like *sunk* or *dead* were never mentioned, at least not during the early part of the afternoon.

George had placed two calls to Cheryl, updating her in similarly evasive language. "Some indications of a sinking," he had advised her, "but certainly nothing definite. And nothing that points directly to *Siren*." He had called Cramm's bankers, minimizing the implications to the financial situation of the company. And he had called Philip McKnight.

"In view of our conversation . . . and your . . . revised offer, I feel it's my personal responsibility to keep you up to the minute," he had whispered.

"I'm following developments, George, with a sinking heart," McKnight had answered. "I can't imagine what might have happened. I can only hope that they both got off."

"We're trying to keep our own hopes up, Philip. And we've certainly had the support of everyone in the industry. All the builders and designers have called. Like you, they're friends first and competitors after."

"Of course," McKnight had hastened to agree. "The business is unimportant until we know about Robert."

They said kind things about Robert, shared their relief that Cheryl had not been aboard, and promised to keep in touch while the search was continuing. Both hung up carefully.

They had used all the proper words. But the real conversation had been subliminal. George had informed Philip that he was now running the company and would be the point man for further discussions about the fate of Cramm Yachts. He had also hinted that the other yachting companies were already rushing to feed on *Siren*'s carcass. It was important that McKnight not get the impression that Cramm Yachts was falling into his lap.

For his part, McKnight had carefully avoided mentioning his offer, and had indicated that there would be no further business discussions until the situation had sorted itself out. He was paving the way for a reduced offer if Robert's pride, and the added value of *Siren*'s victory, were no longer economic values.

Both men knew that they were closer to a deal now than they would have been if Robert Cramm had sailed victoriously into Hamilton. When they met again, they would be discussing a straightforward takeover, without the emotions involved in deciding who had triumphed over the other. They would be pricing a business rather than a century of tradition. It would mean a much more workable number.

21 CHERYL WAS DEEP BELOW THE SURFACE, BREATHING easily through her mask, when she saw the boat passing. It was *Siren*, unmistakable with her blade keel and enormous counterweight. She had been coming toward her, but now she was turning away. Cheryl kicked with all her might, afraid that she was being left behind.

She couldn't remember boarding the boat, or even leaving the pier. She had no idea why she was wearing her wet suit. They never took a sailboat when they were going out diving, but always the power launch. Certainly they would never use *Siren*. She remembered standing by the lifeline in her slacks and jumper, looking up at the sails, which were bent under a heavy breeze. And then she was toppling over the edge and into the sea.

Someone had pushed her. At least that's what she thought. She had felt hands against her back. Or had the boat suddenly pitched over a wave? Maybe the hands were grasping to keep her from falling. She couldn't be sure. But somehow she had found a scuba tank and changed into her wet suit. Now she had to get back to the surface where they could see her and turn the boat around.

When she broke into the daylight, there was nothing around her except the sea. She seemed to be in the trough between towering waves, looking up at the whitecaps that were exploding into spray. And then she was rising, carried up by the water cresting into the next wave. She went higher and higher, through the salty spray and into the howling wind. Suddenly, she was looking down on *Siren*, the yacht flying all her canvas despite the storm. Robert was at the helm, looking ahead, concentrating on holding his course. He had one hand on the wheel and the other wrapped around Beth's shoulder. Beth was leaning against him, following his gaze out over the boat's prow. Robert was wearing a blazer, with a white yachting cap set jauntily on his head, apparently unaffected by the wind. They were completely absorbed in their work and in one another, and didn't seem to notice that Cheryl had fallen over the side.

She called to them, but her voice made no sound. She was weakened by her struggle back to the surface, and didn't have the strength to shout over the wind. And then she was falling, sliding down along the edge of the next trough. She screamed Robert's name just as *Siren* dropped behind a wave crest. He disappeared without ever looking toward her.

She dove back under, caught up with the boat, and held on to the keel. They wouldn't get away from her. If they wouldn't take her back aboard, she would snap the keel off their boat, and then they would fall into the sea with her. Cheryl kicked out ahead and came to the surface right next to the boat.

Robert and Beth were still at the helm, both staring straight ahead.

"Rah . . . bert!" She screamed his name and was thrilled to hear her voice rising over the roar of the air and the thrashing of the sea. "Rah . . . bert!"

His chin rose as if he were faintly aware of someone calling his name. But he didn't seem particularly concerned. Beth's face turned to look back over his shoulder. She looked directly at Cheryl and then, with no change in her expression, turned back to her vigil over the prow.

Cheryl swam alongside, looking up at the yacht's shiny white flank and at the top of the mast that towered above.

"Rah . . . bert!" Her voice roared above the wind. He had to hear it.

His face was suddenly there, looking down over the side. He was staring curiously as if he wasn't sure exactly what he was seeing. Then Beth stepped up next to him, and they both looked down at her.

Cheryl reached up, but neither of them reached down to catch her hands. Instead, they began to smile and then shook their heads in sympathy. Cheryl knew why. She was ridiculous, swimming alongside like a dolphin, begging to be asked aboard. Of course they wouldn't reach down to her. Obviously she was mad. If they brought her aboard she would only be a problem. She was a fool to think that they'd help her.

Robert and Beth turned away and disappeared over the edge of the gunwale. And then *Siren* began to move, accelerating away from her. Cheryl reached up, trying to grasp the edge of the deck, but her reach kept falling short. Each time she kicked up out of the water, her fingertips came closer, but then slipped away down the polished side of the hull.

Siren's stern rose above her, and then the boat pulled away, leaving her thrashing in the wake. Over the transom, she could see Robert and Beth back behind the wheel, his arm around her shoulder, their faces pressed close together.

"Rah . . . bert!" she screamed with all her power. But he wasn't looking back. "Rah . . . bert!"

There was a flash of light, and then Gretchen's voice calling her name. She saw the young au pair rushing toward her, dashing across the surface of the water, and reaching out to drag her away from the boat. Angrily, she slapped Gretchen's hands away. "They're leaving me!" she screamed. "Robert and Beth are sailing away. Stop them! Help me stop them! They'll be killed!"

She jumped up and tried to run across the water after the fleeing yacht, but Gretchen was holding her back. She struggled violently, but as she broke free another pair of hands wrapped around her.

"Cheryl! Cheryl!" Everyone seemed to be screaming her name.

"Robert and Beth are sailing away," she tried to tell them. "But they'll be killed. They have no keel. . . ."

They were shaking her. She heard Gretchen shouting, "Cheryl! It's all right! It's all right!"

She froze, suddenly aware of the familiar surroundings of her bedroom. She was sitting on top of her bed, Gretchen holding her from behind, and Mrs. Callen, the cook, was standing directly in front of her. "They're alive," she tried to explain logically.

No one answered. As she looked from face to face she saw eyes soft with sympathy. "Oh, God. I was having a nightmare," she explained.

"Of course," the au pair said patronizingly. "It was just a nightmare. You're going to be fine, Cheryl. Just fine."

"Mommy." It was Rachael, standing in the doorway in her nightgown, her face white with fright. "Are you going away again?"

22 BETH HARDAWAY'S BODY WAS FOUND IN THE morning, floating facedown, spread-eagled across the top of the waves. One of the boats, resuming the search as soon as there was new light in the sky, had nearly run over her. The helmsman just happened to glance up as the corpse rose over the white water from the bow wake.

She was fully clothed, wearing the jeans and weather jacket that she had on when *Siren* sailed out of Ft. Lauderdale. There was no life jacket, which indicated that she had been below when the boat broke up. The body was snowy white from its exposure to seawater, and bloated from the early stages of decomposition. Apparently, it had gone under with the wreckage and floated free. Then gasses caused by decay had carried the remains back to the surface.

"Kind of gruesome," the captain reported after he had lifted the body aboard. "But at least she wasn't hit by sharks or barracuda. The only disfigurement is the burns on her back."

"Burns?" Sean Patton was stunned by the information.

"That's what I was told," Thomas Greeley of the racing committee explained. "The Coast Guard has the body, and they're in contact with the Ft. Lauderdale police. As soon as they decide who has authority, someone will order an autopsy. Maybe they'll come up with an explanation."

"*Siren* couldn't have burned," Sean blurted out. "At least not enough to sink her." Then he asked, "What about the seat cushions and the sail cover? Were they burned?"

"Not that anyone mentioned," came the answer. "Just the clothes she was wearing. But the Coast Guard has everything. They'll put it all together."

The reaction was the same among the industry people on Bermuda. Even though they had kept offering George words of encouragement, their private conversations were more realistic. The search had been thorough and had confirmed that *Siren* was nowhere near the race course. Given that, the floating cushions and sail covers provided the only logical explanation. The boat had suffered a catastrophic hull failure and had sunk instantly.

"The design was too radical," one of the corporate executives said, putting into words what they were all thinking.

"Sean Patton takes too many chances," another answered, shaking his head gravely. "You can't just throw away the proven principles of yacht design."

George Williamson voiced the same conclusion in the morning. "She sacrificed everything for speed," he agreed. "I told Robert . . . the first time I saw the sketches . . ." His eyes filled and the words choked in his throat.

The burns on Beth's body interrupted the rush to judgment. If the hull had shattered and sunk in an instant, how could there have been a fire? What would have burned? George speculated that there might have been something cooking on the stove. It was, after all, daybreak. Someone would have been getting breakfast.

"They may have been running the engine," another yacht company executive suggested. "The lights had been on all night and quite logically the batteries needed charging." So, the thinking went, fuel lines would have parted when the hull broke up. Gas fumes could have been ignited by the generator.

Neither explanation was likely. In a two-handed race, it didn't make sense that they would have been cooking an elaborate breakfast. Nor was a broken fuel line an obvious answer. *Siren*'s diesel fuel probably wouldn't have caught fire. It had to be compressed before it could be burned even in the engine.

But there was no denying the facts. The boat had sunk quickly, indicating that the hull was breached. And there were burns on the body, pointing toward fire or an explosion. There had to be some explanation for both facts.

Sean had *Siren*'s plans spread all over his office when George returned from Bermuda. His desk was piled with the computer runs of all their simulations and tests. He swept papers off the chair so that George could sit, and then took him through all the data he had developed. "It doesn't make sense," he kept repeating.

George looked patiently to figures and graphs that he couldn't pretend to understand. He listened as Sean kept demonstrating that *Siren* couldn't have broken up in such light seas. "It had to be an explosion!" Sean kept concluding. "But there's nothing on the boat that would have exploded."

Williamson nodded gravely at the conclusions, stood and wiped his glasses with his tie as he walked to the window that overlooked the harbor. "No one is blaming you, Sean," he finally said. "The boat was . . . highly experimental." The word sounded less demeaning than "radical."

"There was nothing experimental—" Sean started to protest, but George cut him off.

"Certain risks were involved in *Siren*'s design, and Robert was fully aware of those risks. God knows I warned him dozens of times. I told him there were all sorts of arrangements I could make to save the company. But he wanted one last chance to save it in a dramatic fashion . . . on the high seas."

"He didn't want Cramm sold out from under him," Sean contradicted. "And he believed in *Siren*."

George nodded knowingly. "Yes, he did. He made his own decision. He wouldn't blame you, and neither do I."

Sean looked down at the scattering of drawings and printouts. "I'll build her again. And I'll sail her myself." He turned to George. "We've done all the studies. We have the plans. We could build her for a fraction of the cost of the original."

George paused thoughtfully. "I'm sure you could," he concluded. "I don't think anyone would object to your taking your design work with you."

"With me?" Sean jumped to his feet. "I didn't mean on my own. I meant build it right here. And do the same thing that Robert wanted to do. Race her, and prove to everyone that Cramm is still the champion."

George's response was a grim smile. "Cramm Yachts went down with *Siren*, Sean. Nothing else is going to be built here."

"You're closing it down?"

"No. Merging it with a larger organization."

"Vector?"

"Yes, Vector."

"Vector builds shit!"

"Whatever they build, they're earning money. And the price is more than I would have dared to ask."

"But that's not what Robert wanted," Sean begged.

George put a comforting hand on the young man's shoulder. "Robert is gone. We have to do what we can without him."

It was the first time they had both acknowledged the inescapable. Robert Cramm had gone down with *Siren*.

23   THE SEARCH WAS ABANDONED THE NEXT DAY. BOTH American and British helicopters had run exhaustive patterns over the area. Cutters and other powerboats had joined the sailing fleet, formed a line of bearing that was over five miles long, and moved slowly in the direction of the tide and the prevailing wind. Had Robert been afloat, it was impossible that they would have missed him.

George brought the news to Cheryl personally, sitting opposite her in the library of the house. "Of course, this doesn't prove that Robert is . . ."

She took her hand from between his. "He's dead, George. There's no point in dragging this out forever, is there?"

"No, I suppose not," he admitted. "All the evidence points to a sudden disaster. Something that happened so quickly that they couldn't even get off a radio signal." He looked up into Cheryl's face. "If it's any comfort, I'm sure neither of them knew what happened."

"What do you think happened?" she asked.

"Broke in half, I guess. And something ignited the diesel fuel. Or the propane. The design put enormous stresses across the hull. I think when the keel went, it tore out the bottom. I think they were gone in an instant."

"Robert and Sean were so sure of the design," Cheryl said absently.

"Sean still is," George told her. "He's moved into the design shed and he keeps going over the plans. It's as if he's building her all over again. But"—he stood as he spoke, indicating the end of his visit—"we have to face the facts. It was a risky design. Maybe even desperate. A regular boat wouldn't have been nearly as fast. But it would have stayed afloat."

24

THE DIRECTORS CONVENED IN THE CRAMM LIVING room immediately after the memorial services. The setting, with its casual arrangement of soft chairs, had been carefully chosen by George. Nominally, Cheryl was the company's new chairman and would have been seated at the head of a conference table. By eliminating the boardroom setting, he was hoping to spare her from presiding over events that she didn't understand.

The timing, too, had a purpose. The directors were members of the Cramm family, two of Robert's first cousins, who had each retained 10 percent of the shares. Thomas Cramm had converted most of the stock he inherited back to the company for cash, and then converted the cash to gin. Watery eyes and a vein-lined nose were his heritage for the family's hundred years of seafaring. His sister, Theresa, had turned her shares over to her husband, a Wall Street broker, who had traded most of them back to Robert for shares in a marine electronics company that had done quite well. Neither cousin kept close track of the company's affairs. In fact, they had never personally attended a board meeting despite the astute observations credited to them in the official minutes. Their attendance at this meeting was in response to a promised cup of coffee at the end of the memorial service.

The two outsiders were James Darby, a representative of the company's bank, who had received his seat on the board as part of a loan covenant, and Whit Hobbs, partner in the company's law firm. Hobbs had stood on the dock with the family as prayers were recited and a wreath was placed on the water, the simple service that Cheryl had requested. Darby had been waiting in the house when the family returned from the water's edge.

George opened the meeting, as coffee was being served, with consoling words to the family, and with a tribute to Robert's leadership. "It's because of his achievements that Cramm Yachts is held in such high value," he said, and then he put a figure on that value: the $90 million buyout he had negotiated with Philip McKnight.

A pleasant murmur swept the room. The news represented found money for the two cousins, and assurances of repayment for the banker. Hobbs's law firm, which had reviewed the proposal, was already billing time against the proposed merger.

Williamson then explained the key-man insurance Robert had insisted that the company take out only weeks before he had sailed. It would be used to retire some of the company's debt prior to the merger. And he took a few moments to explain the sweeteners he had negotiated for Cheryl: a long-term contract as a consultant to Cramm Vector, and bonuses on the purchase price based on the profitability of the new venture.

"It's the kind of arrangement that Robert was hoping to negotiate after *Siren*'s victory," he told Cheryl. "So, in a sense, he achieved everything he had set out to accomplish."

The attorney passed out copies of the documents, noting that there was a time limit on the Vector offer. "If you see any serious problems, you should bring them to George's attention at once. If not, we'd like to have the signed agreements back in a week."

Cousin Thomas was already unscrewing the cap from his fountain pen.

Cheryl folded the documents without sparing them a glance, thanked the mourners and the other directors, and stepped out through the French doors into the gardens. Sympathetic eyes watched her as she walked off into her private silence, following a flowered path until it disappeared behind the garden wall.

"Is she going to be okay?" James Darby asked, leaning toward Whit Hobbs.

The attorney shrugged. "Terrible tragedy. And just when she seemed to be making progress."

Thomas Cramm conferenced with his sister. "Robert turned a tidy profit," he observed. "Wish I'd held on to a few more shares."

"It's all paper," Theresa said, and with a nod toward the still open French doors, "unless she goes along with the sale."

His eyes widened as he realized the money wasn't yet his. "Why wouldn't she go along?"

"I really couldn't say, Thomas. I don't know the girl at all. She's not of our class."

.   .   .

GRETCHEN SAW CHERYL from the nursery window. She had disappeared behind the wall for a moment after she left the garden. But now she was visible again, emerging from the cover of the trees, onto the driveway. She was wandering down the road, still in the black dress and high heels she had worn to the funeral service.

The au pair girl clutched Rachael closer to herself. There was no way she could go back to her own country and leave the helpless child with Cheryl. Everything had gone wrong! If only Robert had been the one to race home to Rachael's sickbed!

Cheryl kept walking, the folded contracts hanging from her hand. She was through the front gate and out onto the path that led to the boatyard before she became aware of her heels digging into the soft gravel. She hesitated, looking back at the house, and then toward the water, puzzled as to why she had come this far. And why was she still carrying the damn legal papers?

"Where you heading?" Sean's salt-eaten pickup truck had rolled up next to her and he was leaning out the open window. With his hair pulled back and a shoulder showing through the stretched neck of his T-shirt, he looked primitive.

She smiled. "I was just wondering the same thing myself." She looked out at the water. "I suppose I was going back out on the pier . . . although I never did believe in visiting graves."

"Get in," he invited. "You can't walk around in those things." She looked down at the shoes and then hobbled around the tailgate to the passenger side. "Which way?" he asked, and when she seemed puzzled, he added, "Back to the house, or out to the pier?"

"Could we just drive around the yard?" Cheryl finally asked. He shifted into gear and drove onto the boatyard property.

Cramm Yachts now occupied just the southern end of what had once been a sprawling shipyard that stretched for half a mile up the bay. There had been three large assembly tracks, each served with its own overhead crane. They had now been dismantled, the land turned over to the state for a waterside park. The metal-cutting shed had been replaced by a carpentry shop where the wooden fittings and deck components were still made by hand. The old forge had been converted to a molding area where the fiberglass was formed into hulls. And then there was an open yard where boats were assembled and finished.

The gate led directly into the yard, which had a launching ramp, and a long pier reaching out into the harbor. To the other side of the gate was the design shed, which was really the basement of the business offices that faced out to sea.

Sean stayed in the truck while Cheryl walked out on the dock in her stocking feet, holding her shoes in one hand and the papers in the other. He watched as she stood staring out over the water, like a woman on a widow's walk. He wanted to look away, to give her a moment of privacy, but he knew that she wasn't herself. Without admitting it, he was afraid that she might throw herself over the edge. She seemed to compose herself, and when she turned, straightened her shoulders, and started back to the truck, she was a different person. He said nothing when she climbed in, but simply backed into a U-turn and headed up to the house.

"I watched the service this morning," Sean told her. "I felt terrible for all of you."

"You should have been there," she answered. "The last few months you were closer to Robert than any of us."

"I said my own prayers. All I've been doing is praying that it wasn't my fault."

"Jesus! Don't even think such a thing."

"The design was—"

"Whatever happened, it wasn't the design. All kinds of boats run into trouble. Robert believed in it. We all believed in it."

"George didn't," Sean answered without taking his eyes off the road.

Cheryl seemed shocked, but then her eyes showed understanding. "George is always looking for the sure thing. Not that there's anything wrong with him. He's always had the interests of the Cramm family and the Cramm business at heart. But the business is about the sea, and there are no sure things out there. Robert could never get him to understand that every day was a risk."

He nodded. "Thanks. But I can't help thinking—"

"We'll build another one," she said as if that were the obvious solution.

Sean smiled. "George didn't tell you that I was leaving?"

"No! Why?"

"I guess we've agreed to disagree," Sean said.

"When?" Cheryl asked.

"I'm packing right now."

They had passed through the gate and were heading up the hill to the house. Sean was still staring straight ahead, even though he could feel Cheryl's eyes fixed on him. As they neared the house she asked, "Could you stay on for a couple of days?"

"I don't think that's a good idea."

"A week at most." She held up the legal papers as if he should understand what they were. "I've got some decisions to make. I may need a little professional advice."

"About the business? I don't know. . . ."

"About Cramm Yachts and Vector Yachts. And no one knows boats any better than you."

He looked in her direction for the first time. "You're going to be okay, aren't you." It was a statement rather than a question.

"I think so," Cheryl said.

Sean nodded. "Okay. I'll move my stuff into the design shed. I'll be away for a day . . . two at the most, and then I'll be back."

25 SEAN SPREAD HIS DRAWINGS ACROSS BLADESDALE'S desk and then began stacking the bound folders of his computer tests. The professor watched through the haze of smoke that was constantly fed from his pipe. They were both silent, the mood funereal, as if they were gathered beside the corpse of a dear friend. When he was finished, Sean didn't even look up, but simply slumped into the chair across from his mentor. Only his face was visible over the mountains of data.

"I've been through everything," Sean finally allowed. "I don't even have possibilities of what might have gone wrong."

Bladesdale's answer was an explosion of hot embers and a puff of smoke. He leaned forward, lifted the corner of the full-hull drawing, and searched the design. "As soon as I heard she was lost, I went down to the basement and reran all the data from the tub tests," he said. Then he shook his head and sighed in despair. "Last boat I would have expected to break up. The hull hardly generated any pressure. Went through the water like a knife through butter." He tapped the plan with the back of his hand. "And this . . . it's built like a German battleship. Strongest glass hull I've ever seen." He leaned back with his hands folded behind his head, his eyes turned up in thought.

"But she did sink," Sean reminded him. "Broke up and maybe burned."

"Never burned," Bladesdale mumbled. "Not enough fuel aboard her to burn a steak. And to my mind, never broke up. Not in those seas."

"She sank," Sean repeated.

Bladesdale was up, circling the desk with his pipe belching like a steam engine. "I think we're looking for something very, very big . . . or something very, very small. Something that wouldn't be covered in any of engineering data."

"Start with big," Sean suggested, trying to get the conversation on track.

"Oh, like a floating mine. Something designed to sink a warship, that simply would have exploded through the hull like a rock through a plate-glass window."

Sean winced. "A mine?"

"Yes."

"Professor, she was sailing off Grand Bahama, not in the Persian Gulf. How the fuck would she hit a mine?"

"You get my meaning, don't you, Sean? An external force. Something that has nothing to do with the wind or the sea." He gestured at the desk. "It wouldn't be in any of our studies."

"How about something small?" Sean asked.

"A sea cock," Bladesdale answered. "A two-dollar fitting that no one ever thinks to stress-test. So it pops open and the boat fills."

"I figure two experienced sailors would have noticed if their boat was filling with water," Sean said sarcastically.

"Or a turnbuckle. I remember a boat running under power in heavy seas. A turnbuckle parted, releasing a shroud. The mast fell. The end of the mast caught in the sea and the whole thing rolled back across the cockpit, knocking the captain overboard. The boat broached and sank, and the captain spent two days in the water clinging to the mast."

"What are you saying?" Sean asked, hoping that the story had a point.

"I'll go through your data," Bladesdale answered. "I'll analyze every one of your materials tests. I'll share the numbers with my colleagues, many of whom would delight in pointing out your design flaws. But I don't think we'll find an answer. Your keel didn't come off, and that boat never broke up. It was either something extraordinarily powerful that you'd never figure on, or something so small and insignificant that you'd never find it."

26 THREE DAYS LATER, CHERYL APPEARED AT THE DOOR of George's office. He sprang from behind his desk the moment he noticed her, and led her to the corner sofas that were angled around the coffee table.

"Can I get you something? A soft drink? Or a glass of wine?"

She settled for coffee and glanced around his office while he was relaying her order to his secretary. She saw the chart of the race course, with the pins still fixed as they had been the last time *Siren* had reported. The Cramm yacht's pin was off by itself, far ahead of the competitive field.

"I thought you'd have taken that down by now," she said as soon as George stepped back into the office.

He followed her eyes to the chart. "I tried to a half dozen times. But the pin seemed to say that Robert was still out there. It would have been . . . final . . . if you know what I mean."

She nodded. "I know. I still walk out on the dock as if I expected him to sail into the harbor. But it's final. It was final when we put the wreath into the water. We have to get ourselves going again."

They sat silently while the secretary brought in Cheryl's coffee and set a glass of wine in front of George.

"You're right, of course," he said as soon as they were alone again.

"And I have moved on . . . with the details of the Vector deal. I hope you've had time to look it over. If there are any questions . . ."

Cheryl smiled. "The only question is how you were able to pull it off. It's far more generous than I would have imagined."

George beamed. He mumbled a few words about the high regard Robert commanded in the industry. Then he modestly allowed that the terms he had negotiated with Vector were a tribute to the company rather than a personal triumph.

"But it *is* the end of Cramm Yachts," Cheryl observed. "At least as anything more than a logotype on a Vector hull."

"Oh, I wouldn't feel that way . . ." George started, but Cheryl continued talking right through his protest.

"I appreciate your thoughtfulness in insisting that Cramm be perpetuated. But niceties aside, complete control and all the assets are handed over to Vector. Philip McKnight will be making all the decisions about Cramm's future."

"I suppose that's true," George admitted, "but if I may speak plainly . . ."

Cheryl nodded.

George sipped his wine and set the glass on the table. "The plain fact is that Cramm is in desperate straits. The company long ago lost control of its future, and most of the assets are already pledged against loans. We're really out of room to maneuver."

"Robert thought he could save it," she reminded him.

He sighed sympathetically. "I'm not sure whether he really believed he could save it or was simply determined to go down fighting. He hoped that *Siren's* victory would bring a flood of orders. I didn't see any evidence that it would. But that's a question that will never be answered. All I can tell you for certain is that there is no flood of new orders, and some of our dealers are already talking to other manufacturers."

She turned through her papers, looking for the financial figures. "I thought the insurance money might buy us a bit more time."

"It's already committed," he said. "There are debts. . . ."

She found the balance sheet and began scanning the liabilities. George reached out his hand and placed it on hers. "Debts that aren't in the records . . ."

She looked up, her expression puzzled.

"Robert had . . . certain commitments. I don't think I should say more."

Cheryl smiled. "George, don't be so damn chivalrous. I'm a big girl with some big problems. If these numbers aren't real, I need to know."

George took back his hand. "Robert had generated . . . certain entries. He covered up the cash he needed to build *Siren*, and in the process created substantial tax liabilities. The insurance covers the liabilities."

"Robert knew this?" she asked.

George nodded.

"Then," Cheryl continued, "he knew he needed the insurance money. He was betting his life on *Siren*. There was no fallback."

"I'm afraid so," he answered.

The papers fell from her hand. He had done everything. Even stolen from his own company. So if something happened to the yacht that would snatch away the enormous victory he needed, then his life was Cramm's only collateral.

"Oh, Jesus," she prayed. "He wouldn't have . . ."

"He wouldn't have, and he didn't," George snapped angrily. "Robert wouldn't have killed himself. Certainly not if it meant taking Beth with him. Don't even consider such a thing."

Her face was in her hands, but she was still able to nod. Robert would never have killed himself.

"But we don't want to give an insurance company any reasons for second thoughts," George added. "And we need to have this covered before we merge our books with Vector's. So there's really no choice. This deal is a godsend."

He leaned back to his desk and retrieved a pen from the ornate writing stand. "If you're up to it," he said quietly, offering the pen to Cheryl.

She glanced at the papers on the table, but didn't reach for the pen.

"Like you said, it's so final," she managed.

George nodded. "It is over, I'm afraid. All the others have signed."

Cheryl took the pen and thumbed through to the Vector agreement. The place for her signature was already highlighted. But she set the pen down.

"Let me think this through once more," she asked.

"Of course," he said. "I know how difficult this is." He took the pen and helped Cheryl to her feet. "But there is a time limit on the Vector offer. And it is our best chance."

He watched her as she crossed the reception area and disappeared through the front door. "It's so sad," he heard his secretary say.

George looked at the woman, and then his eyes dropped. "It's like before," he agreed. "She seems to have just let go of reality."

She spent the rest of the day with Rachael, reading to her and taking her through her naming games. "Let me take her," she said to Gretchen when the au pair had the toddler in her running carriage.

"For a run?" Gretchen had never seen Cheryl run, or even jog.

"Just for a walk," Cheryl said. "If I tried to run, she'd have to push me back."

She strolled down the front driveway with her daughter in the carriage. Gretchen and most of the staff watched her until she was through the gate. "If anything happens to that baby . . ." the housekeeper whispered, putting words to the fear they all shared.

At night, after Rachael was asleep, Cheryl closed the door to her bedroom and sat against a propped-up pillow with the financial papers and the Vector contract scattered across the bed.

The light was still bright under her door when Gretchen got up to check on Rachael. She paced outside for a few minutes and then pressed her ear to the door and listened to the deathly silence. Finally she knocked, and was surprised when Cheryl's clear voice told her to come in.

"I saw the light. I thought, perhaps—" She stopped when she saw the stacks of papers on the bed.

"Gretchen, did you know that Robert had gotten an extension on your visa?"

The young girl's eyes widened as if she had been caught in a lie. "He mentioned that he might need me for a few more months. . . ."

"You're approved for another six months," Cheryl said, handing her a document.

The au pair squirmed. "I hope you're not angry. But Robert thought—"

"Angry? I'm thrilled. I'm going to need all the help I can get for the next few months. I hope you're planning to stay on."

Gretchen blinked. Was Cheryl blind? Didn't she know why Robert wanted her to stay longer? "He thought I might be needed," she managed. "But with all that's happened . . ."

"With all that's happened, I'll need you much more." Cheryl held out her hands. "Please tell me you'll stay." Gretchen nodded and then Cheryl swept her into an embrace.

27 THE NEXT MORNING, CHERYL KNOCKED ON THE door of the design studio and peered in through the window. There was a big room with rows of cubicles, their furnishings evenly divided between drawing boards, and desks with computer workstations. The walls were covered with white boards, and there was a round conference table in the center. As she looked in, overhead fluorescent tubes flickered on. Sean came through a back door that connected to the storeroom he had converted to a bedroom. It was only a cot and a footlocker, but it kept him close to his work.

He unlocked the door and stepped aside so that she could enter.

"Coffee?" He went straight to the coffeemaker and put on a full pot.

"I have some numbers I'd like to go over," she said, spreading her inventory figures across the center conference table. He picked up his discarded shirt and pulled it over his head as he crossed over to join her. Cheryl looked at the faded design across his chest. "What's that?" she asked.

He had to twist the shirt so that he could see the remnants of the missionary position, represented by two small feet pointing downward between two larger feet pointing upward. "Baron Murot's fleur-de-lis. It was painted on the stern of his Cup boat until the committee made him take it off."

Cheryl shook her head with a smile, then pushed her papers in front of Sean. "This is the completed inventory," she began explaining. "Yachts sitting in the yard waiting to be delivered. Others in the hands of dealers, on consignment."

"Twenty million," he said, looking over her shoulder at the number.

"It may be a bit inflated," Cheryl mumbled, not wanting to get into George's warning about her husband's overcharges, "but it's still substantial."

"Twenty million," he repeated.

"What I need is to have you verify the numbers. Check out the yard and the docks. Visit the dealers. Get me a figure if we wanted to convert it all to cash."

Sean looked up and smiled at her. "You're not selling."

"I don't think so."

"Christ," he said, "you're tougher than Robert."

"Certainly crazier. But I think it can be done. We can use the insurance money to make a down payment on the debt, and get an extension on the principal. The inventory will give us our working capital. And we'll concentrate on our lowest-cost, fastest-moving boats to keep the factory running. Meanwhile, we'll put together a new *Siren*, just like the first one. We'll campaign her to generate our publicity—"

She stopped. He was looking down solemnly. "What's the matter?" she asked. "Don't you think it can work?"

Sean nodded. "I liked it until you began talking about a new *Siren*. I'm not sure that's the smartest—"

"Sean, do you believe in the design?"

He stared at her, the fire in his eyes dimming. "If I could only find out what went wrong."

"Your experts at Hoboken couldn't find anything."

"They're still looking," he answered.

"If they come up with something, you'll fix it. You're the only yacht builder Cramm has left. This plan won't work without you."

Sean walked away from the table, then turned to look back at her. "They'll fight you, you know. The relatives. The banks. The lawyers. Even George."

She nodded, and then demanded an answer. "Will you stay with me?"

Sean shook his head and chuckled. "It's not as if I were buried in offers."

. . .

WHEN GEORGE HEARD Cheryl's decision, he slumped into his chair. "This is a terrible mistake," he warned her. "Robert was completely reconciled to the fact that the company would have to be sold."

"He never told me. He seemed certain that he could save it."

"Cheryl, please. The last thing Robert wanted was to give you cause to worry. He wouldn't tell you how bad things have gotten."

"But I think we should try," she persisted.

"I think we should try to honor Robert's wishes. What he wanted was to make certain that you and his daughter would be protected. And that's exactly the way this deal has been constructed."

"I don't need to be protected. I've had people protecting me for the past two years."

"Provided for, then," George corrected. "I'm simply doing what Robert wanted."

"Please, George. Help me do what I want."

His shoulders hunched, and then he threw up his hands. "I still work for Cramm Yachts, and you're the new chairman. Of course I'll help you, as long as I'm free to speak my mind."

She smiled. "I'll always want your opinion."

He jumped to his feet and began pacing. "I can get us a bit of time," he pondered out loud. But then he turned on her abruptly. "I'm talking weeks. Not months. Vector . . . the banks . . . they'll understand that you're not yet ready to think about the business."

He paced again. "Probably best if you let me handle them. I'll explain that you're not quite yourself. If one of them happens to get through to you, try to be vague about your intentions."

"Whatever you think," Cheryl agreed.

He paused and slipped slowly back behind his desk. "What I think is that you should evaluate your situation quickly. I can pretty much assure you that if we let this offer slip away, the next one won't be nearly so generous."

As soon as Cheryl left, George lifted the phone and punched a speed-dial button. Philip McKnight picked up on the second ring. "We need to talk," Williamson said. "I'm having a bit of difficulty getting Cheryl Cramm's attention. . . . Yes, of course it's all been a terrible shock, but I think she'll weather it. We just may need to push your deadline back a bit. . . . No! Nothing like that. I'm talking weeks, maybe a month. . . ."

28 CHERYL AND GEORGE FLEW TOGETHER TO THE coroner's inquest, held in Ft. Lauderdale. George had protested that Mrs. Cramm was still not sufficiently recovered and that he would gladly represent her at the inquest. He had been surprised when the clerk told him that Mrs. Cramm's testimony would be absolutely essential and that she would be deposed if she couldn't travel. They had decided that she should make the trip.

The hearing attracted no outside attention. Present were Thomas Greeley of the race committee, the captain of the yacht that had recovered Beth Hardaway's body, a Coast Guard lieutenant, and the Broward County medical examiner. As they gathered around the conference table in the coroner's office, the hearing promised to be perfunctory. George was annoyed that he and Cheryl had been summoned when the legal niceties probably could have been handled by mail.

The coroner began with an expression of condolence, which Cheryl acknowledged with a nod. Then he announced the purpose of the hearing, which was to rule on the cause of Beth's death, and of the presumed death of Robert.

Greeley was the opening witness and explained the procedures for the race. He produced the copies of the Coast Guard inspection of each of the participating yachts and the qualifications of the crews. His message was simple: The boats were seaworthy and the crews were competent. There was no negligence on the part of the sponsors.

"I'm curious that Miss Hardaway was not listed as *Siren*'s crew member," the coroner remarked, and then he listened to the last-minute details that had taken Cheryl Cramm off the doomed boat and put Beth Hardaway in her place.

The Coast Guard officer spoke next, listing the search procedures and describing the sparse wreckage that had been recovered. In addition to the cushions, mattresses, the sail cover, and the deck planking, numerous pieces of flotation material had been found. These, he explained, were slabs of light polyurethane that were blown into the hull during construction to assure that the boat would float even when filled with water.

"Was there anything unusual about the debris?" the coroner asked.

"Yes," the officer answered, causing George's eyes to snap up from their fixation with the table. "They were scorched, indicating that they were subjected to considerable heat. And they were impregnated with residue of nitrates."

"What conclusions did you draw?"

"That the boat was destroyed by a violent explosion, and that the cause of the explosion was an unstable nitrate compound."

"Dynamite?" the coroner asked. His calm demeanor indicated that the testimony wasn't a surprise to him. He had undoubtedly already read the laboratory reports.

"Possibly. We can't be positive exactly what the substance was."

"Dynamite?" It was Cheryl's voice, gasping as much as asking a question. She looked at George, who swung his glance to her and then back to the Coast Guard officer.

"Dynamite?" he said, echoing Cheryl. "That's impossible. There was nothing like that aboard *Siren*. Perhaps some rifle cartridges . . . flares . . . normal equipment . . ."

The coroner turned to the officer, who shook his head, dismissing George's suggestion. "This was a big yacht, blown into very small pieces. It couldn't have been flares or rifle shells. If I didn't know better, I'd swear that she was torpedoed, or that she sailed into a mine."

"Could that be the cause?" the coroner wondered aloud.

"The flotation material was scorched on the inside. I think that whatever sank *Siren* was something that she was carrying aboard."

Cheryl listened open-mouthed. Torpedoes . . . mines . . . dynamite . . . why did it sound familiar? Where had she seen all this before?

"Impossible," George was saying. "We knew every item that she was carrying aboard." He looked at Greeley. "Everything was checked to assure that the boat wasn't carrying even an extra ounce of weight."

Greeley was nodding. "That's certainly true," he said to the coroner, and then to the Coast Guard officer, "Hardest time to slip something aboard a yacht is when she's fitted out for a race."

"Who would have checked everything?" the coroner asked.

"The captain," George said. "Robert Cramm. But I also know for a fact that she was completely inventoried by the designer, and I had been over her several times myself."

Cheryl wasn't listening. She remembered her dream and recalled clearly diving under the yacht and holding on to her keel. And then, when she awoke, she had been positive that *Siren* was taking Robert and Beth to their destruction. Of course, that was after the events. And it was a dream. She had awakened in her own bed. But it was all so vivid, and seemed to fit perfectly with images of mines and explosives.

Next the medical examiner leaned forward and described the condition of Beth's body when it had been brought to him. "Drowning," he stated, was the cause of death. Then he described the burns to Beth's back and legs, and added a detailed description of the bones that were broken.

"And your conclusion?" the coroner asked.

"I would support the probability that there was an explosion aboard the yacht, and that the deceased suffered severe trauma prior to going into the water. She was alive, and she did drown. But there were substantial internal injuries that would have been a threat to her life in any event."

"Was there anything else unusual about the deceased's body?"

"Well, not unusual," the medical examiner said. "But Beth Hardaway was about three months pregnant."

The coroner turned to ask Cheryl and George whether they knew that Beth was expecting a child. Their stunned expressions told him that he didn't have to ask.

NARRAGANSETT BAY

29

SHE HAD TO KNOW. BECAUSE IF THE BABY WAS ROBERT'S, then her coordinates were gone and she had no fix on her direction. His business failing. A scandal about to destroy his marriage. Suddenly, it was thinkable that he might destroy himself and take Beth with him. He might have chosen the more northerly course not for the currents but to take *Siren* away from the other boats, to a point where there was little possibility of rescue or salvage. And then he could have put an end to the problems that were closing in around him.

Cheryl tried to banish the thoughts, but details kept pushing their way into her mind. It was Robert who had mentioned "hospital" in the telephone call to Gretchen that he knew his wife was overhearing. Had that been a ploy to get her off the boat and force Beth to sail? Was that why Gretchen had been surprised that she had rushed home? Because there was no emergency other than the one that Robert's choice of words had created?

Then there were the images of Robert and Beth working so closely together as the new yacht was taking shape. She had been no help to her husband. Beth had been sharing his dream. It took no great leap of fancy to imagine them falling in love.

There was another possibility. She remembered Robert's abrupt decision to have Cheryl sail the race even though Beth had handled all the shakedown cruises. Had he been *ending* a relationship with Beth? And if he had, perhaps Beth had been the one who decided to close off their problems.

That was certainly one of the avenues that the coroner had been exploring. George, who had outfitted the boat, was certain that there were no explosive materials aboard. Sean and others from the Cramm yard had *Siren* under constant guard whenever she was at the pier. The only person who had brought anything aboard after the stores were loaded had been Beth. She had rushed aboard at the last minute, dragging her seabag.

But all these speculations were driven by the thought that Robert was the father of Beth's child. Cheryl could admit that possibility. What she couldn't conceive was the possibility of either of them doing something so drastic. They were responsible people, each accepting the consequences of their actions, neither given to looking for the easy way out. She had no idea how they would have coped with the mounting problems. But *Siren*'s destruction wasn't the kind of solution that either would have considered.

But, still, she had to know. Were Beth and her husband simply a racing crew? Or was there something more? And if there were, how was it connected with *Siren*? She could feel her heart beginning to race as she stood by the side of the design shed, waiting for Sean Patton. He might not be able to tell her anything. He might not want to. But he was the only one who had worked together with the two of them.

She started to retreat into the shadows as soon as his truck turned through the yard gate. But she forced herself to step up to this parking area, and she was standing beside him when he stepped down.

"I've got some numbers for you," he said.

Cheryl was taken off guard, and her expression went blank.

"For the inventory," he explained. "You wanted to know how much we could raise. I'm not certain because I haven't talked to all the dealers and distributors. But I can give you a pretty fair estimate."

"Oh, yes, of course." There was no life in her voice.

"It's not great, but it isn't all that bad," Sean told her. He stepped around her and fitted his key into the door of the design shed. He reached in and snapped on the fluorescent lights, and then stepped back so she could enter ahead of him.

"Basically, the boats still in our yards *could* be used for a fire sale." He pulled out a chair at a small, round conference table, and she settled into it dumbly. He took some files from his desk and then sat down next to her. "The dealers won't take them for anything close to what they're worth until they know what's happening to Cramm Yachts. But they'll pounce on them like vultures if you have to auction them off. I'd try to hold on to them as long as you can."

He began arranging papers in front of her. "Now, the boats already delivered to the dealers are a different story. They'd put up cash for those at even a modest discount. . . ."

"Sean?"

He looked up from the papers he had been arranging.

"You heard about Beth?"

Sean studied her before he answered. "Yeah. I heard." He dropped his eyes back to the inventory figures. "As if there wasn't enough tragedy."

"I have to ask you. . . ."

"Was I the father?" he said quickly, finishing the question.

Cheryl turned her face away. "I'm sorry. I have no right—"

"I already told you. We tried being lovers almost a year ago. It wasn't right for either of us. I liked Beth. I respected her talent. That's all there was."

"Could . . . Robert?" She was hardly able to get the words out.

"She didn't tell me she was pregnant. So I didn't do a lot of guessing. As far as I knew, we were all working to build a boat."

He could see that his answer wasn't satisfying her.

"Personally," he continued, "I don't think there was anything between them. But I'm not going to try to figure it out, and I don't think you should either."

Cheryl got up from the table and turned her back as she looked out the window. "The Coast Guard and the police think that Beth might have brought explosives aboard," she said almost idly.

"Christ," Sean groaned. "That's the craziest thing I ever heard. What are they trying to prove? That she blew herself up because she was pregnant?"

Cheryl answered, "Or that Robert blew them both up. Or that they were in some sort of suicide pact. They're pretty sure that *Siren* was blown apart by a bomb."

"That would be comforting," Sean allowed.

She turned abruptly, almost angrily.

"It would mean my design didn't tear itself apart. It wouldn't be my fault. But that's too easy. I think she exploded from the stresses on the hull, and then something blew up. The flares . . . the oil in the fuel lines . . ."

Cheryl nodded. "That's what George says. He thinks talk about bombs and mines is ridiculous. But it's just as illogical to think that *Siren* simply broke up in such light weather."

"I'm not discounting sabotage," Sean admitted. "I've been calling friends with the other companies and some of the crews that Beth sailed with. I figure if there was a bomb, somebody would have heard something."

She looked at him hopefully.

"There's nothing," he said. "Not even a rumor. As far as everyone is concerned, I screwed up. The keel snapped off—"

Cheryl started to protest, but he waved her words away. "Unless something else turns up, that's what happened." He picked up the papers they had been reviewing. "Now let me tell you what I think you can raise on the inventory."

30 GEORGE LOOKED LIKE A PALLBEARER WHEN HE called at the house that night. He was hunched over with his head sunk between his shoulder blades, his gait more a shuffle than a step.

"We're losing the deal," he said heavily as soon as Cheryl joined him in the library. He was already at the bar fixing himself a drink.

"I've got some numbers that Sean worked up," she responded. "We should be able to raise ten million. Maybe even a bit more."

"You better sit down," he told her. It was almost an order. She settled slowly into a soft chair, her eyes fixed on George's back. When he turned, he held two glasses and he crossed the room to hand one to her.

"Vector is concerned about the hint of scandal," he said, and then while shaking his head, "as if the women Philip McKnight brings aboard his yacht don't qualify."

"Scandal?"

"There may be a crime involved in Robert's death. There's a suggestion that you may not have clean title to Cramm. Which would mean that you couldn't enter into a—"

"They think I blew up *Siren*?" Cheryl gasped.

"No, of course not. But people are talking, and the Vector attorneys—"

Cheryl was on her feet. "What people? What are they saying?"

"It's all nonsense. . . ."

"What are they saying?" she demanded again.

George sighed and then deflated into the chair opposite Cheryl's. She took the signal and sat back down, watching George as he sipped at his drink.

"Everyone in the business has heard that Beth Hardaway was pregnant," George began. "So, of course, the question on everyone's mind is who she was sleeping with."

"That's none of anyone's business—" she started, but he held up a hand to silence her.

"Didn't you ask me on the plane back who I thought the father was?"

She blushed in embarrassment, knowing that she had asked the same question only a few hours ago.

"Well, you're not the only one who's wondering. And the list of candidates seems to have boiled down to Sean . . . or Robert."

This time Cheryl made no pretense of being indignant. She simply nodded.

"If it was . . . Robert"—he said the name softly—"then there are two prime suspects. Sean, because Robert would have taken Beth away from him—"

"And me," Cheryl snapped, "because Beth would have taken Robert away from me."

He nodded gravely and then took a slow swallow of the drink. He watched as Cheryl drained her own glass. Then he took the two glasses back to the bar.

"Why did you leave the race and come back to Newport?" he asked almost absently as he added the ice cubes.

"You know damn well," she snapped.

"Yes, I remember clearly. We were all concerned. But there was nothing wrong with Rachael. I mean, when you got home, everything was fine."

"It wasn't as serious as it sounded," Cheryl agreed.

He handed her the refreshed drink. "The last-minute change of crew. The secret child. It's just the sort of coincidence that fuels a rumor."

Cheryl's anger rang in her voice. "Is that what Philip McKnight thinks? That I found out my husband was having an affair, so I murdered him and his mistress?"

"Of course not." George laid a comforting hand on her shoulder. "No one who knew you and Robert would ever think that you could intentionally . . . have anything to do with his death."

"*Intentionally?* So that's the story? Cramm's crazy wife killed him in a mindless rage?"

George walked back to the bar and set down his glass. "Forgive me, Cheryl. I never should have brought this up."

She stood and went to join him. "You *had* to bring it up. It affects the whole outlook for the company. And God knows I've given them enough ammunition. But I never hurt anyone."

"I know that," he reassured her.

"But McKnight and his friends don't?"

George led her back to her chair and pressed her glass back into her hands. She took a drink and then gave herself a moment to cool down.

"You had blackouts, Cheryl," he reminded her in a sympathetic tone. "There were days, even weeks, when you didn't know who you were, much less what you were doing."

"I'm over all that. For the past eight months . . ." She felt guilty in just defending herself.

"I know. But people who knew about . . . your problems haven't been with you since your recovery. It's easy for them to imagine you lapsing back. Particularly if it makes for a nasty rumor. I don't know why we all find it so much more satisfying to believe the worst."

Cheryl sat quietly. As ugly as it was, the scenario was possible. And there was that dream. Why should her mind flash images of her swimming under *Siren* and hanging on to her keel? Unless her dream had really been a memory. She could imagine the people in the industry mourning with one another. Poor Robert. And what a terrible thing to happen to Beth. It would never occur to any of them that she knew nothing about planting a bomb.

"Is that what McKnight believes?" she asked.

"I'm sure it's not," George assured her. "But the fact is that Philip is paying a very hefty premium for the Cramm name. He's a businessman, Cheryl, and he doesn't want to buy damaged merchandise. He's concerned about the innuendos he's hearing."

He settled back into his chair and pulled thoughtfully on his drink. Then he asked, "You're determined to try and keep Cramm independent?"

"More so than ever. Particularly if the industry wags would interpret a quick sale as an admission of guilt." She tossed down the rest of her drink.

31 WHEN SHE REACHED THE BOTTOM OF THE STAIRS, she couldn't remember where they led. They seemed to climb into the mist, curving gracefully, first to the left and then to the right. But eventually they just disappeared.

There was the sound of the sea. Waves seemed to be crashing all around her, the lacy white foam gliding in the wind. But where? The sea couldn't be at the top of the steps. It was outside. Down the road and through the gate.

Cheryl turned away from the steps and walked to the front door that she had just closed behind George. But when she stepped outside, he was gone. Even the taillights of his car had become invisible. She started down the road, following George to the gate.

And then she remembered that he had left a long time ago. He had reached out with his hands, squared her shoulders, and then given her a kiss on the cheek as if he were a French officer presenting a medal. He had said something but it had seemed too faint to hear. Then she had followed him to the door and watched him dash down the steps to his car.

She felt cold when she reached the gates, and saw that she was in her robe. She looked down and saw that she was wearing her slippers and then understood that she had already dressed for bed. When she looked back at the house, the lights in her bedroom were blazing.

When had she gone upstairs? She couldn't remember. Had she checked on Rachael? She had no recollection of going into the nursery. And what was she doing at the front gate of the estate?

She heard the sound of the sea against the seawall across the road. Of course! She had heard the water and seen the waves crashing around her. She had gone to find the water. Cheryl spun quickly and raced across the road to the gate of the Cramm yard.

It was locked. Someone had locked the gate to keep her from the water. To keep her from finding Robert.

"Rah . . . bert!" she screamed. But she knew that no one would hear her. The yard was shut down. The road behind her was empty. And there was a wind blowing off the water that scattered her voice. She would have to do it herself. She would have to drag the gate open.

Cheryl hooked her fingers through the wire mesh and began banging the gate against its lock. She pulled it back and then pushed it with all her might until the chain clanged against the metal frame. The sound was like an anchor rattling over the side.

Suddenly, she was freezing. The wind was cutting through her robe and nightgown. She was all alone. The gate was not going to open, and the distance back to the glowing light in her bedroom was impossibly far. She would die right here unless someone came to help her. She began screaming with all her might.

She was still screaming when she saw the light flash on in front of her. And then she felt her fingers being unwound from the wire fence.

"Cheryl! Cheryl!" It was Gretchen's voice screaming in her face.

The yard was lighted, and she saw Sean racing toward her.

A dream, she thought. Another nightmare! But why was she freezing? And why were her hands cut and bleeding?

And then Gretchen was holding her. Sean was throwing his jacket over her shoulders.

"What the hell happened?" Sean demanded.

"I don't know. She was in her room, and then she was gone." It was Gretchen's voice talking past her, as if she weren't even there.

"I'll get my truck."

Cheryl knew it was real when Sean's truck screeched up in front of her. Sean pushed open the door, and Gretchen steered her into the seat. Then Gretchen squeezed in beside her, and the truck crossed the road and drove through the gates to the house.

"What happened?" Cheryl asked.

"You walked down to the yard," Gretchen told her. "You were trying to get into the yard."

She looked from Gretchen to Sean. Their faces were set like masks, concealing whatever they were feeling. Both were staring straight ahead as if they were afraid to look at her.

"Why was I going to the yard?" she asked.

Neither of them answered.

"When did I get ready for bed?"

"After George left," Gretchen answered softly.

"Why don't I remember?" Cheryl's voice was more mystified than frightened.

"You've had a terrible ordeal," Gretchen reminded her.

Sean nodded, his eyes still on the road. "You've been through hell."

32 "MONSIEUR SEAN PATTON?" THE FRENCH ACCENT turned his last name into "pa-TON."

Sean blinked at his watch. It was seven-thirty, and he had padded out of his makeshift bedroom into the design shed wearing only his shorts.

"Who is this?" he mumbled.

"One moment please, for Baron Murot."

Murot, Sean remembered. The lunatic Frenchman who was still trying to win the America's Cup.

"Sean," the baron's voice said with a delightful lilt. "I understand you have designed the world's fastest yacht. I wonder if you would like to build one for me?"

"It sank, Baron," Sean answered dryly. "I'm surprised you haven't heard."

"Of course I've heard. But it sank in heavy seas. The Cup isn't raced in heavy seas. If the wind blows strong, they cancel the race. Besides, there are no engines. No fuel. Nothing to explode."

Sean settled into his chair. "You know I work for Cramm Yachts."

"A wonderful company with fine craftsmen. They should be perfect for building a Cup boat, don't you think?"

As soon as he had hung up on Murot, Sean pulled out the plans to *Siren* and began comparing the numbers with the America's Cup formula. His design, he saw quickly, was at odds in every ratio. It would have to be a completely new boat. But the principles could be applied with a smaller, less radical keel. He spent most of the day with rough sketches, changing the dimensions over and over again until he was close to the regulation numbers for an America's Cup contender. Then he rolled the drawing under his arm and rushed up to the office area, where he charged in on George.

"How would you like to do a Cup boat?" he asked as he crossed to Williamson's desk and began spreading out his drawings.

"A Cup boat?" George smiled and reached into his desk drawer for his bottle of Scotch. He nodded in the direction of his credenza. "Get yourself a glass." George poured for both of them. "You have any idea what that would cost?"

"No, and I don't give a damn. Because Baron Murot will be footing the bill."

The glass slipped from George's lip. "Murot?" His eyes narrowed suspiciously.

Sean reminded him that he had once designed a boat that the baron campaigned, and then he repeated the telephone conversation from the morning. "We call the shots, we get to build a Cup version of *Siren*, and we can even manage the campaign. It's a godsend. We can put Cramm Yachts back on the map."

"The man is a crackpot," George pronounced. "A public fool!"

Sean nodded. "Yeah, but a rich crackpot. And he pays his bills in thirty days."

George leaned back and balanced the pros against the cons. There was no question about it. The design and construction fees would keep the company going for several months more. And the prestige of designing a Cup boat would probably deliver some additional business. But joining up with Murot would make Cramm look ridiculous. And it would be almost impossible to have a strong campaign with the baron interfering at every turn. "Terribly risky, at best," he concluded. "But Vector might like it. It could be your first assignment with the new company."

"I thought we could do it here, as Cramm. We might be able to help Cheryl keep the company. . . ."

George looked suddenly saddened. "You heard about last night, I suppose."

"I was there," Sean answered. "It's been too much for her."

George poured himself another drink and held the bottle out to Sean. Sean waved it away.

"Trying to save this company will put her in an asylum," George went on. "I'm willing to help her any way I can, but at the same time I don't want to help her back into her madness." He told Sean what Cheryl had been like, constantly suspicious that her daughter was dead, and certain that everyone in the household was plotting against her. "It will only get worse if she has to deal with the strain of running Cramm Yachts. And then, if we bring a lunatic like Baron Murot into the picture . . ."

George's secretary stepped into the office and handed Sean a manila envelope. He opened it absently as he listened.

"We have a deal on the table that will make Cheryl a wealthy woman without a care in the world. It will keep Cramm up and running. And it will give both of us exactly what we want. For me, a bigger company to run. And for you, a chance to design high-performance yachts. We should take it, Sean. And I'd appreciate it if you would help me persuade Cheryl that there's no way anyone is going to save her husband's company."

"I'd like the chance to rebuild *Siren*," Sean admitted. "It's the only way I'll ever satisfy myself that the design wasn't flawed."

He slid a large, blurred photo print out of the envelope and squinted as he tried to decipher the blurred image. The print had a blue cast with a darker shadow in the background. It was cropped by a clean, dark area down one side and a ragged, gnarled shape on another edge. He couldn't tell the top from the bottom.

"What is it?" George asked. "Who is it from?"

"Damned if I know." Sean pulled the envelope out of the wastebasket. There was no return address. The only identification was a Ft. Lauderdale postmark. The back of the print showed the logotype of a photographer, a killer whale plunging through a circle, and a five-number print identification code.

He walked around the desk and laid the print in front of George. Together, they studied the image, turning it slowly so that each edge would become, in turn, the bottom of the picture. Suddenly, Sean stopped, his eyes blinking in disbelief. He was looking at an underwater shot of *Siren*'s keel, the torpedo-shaped weight completely distinctive at the bottom of the knife-shaped blade. He reversed the picture so that the blurry image of the keel seemed to be standing straight up from a rocky bottom.

"The sunken hull," George gasped.

Sean was about to agree, but he noticed that the light was filtering up from the bottom instead of down from the top. He reversed it again, so that he had a photo of the keel sticking down into shallow water. And then, like an optical trick, he recognized the dark areas. He was looking between the pilings of a dock that *Siren* was tied to. One of the wooden braces, covered with saw-edged barnacles, blocked the image of the hull. But details of the keel were visible, even though there was no sign of an underwater light source. The photographer had made do with the available light that was filtering down from above.

"It's taken at a dock," he told George. "It's *Siren* tied to a pier."

Sean studied it intensely. Someone was trying to tell him something about the boat. That it hadn't sunk, and was now tied up to a dock? Or maybe they were showing him a defect in the keel, or something attached to the keel that would explain why the boat had broken up.

"When was it taken?" George demanded.

"I don't know." Sean told him that he had been calling his contacts throughout the industry for any information on why the boat might have blown up. Now someone was replying. Someone who knew that the picture would mean something to him. But who? What?

He turned the print over to the photographer's logo, and then picked up George's phone and dialed Information in the Ft. Lauderdale area code. When he got the information operator on the line, he made up names to go with the logotype—Shamu, Orca, Killer Whale—asking for listings under each name until he had exhausted the patience of the operator. He was fuming when he hung up.

"Try another operator," George advised. He picked up the phone himself and this time described the logotype, hoping that the operator could find it in the Yellow Pages listings. The operator explained that he was at a computer terminal and that the logotype was meaningless. "Call someone in the area. Or try your library. Some of them have a complete set of Yellow Pages directories."

Sean snatched the photo out of George's hand. He raced out of the building, jumped into his truck, and headed into town to the library.

33 CHERYL STOOD SILENTLY OVER RACHAEL'S BED, watching her daughter give up her nightly struggle and settle into sleep. She lifted the hand that the child was holding and carefully separated the little fist from her fingers. Then she backed away to the door, setting each foot down gently so as not to make a sound. Only when she was outside the nursery could she be sure that Rachael was down for the night.

She was startled when she bumped into Gretchen, who was standing just outside the door. "Oh, God, you frightened me," Cheryl whispered.

"I just came up to see if you needed help," Gretchen said, keeping her own voice low. They crossed the hall to Cheryl's bedroom and closed the door behind them.

"It gets harder and harder to get her to sleep," Cheryl said.

"Maybe she's getting too old for a bedtime. We could just let her stay up until she tires herself out."

Cheryl laughed. "She'd tire the two of us out before she even began to yawn."

They spent a minute smiling at some of Rachael's antics, taking turns remembering something that the little girl had done during the day.

"I better let you get some sleep," the au pair finally said, and began to open the door.

"Gretchen?" Cheryl's tone had changed from light to serious. "You're not worrying about me, are you?"

"Of course not. Why would—"

"I know I've done some ridiculous things. I still don't know what I was doing at the boatyard gate. But I feel fine. I know what I'm doing."

"I know you're okay. I'm not worried," Gretchen protested.

Cheryl looked at her skeptically. "Every time I turn around, I'm stepping on your toes. You're watching over me like a hawk."

"Oh, I'm sorry. It's just . . ."

"You're worried that I might hurt Rachael."

"Oh, no," the girl insisted. "You'd never do anything to hurt her."

"Well, *I* was worried," Cheryl admitted. "I thought, What if I had taken her with me? What if I carried her out to the pier?"

Gretchen's hands came up to her mouth. She nodded and whispered, "I did think about that, too. I'm sorry, but I worried that, if you had one of your spells—"

"I'm not having spells," Cheryl interrupted. "It's not like when I was sick. I feel fine. Really." She was almost begging to be believed.

"I know," Gretchen said, but Cheryl could read the disbelief in her eyes. There was no purpose in trying to explain. Gretchen had seen her climbing the fence. The more she insisted she was sane, the crazier she would seem.

"But I do want to say thank you," Cheryl finished. "I know you're concerned for both of us, and I appreciate it."

Maybe it is too much, she thought as she laid out her nightgown. It would all be easier if she just signed the papers and let Cramm Yachts slip away. Sean had shown her how she could raise the money to keep the company going another few months. But not much would change in a few months. And the deal that George thought was the best they could hope for might slip away.

She heard a telephone ringing as she slipped the cotton gown over her head. She listened curiously and then realized that it was coming from Robert's office in the next room. The phone hadn't rung since he had moved back into the room they had shared. Cheryl had assumed that the line was disconnected.

She hurried to the door that connected to the office and stepped into the room, now lit only by the shaft of light that came from her night table. She found the wall switch and then rushed to the desk, snatching the telephone handset from the cradle.

"Hello."

The line was live. She could hear the faint, airy sound of the line current, and could barely make out the sound of breathing.

"Hello, who is this?"

There was no response. Just the sound of a presence at the other end.

"I think you have a wrong number," she said with much more self-assurance than she felt.

"No!" The voice at the other end was muffled. It had a metallic quality, as if it were being played from a cheap speaker.

"Who *is* this?" Cheryl demanded.

"It's me. Robert."

The phone dropped from her hand and clattered to the floor. Cheryl's piercing scream cut through the nighttime quiet as she stumbled out of the room.

34 GEORGE AND SEAN WERE WAITING IN THE LIVING room when the doctor came down the stairs. George had been summoned by Gretchen when Cheryl hadn't snapped out of her hysteria. Sean had seen the cars racing through the gate and realized that there was a problem up at the house. Now they both sprang up from the chairs

where they had been sitting morosely, but the doctor was shaking his head before they even reached him.

"There's nothing I can add," he told George. "She's very upset, as you can imagine. I've given her something to relax her, and she should feel better in the morning."

"Did she say anything more about the call?" George demanded.

"Just that it was Robert."

"She should be in a hospital," Sean said.

"Not if you want to keep this confidential," the doctor answered. "And I don't think it's necessary. She's sleeping now, and I'll check back in the morning." George saw him out.

"Who could do something like this?" Sean asked when George returned from the doorway.

"We should check with the phone company," George answered. "They can tell us the number where the call came from."

"It will be a phone booth," Sean guessed.

"If there was a call . . ." George seemed to be thinking out loud.

Sean's anger flashed. "You think she's making this up?"

"No! No, of course not. It's all very real to her. It's just that Gretchen didn't hear a telephone ring. And the phone in the office is private and unlisted."

Sean groped for an answer and then looked hopelessly toward George. "Could Robert be alive?"

"Sean, for Christ's sake—"

"The photo," Sean interrupted. "It's a shot of *Siren* floating at a dock. Suppose someone was telling me that *Siren* is still afloat."

"Absurd," George snapped, turning away in anger.

Sean kept on him. "If the boat is still afloat, then Robert could be alive. And that would explain the phone call, placed to his private office where Cheryl would be the only one likely to answer."

George turned on him. "There's another far more likely answer, and we both know damn well what it is. Cheryl is out of touch. She's fantasizing phone calls from her husband because she wants him to be alive. But he's dead, and it would be very dangerous for you or I to feed her fantasies."

"But the photo . . ."

"Sean, we don't know when that picture was taken. We don't even know who took it."

"I found out," Sean interjected. "A guy in Miami, named Whaley. I called but there was no answer. I'll keep trying. The picture *has* to mean something."

"All right," George agreed. "Check on the picture, and see what the phone company can tell you about the call. But if there's nothing to be learned, then help me convince Cheryl to give up the company. Because if word gets out that she's hearing voices, this whole deal could get away from us. And then everything is lost."

35 WHEN HE WOKE IN THE MORNING, SEAN FOUND that he had fallen asleep in his clothes. He peeled off his T-shirt, changed his jeans for an even older pair that was cut off above the knees, and carried his shaving kit out to the dock. He dropped the kit at the foot of the gangway and then dove into the space between the antique steam yacht and the modern cruiser that were tied to the pier. For a while, he played dolphin, diving down deep into the channel until the water lost all trace of light, and then kicking up until he blasted out into the open air. Then he rolled onto his back and floated, his hair spread out like a halo, the morning sun turning the insides of his eyelids pink.

Sean used the swim ladder on the back of the launch to pull himself out of the harbor, and then held the freshwater hose over his head for an icy shower. He shaved, tied his hair back with a rubber band, and went back to his home in the design shed.

He picked up his telephone and called the phone company. When he told the first clerk what he needed, he was bumped to another clerk and then transferred two more rungs up the ladder.

"Look, you're the fourth person I've spoken to," he said, trying to sound irritated. "It's a simple enough request. I got an important call last night and I didn't write down the phone number of the caller. I need the number."

"You want the calling number ID of a call you received last night?" the telephone representative asked.

"That's right. And please don't tell me that you have to transfer me to someone else."

"No. I just need some information." Sean answered a series of questions to identify himself and the company. Then he gave Robert's private number and the time of the call.

"Have it for you by the end of the day," the voice promised.

"Sooner the better," Sean said as his parting shot.

Cheryl was sitting on the sunporch when Sean burst into the house. She barely managed to smile as he sat down next to her.

"You're not ready for a rocking chair," he said.

She looked at the chair, and the blanket that Gretchen had tucked in over her bathrobe. "This was my place. They parked me out here for over a year," she said bitterly. "I don't remember most of it, but what I do remember scares the hell out of me."

"Then let's get out of here. We can take the launch down into the bay. I've got things to tell you."

Her eyes dropped. "I guess you didn't hear about my performance last night."

"Sure I did. Some son of a bitch placed a crank call and scared the hell out of you. Anyone would have run out of the room screaming."

She looked up and smiled. "Thanks for trying. But it came in on Robert's private line. Apparently I'm hearing voices."

"I'm betting you heard a telephone. I've called the phone company. They'll be back to me before the end of the day with the number where the call was made. Then we'll go looking for the bastard."

Cheryl brightened. "They can do that? I thought you had to keep them on the line."

"Not anymore," Sean said. "Now get yourself dressed. There are things I have to tell you. We're back in the racing business."

The family boats were docked at the end of the pier, usually with one or two of the finished yachts that had been custom-outfitted and were awaiting the inspection of the new owner. The old steam cruiser was the *Solomon Cramm*, a turn-of-the-century wooden yacht that could accommodate three or four couples for summer cruising in splendid style. She was sixty feet long, with a tall stack that used to serve her coal-burning boiler. The boat had been overhauled in the fifties, her boiler and reciprocating steam engine replaced by a simple diesel. Although she was completely seaworthy, the *Solomon Cramm* was generally used for conferences and high-level entertainment. No one was quite sure when she had last put to sea.

Just astern was the *David Cramm*, named for Robert's father. She was a forty-foot planing cruiser with fore and aft staterooms, a flying bridge, and two mammoth gasoline engines that could drive her at thirty knots. This was the boat they used for their diving trips, for accompanying yachts on extended sea trial, and for trips out to the cottage on Buzzard Island. Sean threw the lines aboard while Cheryl fired up the engines.

As they cruised south, following the channel past the old navy piers toward Castle Hill and the open sea, Cheryl's spirits lifted. The sunlight, sparkling off the water, seemed to penetrate the frightening darkness. She tossed her head, smiled easily, and enjoyed her hair blowing freely in the breeze.

Sean told her about Baron Murot, whom she knew only by his eccentric reputation. "He never mounts a full campaign," he laughed. "Just gives some boatyard a couple of million to build him a boat, puts his own crest on the sail instead of getting sponsors—" Cheryl interrupted with laughter and Sean remembered that she had seen the baron's missionary-position crest on his shirt. "He throws together a crew from among his sailing buddies," Sean continued. "His crew was so hung over when he missed the finals by less than a boat length that they didn't realize the race was over. They turned around and started sailing another leg. I swore I'd never get involved with French sailors again."

"What's different now?" she wondered.

"He wants Cramm to run the show. Design the boat, build it, outfit it, even get a captain and crew. And he'll upfront half the money. That, plus the inventory, could keep Cramm afloat for nearly a year."

Cheryl was pleased at the news, but before she allowed herself to get too enthusiastic she asked, "What does George think?"

Sean relayed Williamson's appraisal of Murot and agreed that nothing was ever certain when dealing with the baron. He presented George's concerns about the danger of losing the Vector deal, but steered clear of his appraisal of Cheryl's health. But she saw through his evasion.

"George doesn't think I can handle the stress of keeping Cramm afloat," she added. "And, with the way I've been carrying on, I guess I'd have to agree with him."

She gunned the engines as soon as they had turned Castle Hill, letting the cruiser lift her bow and begin to plane.

"Where are we headed?" Sean wondered.

"How about Buzzard Island? I haven't been there in months."

Sean nodded, and Cheryl headed out into Rhode Island Sound, southeast toward the mythical line that separated the sound from Buzzards Bay.

They cruised in silence for a few minutes, enjoying the rush of salt air and the thrill of speed. Then Sean eased into a subject that he hesitated to raise. "The phone call last night . . . are you certain it was Robert?"

She seemed surprised that a sane person would even consider the possibility. "No. The voice was muffled and scratchy, like an old phonograph record. It was more the phrasing that seemed familiar. The more I think about it, the more convinced I am that it wasn't."

"But at the time . . ."

"At the time I was damn sure it was him. Why else would I have carried on so?"

He nodded. "Well, we'll have a better idea when I hear from the phone company."

Cheryl glanced across at him. There was more. Something he wasn't telling her that was connected with the call. "Do you have any idea who it might have been?" she finally asked.

"No . . ." He hesitated, but then decided to tell her. "I got a photo in the mail. I don't know who sent it, and I haven't been able to reach the photographer. But it's an underwater shot of *Siren* tied to a dock."

Her mouth slackened. "When?"

"The photo came in yesterday, mailed just the day before. But I don't know when the shot was taken. It's just that if *Siren* is still afloat . . ."

"Robert could still be alive," she completed.

They tore into the possibilities, always concluding, as the Coast Guard had, that the boat had gone to the bottom. But there was the tantalizing suggestion of the photo, which recalled Cheryl's darkest thoughts about Robert and Beth, and the possibility that Beth's child was also his.

"What am I doing, Sean?" she asked. "Am I trying to save a company that deserves to be saved, or am I just dragging this out until I have some answers?"

They picked up the island dead ahead, and then the buoy that marked a dangerous ledge that ran northwest from the harbor. They could make out a trace of the low-lying Elizabeth Islands farther out, and to the southeast there was the first hint of Martha's Vineyard and the cliffs of Gay Head.

"I hope you're thinking about what's best for yourself," Sean answered. "It's not your fault that the company is in trouble. And there are no questions that you have to answer."

Cheryl told him about her dream and the vivid image of herself in scuba gear swimming under *Siren* and hanging on to the keel. She wondered aloud if perhaps it wasn't entirely a dream, and if she could have planted an explosive on the boat's hull.

"You know anything about explosives?" he asked. "Or fuses? Or timers?"

"Of course not," she answered. "But I don't imagine it would be very hard to find someone who did. What I'm wondering is whether it's possible to do something while you're blacked out? I mean, to be functioning perfectly normally on one level, that you remember, but to be living a different life on another level that you don't remember."

He shook his head sadly. "Stop torturing yourself. In all likelihood, there was no explosive. And even if there was, you sure as hell didn't set it—"

"Look!" Cheryl interrupted the conversation and was pointing straight ahead. Sean followed her finger and saw a cigarette boat, low to the water, powering out of the tight, rock-encased harbor of the family island.

"You've had visitors."

She pushed the throttles all the way. "Let's find out who they are."

But as soon as the sleek, low cigarette cleared the harbor, the crackle of its airplane engines droned across the water. All they could see was the rooster tail of white water she threw up as she sped off toward Martha's Vineyard.

Sean reached across and eased back the throttles. "No way you're going to catch her. Let's put in and see if they've been into anything."

They negotiated the rocky entrance to the harbor, which posed enough hazards to keep most Sunday yachtsmen from landing. Cheryl eased the boat skillfully up against the small dock.

"Is there a gun aboard?" Sean asked.

Cheryl thought so, but had no idea where it was. They looked up the path to the small cottage and then scanned the light foliage to either side. The island seemed deserted, and they stepped ashore and walked cautiously up the hill.

The padlock was still secure on the front door, but Cheryl had a key on the ring with the cruiser key. Sean went in and glanced around the inside. Cheryl followed when he told her that the cottage was empty.

"Looks as if someone has been keeping the place clean," she said.

Sean smiled. "I guess I'd never notice. But someone did crack the window next to the fireplace. So maybe someone has been sleeping here and using the fire at night."

They circled the shore of the island and convinced themselves that no one else was there.

"What do you think?" she asked.

"Probably a couple of lovers at anchor in the cove."

"But why would they run away?"

"Maybe they thought we were the jealous husband."

They laughed away their anxiety and sat on the dock next to the boat, enjoying the sunshine and the freedom of the island.

But Cheryl's spirits grew heavy as they sped back to Castle Hill. All the troubles that she had so happily put behind her were now back in front of her. Robert's death. Cramm's financial problems. Her own bizarre behavior that hinted she was dropping back into a nightmare world that she had barely escaped. Robert and George had set everything up so that she would never have to worry again. They didn't expect her to try to save the battered wreckage of the company.

"I've been thinking of going through with the sale," she finally admitted. She glanced in Sean's direction, expecting to see shock, and maybe even anger. But his expression told her nothing. "I thought you were going to fight," he said.

"Much as I'd love to save the Cramm tradition, I'm not sure I'm up to it. And I don't want to risk everything on a long shot."

He nodded. "That's the smart play. Vector's money is legal tender."

"I know it will hurt some people. . . . You, I suppose."

"I'll be okay," Sean assured her. "There's a place for me at Vector, if I want it. Hell maybe the baron will give me my own deal. Either way, I'll be able to show that *Siren* was a good design."

Cheryl seemed relieved as she looked straight ahead, over the bow.

"Just one thing," Sean continued. "Whatever you decide, do it for the right reasons. Don't let anything convince you that . . . you're . . ."

"Crazy," she offered, using the word he didn't want to say.

"Whatever. I've been working with you for nearly a year. We've been talking every day over the past few weeks. You make plenty of sense to me."

"Thank you." She wanted to throw her arms around him. He was the only one who wasn't thinking about padding her bedroom.

He dropped her off at the house, where the whole staff was waiting nervously on the front porch. "Jesus, it looks like a burial party," she said.

Sean pushed the truck door open for her and watched as she disappeared into the house with the staff trailing at her heels. He drove back down the hill and went to his room in the design shed. On his desk, he found the call-back message from the man at the telephone company.

"I'm sorry, but we have nothing," the voice told him.

"What do you mean, nothing?"

"No record of a call yesterday. There hasn't been a call to that number during the entire billing period."

"The phone call came in last night," Sean insisted, "between nine and ten o'clock."

"Well, I won't contradict you," he heard. "But if someone called that telephone last night, they didn't call over our network. There was no call recorded."

Sean set down the telephone slowly, trying not to believe what he had just been told. There had been no crank caller. The ringing telephone was in Cheryl's imagination.

36 CHERYL WALKED STRAIGHT FROM HER BEDROOM AND into Robert's office. Now that the connecting door was open, it seemed part of her bedroom. And with Robert gone, its privacy was no longer important.

She glanced at the pictures he had chosen for the walls: hand-colored etchings of the great sailing vessels that Cramm had built over a century ago. The volumes in the bookcase were all histories of great explorations, from Magellan's circle of the earth to the *Apollo* missions to the moon. Sean's test-tank model of *Siren* was mounted on a brass stand and decorated the end table next to the daybed. There was a telescope in the window, pointed down toward the harbor.

It could have been a bachelor's room except for the two framed photographs on the desk. One was of him and Cheryl, taken a few days after their wedding. The other was of Rachael, carefully posed with a favorite doll. That was all there was of their life together: a momentary flash of a happy marriage, and a beautiful child sitting alone. There was nothing of her recovery, nor any reminder of the months they had just shared. It was Robert's solitary cell where he lived while she was alone in her own prison. Apparently he had no use for it once she had recovered.

Cheryl could only guess at the photographs that would have been added. Probably the two of them aboard *Siren* in Hamilton Harbor, each with a hand on a trophy. Certainly both of them with Rachael between them in her ballet costume, on her first bicycle, or even at the cockpit of a day sailer. She felt a knot tightening in her chest. Was she really lapsing back into darkness? Had she really heard his voice?

She settled carefully into the chair, her light pose betraying the awkwardness she felt at invading Robert's affairs. She fitted the small key into the lock, and the desk drawer opened at her touch. She had never thought that Robert held things back from her. But that was exactly what she was looking for: something that he had held back. She knew she was invading the life he had lived while she was unreachable. She knew she was looking for answers as to why *Siren* might have been carrying explosives. Or why Beth Hardaway had been pregnant.

She began thumbing through the file folders. There were copies of business correspondence that he had worked on at home, probably while listening to her sleep in the next room. The enormous volume of the material testified to his determination to watch over her constantly. There was a file of articles about illnesses like her own, and correspondence with doctors and medical editors. He had left no stone unturned in his search to find the cure that would bring her back. There were medical records, with bills attached that totaled to staggering amounts. Half the desk was filled with evidence of Robert's devotion, and proof that he had suffered with her.

She found financial folders, filled with penciled work sheets. She recognized the account number of the cash account, and saw the systematic withdrawals with charges to expenses that didn't make sense. His private accounts, she thought. The ones that George was attempting to cover with the insurance proceeds. There was no question of why Robert would have needed money. The correspondence indicated neglect of his business, and the medical expenses were probably beyond expectation.

There was a folder marked *Sean Patton*, containing the original correspondence between the two men, some preliminary drawings of *Siren*, engineering data, and cost estimates. There was also a handwritten agreement that specified Sean's funding and the bonus he would earn if *Siren* met his speed projections.

Her breath caught when she saw *Beth Hardaway* written in Robert's hand across the tab of a file. Cheryl opened it reluctantly, hoping that she would find nothing personal. Her face eased into a smile as she found a similar agreement for Beth's salary, receipts for bonuses he had given her as the work progressed, and a promised bonus when *Siren* clocked her first record time.

She sat back in the chair, half disappointed, half relieved. There was nothing that began to answer the questions that were troubling her, but also nothing that would link her husband with Beth or suggest any reason why he would kill himself. As she pushed the drawer closed, the files slid back. Buried beneath them she saw the stack of letters on blue stationery. They were clipped together as single sheets. There were no envelopes, nor any signatures that she could see. But even at a distance she recognized the distinctive European style of Gretchen's script.

Cheryl glanced up at the open door to her bedroom, almost expecting to see Gretchen standing there. She felt guilty for invading the young girl's private correspondence. But she had to know.

The letters began at the end of Gretchen's first month in the Cramm home. The first told Robert how well Cheryl was doing, seemingly in response to his request that she keep a close watch over his wife. It also mentioned the joy she was finding in taking care of his child. But she complained of her loneliness and wondered if their arrangement might be shortened. She didn't think she could last a year away from her home country. The tone changed during the second month. She was beginning to feel at home and had developed a happy relationship with Mrs. Cramm. By the fourth month, Gretchen seemed to be completely in charge. She felt that Cheryl was hovering over Rachael and that the little girl was confused and frightened. The chronology continued, expressing growing concern that Cheryl was "smothering" her daughter. And there were expressions of Gretchen's sorrow that Robert was burdened with such great difficulties. There was another change in tone about the time when Robert had become heavily involved with *Siren*'s trials. Gretchen specifically regretted his absence, but promised to protect his daughter. Implied was the notion that Rachael needed to be saved from Cheryl's domination. And then, over the most recent months, Gretchen's undisguised affection for Robert and Rachael, and her only slightly ambiguous suggestion that Cheryl was the only obstacle to the family's happiness.

"I worry terribly what will happen to Rachael after I'm gone," Gretchen had written, "particularly if you will continue to be away from the home. She will miss you even more than I do, and poor Cheryl cannot begin to substitute for either of us."

There was a frightening intimacy in the letters, a supposition by Gretchen that she could say anything to Robert. There was the certitude that Gretchen was the linchpin of the family, and Robert's only safe connection with his daughter. Nowhere did she suggest that Robert would be better off without his wife. But even more terrifying was the fact that such a suggestion did not need to be made. The letters seemed to assume that Cheryl's presence as a rational parent was only temporary, and that Robert would naturally be making decisions for the long term.

Cheryl pushed the letters back into the drawer. She had to hold on to the desk to steady herself as she climbed to her feet. How could Gretchen have felt so much in control of the household? How could Robert have let her go on when her fantasies were so clearly spelled out in the letters? Knowing the au pair's state of mind, how could he have arranged for her to stay on? Unless he believed what she had written in her letters. Unless he had given her reason to think that these were the kind of letters he wanted to receive.

She shut off the light and closed the door to the office. Then she started across her bedroom, headed into the hall and straight to Gretchen's room. But before she was halfway across the room, she stopped short and sat unsteadily on the edge of her bed. Gretchen had the run of the house. She was in and out of Cheryl's room and probably in the office frequently. She would know the telephone number of Robert's private line. And she was the one who had claimed not to hear the telephone ringing. Oh, sweet Jesus, Cheryl thought. If she were suddenly to accuse Gretchen, she would be giving everyone just one more scene that proved her insanity. And if she sent the au pair away, she would drive a wedge between herself and Rachael.

She felt like a prisoner with no way to escape. Gretchen was trying to take her place, and the more she fought back, the easier she would make it for the young girl to drive her away. Oh, Robert, I need you, Cheryl started to pray. But just the mention of his name reminded her that she wasn't sure whose side he would be on.

37 SEAN WAS WAITING AT THE DOOR OF WHALEY Photography when the owner and principal underwater photographer stuck his key in the lock. Glen Whaley was just about what Sean was expecting, a great shock of bleached blond hair on top of deeply tanned swimmer's shoulders. He had lifted his air tanks and his camera

cases out of the car with an easy motion that demonstrated a reserve of power in his arms and chest.

"A killer whale," Sean commented as he followed Whaley into the studio-office. "I looked up everything connected with killer whales before I hit on a photographer named Whaley."

The photographer came to an abrupt halt in front of the countertop that served as his secretary's desk and set his equipment down gently. He seemed menacing when he turned around to his visitor. "You the guy that's been calling from Newport?"

"Yeah, that's me. Sean Patton. And this is the picture." Sean slipped the photo out of the envelope. He held it out to Whaley, but the photographer didn't even spare it a glance.

"You a cop?" His tone made it clear that he didn't like policemen.

"Nah! I'm a boat designer." He offered the photo again. "This was one of mine."

The photographer recognized his work immediately. But he didn't look pleased when he turned his eyes back to Sean. "Like I told you on the phone, I got nothing to say to you. If you listened, you'd have saved yourself a long trip for nothing."

"I need to know when you took this shot," Sean said, ignoring Whaley's dismissal. "And I need to know who you gave it to. Because whoever you gave it to was trying to show me something. Maybe something important."

"I said I don't want to talk to you," he told Sean. He put a hand on Sean's chest and began steering him toward the door.

Sean gave ground grudgingly. "I really need your help. There are people's lives involved."

"Man, you don't hear even up close. So read my lips: I ain't talking."

Sean was still backing away. "Please," he asked.

Whaley mistook the "please" as a sign of surrender. He leaned harder, pushing Sean out onto the street.

In one quick movement, Sean snatched the outstretched hand and swung Whaley's arm behind his back, throwing the big man off balance. He kicked his feet out from under him and Whaley fell like a tree.

"Let me try a different approach," Sean told him. "I'll pay for your time."

Whaley blinked in amazement and then scampered to all fours.

Before he was all the way up, he was rushing forward, his right fist launched like a battering ram. Sean ducked under and used the photographer's momentum to send him cartwheeling through the air. The big man landed on his back across the receptionist's counter. There was an explosion of wood as the counter shattered, dropping him onto the floor.

"Just a couple of questions," Sean said. He pulled a roll of bills from his pocket and held it up in Whaley's field of vision.

"Son of a bitch!" He screamed in rage as he started to his feet, and then screamed again with the pain that shot through his limbs.

"They're easy questions," Sean persisted.

Whaley arched his back just enough to convince himself that the fight was over. He looked at the money. Then he nodded.

"When did you take it?"

"Day of the race. Early in the morning. That's why the lighting wasn't any good."

Sean winced. Whaley's answer eliminated the evidence he had hoped for, proving that *Siren* was still afloat.

"How many pictures did you take?"

"Not many." His voice was soft and his breathing labored. "A couple of angles."

"Where are they?"

Whaley began moving laboriously to his feet. He tried his stance to see if there was any spring left in his legs. He glanced up, trying to figure his chances of taking Sean by surprise.

"I wouldn't," Sean cautioned. "You already made two hundred bucks, and there's lots more to be made."

The photographer kept a respectful distance between them, walking around Sean to get to his files.

There were seven more prints, each shot from a different angle. None was as revealing of the overall design as the one that Sean had received in the mail, but each displayed a portion of the keel in detail. Sean was startled to see blurred images of another diver in the background of two of the shots.

"Who's the other guy? Your assistant?"

"Someone from Vector." He twisted as he tried to stretch the pain out of his back.

"Vector? This was a Vector assignment?"

"That's who paid the bill. The guy was an engineer or something. He was scraping material samples off the keel."

"How do you know?" Sean held the photos so that Whaley could see them. "In both these angles, he's on the other side of the keel. You can't see what he's doing."

"Because that's what he told me. He took me under the piers to the boat and told me to get all the angles while he scraped some samples. He had the tools in his belt."

"Could he have attached something to the boat?"

"Sure," Whaley said. "I wasn't watching him. I was busy taking pictures."

Sean studied the prints carefully. None of them was clear. The photographer wasn't able to use a flash because the light would have been visible on the surface. He had to make do with the inadequate morning sunlight that penetrated down into the murky water. It was hard for Sean to pick up details, and impossible for him to tell exactly what was going on.

"Is there any way you can make these sharper?" he asked.

"I can clean them up a bit on a computer. But it won't do much good. If the camera didn't see something, I can't bring it back."

Sean picked two of the shots, showing both sides of the keel. When he handed them to Whaley, there were five one-hundred-dollar bills resting on them. "Get these as sharp as you can. Then send them to me COD for another five hundred."

Sean never saw the fist that came flying at him over the pictures. It struck like a club across the left side of his jaw, spinning him completely around. He wasn't sure what had happened until he found himself sitting on the floor staring up at the photographer.

"I'll bill you four hundred," Whaley said. "I just took a hundred bucks out in service."

Sean examined his jaw with his fingertips. "Deal," he said. He reached up a hand so that Whaley could help him to his feet.

38 IT WAS LATE AFTERNOON WHEN SEAN'S FLIGHT landed in Providence, and already dark when the limo dropped him at the Cramm offices. He saw that George's light was still on, so he let himself in and walked to the lighted office. George was in his shirtsleeves, a drink in his hand and the telephone resting on his shoulder. He seemed cheery, enjoying a joke with whoever was on the other end of the line. Sean took the Scotch bottle and fixed himself a drink. Then he sat across the desk, listening to half the conversation.

"Well, I'll call you if we ever have a fire sale, but right now we're still charging a premium . . . right . . . right. . . . We'll talk about it at the convention. . . ." He roared with laughter, smiling broadly. "Take care of yourself, Elliot."

His expression turned sour the second he put the phone down. "What in hell have you been doing talking to our dealers about discounts on the inventory?"

"Trying to see how much cash we could raise," Sean answered.

"Christ," George cursed, "Elliot is trying to close sales, and dealers are hearing that we're cutting prices for cash."

"Cheryl wanted to know—"

"Cheryl? Damn it, Sean, she knows even less about our dealer network than you do. Now I don't want any more of this unless it's cleared with me, do you understand?"

Sean was truly contrite. "Yeah . . . I'm sorry. . . . She was looking for alternatives to selling to Vector."

George's anger was beginning to color his skin. "Much as I'd like to accommodate Mrs. Cramm, there is no alternative to Vector."

"Not even if Vector blew up *Siren*?"

The older man's face froze. "What the fuck are you talking about?"

"The underwater photo of the boat. It was taken just before we towed her to the starting line. The photographer was hired by Vector, and there was a Vector guy diving with him. They were all over the bottom of the boat."

"Oh, for Christ's sake. That means nothing! They were just doing a bit of routine industrial espionage." George knocked back what was left in his glass and began pouring a refill. "I'd hate to admit how many times we took shots of other people's designs."

"And how many of them blew up and sank forty-eight hours after you were underneath them?"

George stopped pouring and listened intently while Sean continued.

"We've been looking all over for some explanation of why *Siren* would have sunk. The Coast Guard tells us it blew up, almost as if it hit a mine. I had the boat out of the water at sunrise and did a complete cleaning on the bottom. There was nothing there. And now we find out that between then and the time we towed her out, divers from Vector were under the boat."

"It proves nothing," George countered.

"It raises some interesting questions, like who gained the most by *Siren*'s loss. Robert wouldn't have sold to Philip McKnight, and neither would Cheryl. Put that together with the fact that *Siren*'s victory could have solved Cramm's financial problems, and what have you got? In one disaster, Cramm's hopes are sunk, and the two people who could keep the company out of McKnight's hands are dead."

George frowned. "The *two* people?" he asked.

"Sure. Remember, Cheryl was supposed to be sailing with Robert. It was a last-minute change, and Philip might not have had time to send his diver back to defuse the bomb."

"You're starting to scare me," George allowed. "Not that I think for one second there was a bomb . . ."

"I know," Sean admitted. "It's still more likely that the design failed, and that the boat was already broken up when the fire started. It's just that everything I know about boats tells me that *Siren* didn't break up."

"Okay," George allowed. "Let's go on the basis that you're right. What's the next step?"

"I've ordered enhanced enlargements of all the photos that were taken. I'm hoping they'll show us something."

Williamson nodded his approval. But then he added, "Just don't talk about this to Cheryl. It's just another fantasy she'll jump on. And everything she does pushes down the value of the company."

"I'm not so sure they're fantasies," Sean protested.

George squinted, looking skeptical. "Didn't you tell me that the phone company had no record of the call she thinks she got from Robert?"

Sean nodded.

"And weren't you the one who found her climbing our fence in her nightgown?"

He nodded again.

"Well, everyone in our company knows it. And they also know that Gretchen is putting Cheryl to bed each night. So you can bet that people at Vector have heard the same thing."

39 CHERYL SAT IN HER BED, READING A BOOK TO Rachael, who was already in her nightgown and ready for bed. As she turned each of the cardboard pages, the little girl smiled at the colorful new picture and began telling her mother the names of all the things she saw.

"Window," she said, pointing to the window in the picture.

"That's right, a window. And what's that you can see through the window?"

"The moon," Rachael answered.

"Well, aren't you the smartest little girl," Cheryl said, and the child beamed with pride.

Gretchen stepped into the bedroom. "Is she ready for bed?"

Cheryl pointed to the stack of books that Rachael had dragged into her bed. "I think she's planning on going through the entire library."

"I'll come back," the au pair promised.

Rachael went through one book and then another. By the time she reached the last page, Cheryl was struggling to keep her eyes open. "No more for tonight," she said, and she drew the little girl closer to her.

She was suddenly aware that a telephone was ringing, its tone echoing through what seemed to be a great, dark hall. She blinked her eyes open into the dim light of her bedroom. The phone rang again, and she knew the sound was coming from Robert's office. And then she heard Rachael's voice. "Hello," the little girl said. Cheryl realized that the phone had stopped ringing. And then she saw that her daughter was no longer beside her in bed.

Rachael's voice laughed.

Cheryl bounded out of bed and raced toward the open door.

"You sing it," she heard Rachael say.

When she raced into the office, the little girl was already at the desk, kneeling in the chair and holding the telephone to her ear. Her eyes were bright with delight.

"Daddy," Rachael said.

Cheryl stopped dead. Her hands came up to her mouth.

"When are you coming home?"

Cheryl froze like ice.

"I know how," Rachael said.

Cheryl's breath was the only sound in deathly silence that hung over the room until the little girl's voice shattered it with laughter. Then Rachael began to sing.

"Oh, the buzzing of the bees . . ."

She listened while someone prompted her daughter. Then the little girl continued in a shy voice.

"In the lollipop trees . . . the soda water fountain."

Cheryl's eyes were riveted on the child in disbelief.

"Oh the lemonade springs . . . where the bluebird sings."

She felt weak, her body beginning to fall. Her hands reached out for the support of the door frame.

"In the big Rock Candy Mountain."

Cheryl staggered backward, away from the desk where Robert's voice was speaking to his daughter. As if in a trance, she settled back onto her bed.

Rachael's voice burst into delighted laughter, and then Cheryl's scream cracked like a gunshot through the house.

The door blasted open, and Gretchen rushed into the room, her arms already outstretched to rescue the little girl. She stopped when she saw the terrified look in Cheryl's eyes. "What happened?" she asked.

"Robert called," Cheryl told her.

40 CHERYL WAS POSITIVE. NO ONE BUT ROBERT COULD have shared the little song that Rachael sang into the telephone. But it was obvious that the three men sitting around her didn't believe her.

George was, as always, respectful of her feelings. He never doubted her word, but kept reminding her of the strain she had been under. Clearly George thought she had drifted back into madness.

Detective Sergeant Grattan was completely noncommittal, asking questions but taking great pains to hide his reaction to the answers. He had been summoned by George to investigate a threatening phone call. He was well aware that the Cramms, like most of the families on the hill, had enough political clout to move disrespectful policemen back to foot patrol. He wanted to do whatever Cheryl Cramm thought necessary, and get out of her house as quickly as possible.

Sean wanted to believe Cheryl. But since learning that the photo had been taken before the race, he had locked onto the theory that Robert had been killed by the same explosion that destroyed *Siren*. As much as he hated to be skeptical, he couldn't believe that Robert was alive.

Robert was dead. How could he still be alive? To Sean's mind, the inquest had clearly demonstrated that Beth Hardaway had been the victim of an explosion. So if *Siren* had exploded, then how had Robert escaped? And if he had been plucked out of the water by a rescue boat, why wasn't that fact reported? Even more illogical, why hadn't he returned home or, if he were incapacitated, at least stayed on the line long enough to tell his family where he was?

The sergeant had made detailed notes of Cheryl's comments and had observed the caution displayed by George and Sean. "You're certain that the first call was your husband's voice?" he asked Cheryl with his pencil poised.

"No . . . not the voice," she answered. "The connection was weak, like an old phonograph record or a cheap pocket radio. But it sounded like the way Robert sometimes spoke. The same inflection, I suppose . . ."

"And no one spoke to the caller on the second call."

"My daughter did. She sang a song that she used to sing with her father."

"Right," Grattan said, flipping back through his notes. "And your daughter is . . . three years old?"

"Damn!" Cheryl snapped. "Her age doesn't matter. The caller knew a song that only Robert shared with his daughter."

The policeman watched Cheryl as she answered. The woman was clearly frightened, perhaps even in shock. He could certainly believe that something had stunned her. But he couldn't put much faith in what she was saying. He doubted if she was even sure why he was there. In fact, he wasn't certain himself why he was there. There had been no crime more serious than a crank telephone call. And even that was doubtful, since the telephone company had once again confirmed that no call had been placed to Robert's private number. Whether Robert was dead or not, or whether his boat had sunk or was still afloat, were not matters that concerned him officially. The yacht had sailed from another state. The crime, if any, had occurred on the high seas. The Coast Guard and the Broward County police had already assumed jurisdiction.

"I'm not sure there's much I can do," he told Cheryl. Then he added quickly, "Of course, I'll file a report about the suspicious telephone call. And we'll do what we can to find out where . . . and how . . . it was placed. But generally, in these matters, the best thing to do is change the phone number. If this is some nut who's just trying to give you a hard time, that's the best way to deal with him."

George walked the policeman to the door. As he was showing him out, he said, "There's another aspect to this matter that you should be aware of." Grattan stopped on the steps. "Robert Cramm's company is in the process of a merger with another boatbuilder, a company called Vector Yachts. Any hint that he is still alive, or that his wife who now owns the company is . . . incompetent could destroy the deal."

Grattan nodded. "I understand."

What he understood was that there had better be no police report that an ambitious local reporter could latch onto.

"What if the calls weren't for me?" Cheryl asked as soon as George returned to the room. Both George and Sean stared at her.

"What do you mean?" Sean asked.

"I had a bad connection," Cheryl remembered aloud. "I didn't recognize his voice. Maybe he didn't recognize mine. So he identified himself and then hung up when he heard me scream."

"What about tonight?" It was George asking the question as he made another trip to the bar.

"Rachael answered," she continued. "He wouldn't have any idea who was in the room. If he guessed anyone was with her, it more than likely would have been Gretchen."

Both men squinted in bewilderment. Then Sean said, "I can see that he might want to hear Rachael's voice. But with his daughter singing their song, Gretchen would figure out—" And then he stopped, following Cheryl's logic. "You think he was calling for Gretchen?"

Cheryl was still speaking without emotion, sounding like a recording machine that was playing back her hidden thoughts. "Gretchen has been in that office far more often than I have. We had been together seconds before the phone rang the first time. If the phone had rung a few seconds earlier, she probably would have been the one who answered it. And tonight, she came into my room to see if I was asleep. She also made it into my room within seconds of the time I screamed."

"Gretchen—why would he be trying to reach Gretchen?"

"Because she's in love with him," Cheryl said, "and maybe he is in love with her."

"Christ," George said angrily. "You can't be serious. Your husband worshiped you. Gretchen is only a schoolgirl." He looked toward Sean and raised his eyes in despair. Cheryl, his expression implied, had gone beyond credibility.

"There are letters," Cheryl said.

Sean set down the drink he had just raised. "Letters? Why didn't you tell us . . ."

"Because of the way you're both looking at me right now. You think the notion is insane. And the more I talk about it, the crazier I sound."

George started for the study door. "We can certainly settle this. I'll get the girl in here right now—"

"No!" Cheryl ordered in a tone that cracked like a pistol shot. George stopped with his hand on the doorknob. "I'd rather have him keep trying to reach her. Otherwise I'll have to follow *her* for the rest of my life to see if my husband is really alive."

George walked back toward her. "Cheryl, you can believe what the Board of Inquiry concluded. There's no chance—"

"And I don't want the phone number changed."

Both men looked at her for a long second. Then they nodded.

She stood. "Thank you both," she said. She walked out of the room and turned up the staircase.

41 SEAN WAS STILL PACING THE DOCK WHEN THE SKY began to lighten early the next morning. Gretchen, he thought. Robert and Gretchen? It was impossible. Except that Gretchen had been raising his daughter, and he had probably spoken to the Danish au pair more than he had spoken to anyone else.

Sean's mind began to search for links. Suppose Robert had fathered Beth's child. And suppose that Cheryl was right, and that Robert had returned the adoration that Gretchen seemed to feel for him. That would give him reason to set the charge that would cause Beth's death and suggest his own. And then, having effectively vanished, he might try to call Gretchen. But the whole scheme was monstrous. What could they have planned for Cheryl? An asylum? He couldn't believe that Robert could treat anyone that way, particularly not his wife.

Besides, how could he have pulled it off? Suppose Robert and Gretchen had faked the emergency with the child, knowing that Cheryl would rush home. That certainly would have been the perfect ploy for getting Beth on the boat alone with Robert. He could have put Beth over the side with suitably scorched debris from the boat to suggest an explosion. And then he could have sailed *Siren* to . . . where? Back to the Bahamas? Or past the Bahamas down to some secret rendezvous in the Turks, or even in the Caribbean? That might explain the photograph.

Even if the photos were taken before the race, someone could have sent it to suggest that *Siren* was still afloat.

But why? Why such a convoluted scheme? He had been out on the water with Beth for hundreds of hours of sea trials. Surely he could have found a way to lose her over the side. And if he was calling Gretchen on his private line, why was there no record of the call?

There was a much more realistic possibility. Vector, Sean reasoned, wanted to take over Cramm Yachts. But Robert didn't want to sell, and he had built a boat that would enable him to keep his company out of unfriendly hands. As Sean had suggested to George, Vector would be the beneficiary if Robert and his boat failed.

Suppose the photograph was taken just before the race. And suppose it showed a mine attached to *Siren*'s keel. Vector would have to be the prime suspect. They would simply let the boats leave for Bermuda, knowing full well that Robert and *Siren* would never reach the finish line. So the company, with George Williamson taking the safer course, would fall right into Philip McKnight's lap.

The scenario might even explain the telephone calls. Cheryl had balked at selling the company, hoping against hope that it might be saved. Was someone calling Cheryl in an effort to convince her that she was too ill to save Robert's company?

But how? How would the Vector people know about a private phone? Unless George Williamson was working with them. That was possible. George was certain that selling the company was best for all concerned. Would he try to scare Cheryl off? Would he help Vector drive her away? Sean couldn't believe that George could do such a thing. Even though he might still resent Cheryl, it was impossible that he could be so disloyal to Robert. George owed everything to Robert.

Sean saw the morning sun begin to dance across the harbor. He walked back to the design shed and collapsed into his bunk. He needed some sleep. And then he wanted to have another talk with Sergeant Grattan.

42 HE SAT IN THE HALLWAY, OUTSIDE THE POLICE station booking desk, trying to look inconspicuous. But his long hair, and the T-shirt he was wearing over jeans weren't the uniform of the inhabitants. Each policeman who passed managed a contemptuous stare.

Grattan stepped out and led him into a small and disorganized office. He had planned to resume his respectful demeanor of the previous night, but Sean didn't look at all like a power player from an old-line family. The sergeant put his feet on top of an overturned waste can, lit a cigarette, and filled the small room with smoke. He managed a bored expression while he listened to Sean's suggestion that a bomb could have been put aboard, or even attached to the hull.

But when Sean mentioned Vector, Grattan's shoes came down off the wastebasket. He remembered George's warning about the business deal. "I'll check it out," he said with enough insincerity to cause Sean's temper to flash.

"It could happen," Sean snapped.

Grattan responded by pulling out his notepad.

"Just a couple of things I'd like you to help me with," he said, his bloodshot eyes peering out from behind a curtain of cigarette smoke. "You were watching the boat before it sailed?"

"Right," Sean said. "I slept aboard her."

"And you checked her out real thoroughly. Pulled her out of the water. Searched inside?"

Sean revisited the pre-race routine, which included a final check of the hull and a cabin search to eliminate all extra weight. He had logged everything that was aboard.

"So if any explosives were aboard the boat, they would have to have come past you?"

Sean nodded, but pointed out that there had been an open house between the time he pulled the boat out of the water to check its hull and the time when he searched through the cockpit and the stores. "Lots of people coming on and leaving. And a lot of confusion. Something could have been brought aboard that I missed. And there certainly was enough time for a diver to have connected something to her hull."

The detective flipped the page to his notes on the late switch in *Siren*'s crew. "Did you check Miss Hardaway's gear when she came aboard?" Sean admitted that he hadn't. Nor, in checking out the boat before sailing, did he go through Cheryl and Robert's personal things. "So any one of them could have planted a bomb aboard?"

"Oh, sure," Sean said sarcastically. "But just who the hell would plant a bomb on a boat they were about to take to sea?"

"Right," Grattan shot back. "So I figure I'm looking for someone who had the run of the boat but who wasn't going to be aboard during the race."

"Like me," Sean said, completing the detective's conclusion.

"Or like Mrs. Cramm, if she was going to find a reason not to sail."

"Jesus," Sean cursed, turning away in disgust. He shook his head in despair and then glared back at the policeman. "Why in hell would either of us want to destroy a boat that was so important to us?"

The sergeant ignored Sean's question and fired the next one of his own. "I was talking with some of our guys when I got back last night. Did you know that Mr. Cramm and Miss Hardaway were lovers?"

43 GEORGE WILLIAMSON LOOKED INTO THE DINING room and saw Philip McKnight already seated at a table overlooking the harbor at Mystic. The restored seaport, with its wooden square-riggers and nineteenth-century warehouses, was a suitable background for their discussion, and George had suggested that they would blend in anonymously with hordes of tourists.

"No real point in sneaking around like a pair of criminals," Philip said as they toasted with their cocktails. "The whole fucking industry knows what we're planning."

"I'm sorry all this got out of hand," George acknowledged.

"Everything is so simple and straightforward. There shouldn't have been any trouble at all."

"Exactly what in hell is going on?" McKnight asked. "You've got a guy talking to my people and shaking down my suppliers' records."

"You know about the photograph of *Siren*," George assumed.

McKnight's hands came up in a gesture of innocence. "We'd be criminals for taking a peek at a competitive yacht? For Christ sake, George, we all do it."

"Patton was simply trying to confirm when it was taken. Someone apparently sent it to him, and he took it as proof that *Siren* hadn't sunk."

"*Sean* Patton?" Philip asked.

George nodded.

"I'd just as soon that son of a bitch wasn't part of your entourage."

"We don't have to worry. He had a personal contract with Robert. Cramm Yachts owes him nothing. And he has other plans. Building a Cup boat for the baron, I believe."

McKnight laughed. "They'll make a good team. Murot will sink it, assuming Sean's design doesn't break up first."

They were both in a better mood as they placed their order.

But Philip's concerns were put back on the table just as the appetizer plates were being removed. He wanted to know what was holding up the deal.

George tried to sound unconcerned as he answered. "Nothing that won't work itself out with a bit of patience. Cheryl has had some thoughts about keeping the company in the family. Understandable, I suppose, since Robert died trying to save Cramm Yachts."

"What's this nonsense about an explosion?" Philip demanded. "It's pretty obvious that the boat broke up. What other explanation could there be?"

"You know there was evidence of a fire. I suppose the authorities have to consider every possibility before issuing an opinion. But I have no doubt the coroner will determine that Robert died accidentally."

McKnight sneered. "The breakup probably spilled the propane, or maybe even the fuel."

George anxiously nodded his agreement. "That's exactly what I think." He hoped he had put the issue to bed.

"And what are these phone calls Cheryl is supposed to be getting?"

George was surprised. Even things inside the household were becoming public knowledge. Carefully, he explained that the telephone company had no record of the calls. "Personally, I think they're . . . imaginary. I think Cheryl is trying to hold on to some hope that Robert may be alive. His body was never found, so that leaves the door open for all kinds of speculation."

They chatted through the meal about the synergy of the two companies. George reaffirmed his interest in the deal. "The other shareholders, the banks, and the major suppliers are all onboard. Everyone feels that the best thing for Cheryl would be to get out from under all this." Then he mentioned his idea that Vector might find a place for Cheryl in Florida, or think up a reason for her to take a round-the-world cruise.

Philip was delighted with the idea before George finished his thought. "Anyplace she wants. For as long as she needs."

It was midafternoon when they stepped out into the restoration grounds and began walking along the wooden wharves under the towering masts of the tall ships. The setting spelled out the differences between the two companies better than either of their representatives could. Cramm was linked to a sailing tradition that reached back almost to the Revolution. The pitch and the caulking in the wooden hulls were part of its makeup. Vector's origins were in the 1980s, when tax cuts suddenly created a demand for a boat in every garage. Its traditions were molded in fiberglass.

"You can appreciate that all this nonsense . . . Patton's investigation . . . phone calls from dead men . . . is making Cramm look ridiculous," Philip McKnight said.

George frowned. "I know. It's embarrassing trying to explain to the bank why we're tracing the phone conversations of a three-year-old."

"My point," McKnight continued, "is that *this* is what I'm buying." He gestured grandly at the three-masted whaling ship tied to the end of the pier. "Tradition. History. My directors are starting to ask if the Cramm name hasn't lost its luster."

"I wouldn't go that far," George protested.

Philip interrupted the leisurely walk and turned to face his companion. "To be frank, George, unless we can wrap this up quickly, and without further suggestion that Robert is alive in hiding, or that Vector may have been involved in *Siren*'s loss, I'll have to withdraw our offer. You can understand that we're not interested in buying into a scandal. Particularly at a premium price."

44 "IT'S THE KILLER WHALE," GLEN WHALEY'S VOICE announced over the telephone. Sean had been working late into the night, comparing his own figures on the construction of *Siren* with the charges that Cheryl had found in Robert's desk. He had lifted the ringing telephone reluctantly. Now it had his full attention.

"I reprinted the angles we talked about," Whaley said proudly, "and pulled a few enlargements."

"And?" Sean asked.

"One area looked like it might be something, so I ran it through different color combinations on the computer."

"And?" Sean repeated.

"Did you have a bulge on one side of the keel that you didn't have on the other?"

"No."

"Right at the top," Whaley persisted, "where the keel flared out into the curve of the bilges?"

"No, it was perfectly symmetrical. There were no bulges."

"There was when I took the photos," the killer whale announced. "Looks like it's about two feet long . . . maybe two inches quarter-round. Like some extra epoxy was added after the keel was attached."

"Nothing like that," Sean told him.

"You wouldn't have noticed it unless you were able to look at both sides at once," Whaley went on. "You couldn't see the difference until you compared the two photos."

Sean knew *Siren*'s lines as well as his own face. "I'd have seen it. It wasn't there when I pulled the boat out of the water. You better send them up so I can have a look."

Whaley chuckled over the phone. "Not for any lousy four-hundred COD."

"I said five hundred," Sean reminded him.

"That was for pictures that showed nothing. Now that they make a point, I figure they're worth a bit more."

"How much?"

"More like five thousand."

Sean winced. "My boat sank, Whaley, and my bonus went down with it. I don't have five thousand."

Another chuckle from the killer whale. "I bet Cramm Yachts does. And if they don't, I know Vector can come up with it."

"I'll have to ask," Sean told him. "You'll have to give me some time."

"Ask," Whaley ordered. "And call me back with the answer. Before noon, okay! And you better wire the money because I'm not letting these go COD."

"The murdering bastard!" Sean screamed as soon as he heard the line go dead. He pounded his fist on the desktop. "Fucking Philip McKnight!" He leaped to his feet and began to pace furiously. It was all too obvious. McKnight had killed Robert and destroyed *Siren* in order to get his hands on Cramm Yachts. And now he was playing games with Cheryl's head.

He had sent a bomber under the boat during the pre-race festivities, when crews and guards would be too involved with visitors coming aboard to check underwater. The photographer was probably just a cover. If they got caught, it would look like a bit of industrial espionage, hardly a criminal offense among the builders who were always spying on one another. Who could convict them? If it was legal to take a photograph of the rigging on a boat you were racing against, what was so awful about taking a picture of its keel?

But the picture had been incidental. McKnight would know that he would have the complete drawings on *Siren* and all her material specifications when he took over Cramm. When he got Whaley's photos, he probably never bothered to open them, but just sent them down to his designers. One had probably done computer close-ups to check on how the keel was fixed to the hull. And while he was realizing that the keel *was* the hull, he probably noticed the extra material fixed to one side. Anyone involved with designing yachts would know that it didn't belong there. The difference with this person, whoever it was, was that he was more loyal to a fellow designer than to a greedy and maybe murderous owner. He had taken one of the prints and sent it up to Sean.

He picked up his phone and called George, asking him to meet at the Cramm estate. Then he called Cheryl and told her that he was on the way over.

"I know what happened to *Siren*," he told Cheryl as soon as she came down the stairs. She led him into the library and closed the door behind them.

"Vector put a bomb on the keel just before the race. They blew the boat out of the water."

"I can't believe it. Why?"

"Because they knew Robert would never sell to them once *Siren* had won the race. And they wanted the company."

The door swung open and George walked into the room. He looked angry, and his stride registered his impatience. "What is it now?" he demanded.

"Sean says Vector destroyed *Siren*," Cheryl answered.

"Oh, for Christ's sake," George said, his glance swinging wearily at Sean.

"It's in the photos, something attached at the top of the keel, right along the hull."

His eyes widened. "Let me see!" George's hand was already out.

Sean repeated the details of the telephone call. "I pulled the boat out of the water in the morning for a wash-down and a waxing. There was nothing attached to the keel. A couple of hours later, Vector's diver went under the boat with a photographer as a cover. It was a perfect plan, except that the photographer wasn't in on it, so he took pictures. And one of the pictures caught something that had been attached to the hull."

George was already at the bar, fixing a round of drinks, when Sean explained that the photographer wanted the money in advance. "If the pictures prove something, I think we should send the money," he decided. He handed Scotch splashed over ice to Cheryl and Sean.

"Of course," George added, "even if there is an explosive device, we still can't be sure that Vector is responsible."

"It was their diver," Cheryl argued.

"That doesn't mean that Vector did it. All it would tell us was that something was connected to *Siren* and approximately when it was connected," George countered.

"But . . ." Sean sputtered.

"We're grasping," George said emphatically. He looked straight at Cheryl. "At our last meeting you insisted Robert was still alive, and that he was in some way involved with Gretchen. Tonight, you're willing to believe he was brutally murdered by Philip McKnight."

He turned to Sean. "And weren't you thinking that it might be Robert calling on the telephone? Now you seem to be implying that Philip knew what song Robert sang with his daughter."

Sean reddened with embarrassment. George was right. He was grasping for any answer except the most obvious one—that his radical design had failed.

"Let's pay the goddamned extortion, get the photographs, and see if they tell us anything," George advised. "And if they do, we'll share them with the authorities." He looked at his associates and then sighed deeply. "In the meantime, Cheryl, please try to get some rest. You're stretched out to the breaking point." He swung his glance to Sean. "And for God's sake, let's stop playing amateur detective. Cramm Yachts is beginning to look ridiculous."

He tossed down his drink, set the glass on the bar, and started to the door. "Why don't you come with me, Sean. I think Cheryl has had more than enough speculation for one evening."

George was waiting outside the house when Sean came down the steps. "Stop by my office in the morning," he said. "We'll wire the money down to this . . ."

"Whaley," Sean said. "Glen Whaley."

"And, Sean, please try not to feed Mrs. Cramm's fantasies."

Sean bristled, but George went on, "She's a very troubled woman, and I don't think you're helping her by taking seriously the phone conversations she dreams up, or by offering her cooked-up evidence of conspiracies."

"I'm trying to get to the bottom of all this," Sean began, but George raised a quieting hand.

"I'm not blaming you," he assured. "We all sympathize with her. And I sympathize with you. I know you'd rather believe anything than that your design was some way at fault. But I should tell you, for the record, that the other directors have petitioned me to consult with our attorneys. And they have advised that we begin proceedings to have Cheryl declared incompetent."

"You can't do that," Sean snapped.

"Sean, everything the Cramm family stood for is going to be lost unless we accept this deal and move forward. I can't let that happen to Robert's memory. I can't let it happen to his wife."

Sean sagged and stood speechless. George laid a friendly hand on his shoulder. "Do what you can to get her to sell. The new company guarantees a future for her and her daughter. It also puts you in a position to design a whole line of performance boats."

Sean looked up feebly. "But if Vector . . ."

"Believe me," George said. "No matter what those photos show, Philip McKnight would never have destroyed *Siren*. He was only a few days away from owning her."

Sean stood in shock as George climbed into his car and pulled away from the house. Owning her? he asked himself. McKnight was going to own *Siren*? It didn't make sense unless the Vector deal was a foregone conclusion. Unless Robert was prepared to sell no matter what the outcome of the race. But why would Robert have lied, pretending to everyone, including his wife, that he was determined to save Cramm?

He tossed the possibilities in his mind as he drove back to the boatyard. And then he took them with him as he strolled out onto the pier. Until now, he had been going on a few simple alternatives. One was that Robert was trying to save the company, and that someone who wanted to eliminate Cramm Yachts had sunk the boat. In that scenario, Robert was clearly dead, and the phone calls to Cheryl were intended to break down her resistance to the sale. The logical culprit was clearly Philip McKnight and Vector Yachts. And Whaley's photographs might help prove the case.

Another alternative was that Robert had faked his own disappearance. One reason why he might have wanted to vanish had become apparent when Sean was reviewing the development costs on *Siren*. The company had been charged for millions of dollars' worth of bogus expenses. Robert may have felt the creditors and tax collectors closing in on him. And, if he were the father of Beth's child, he may have feared an unbearable disgrace. Perhaps Robert preferred to die a hero. Particularly if he intended to begin a new life with Gretchen.

But now there was a totally different possibility. If Robert intended to sell Cramm Yachts, then there was a new list of suspects. It included anyone who would have opposed the sale. People in the boatyard crew, who might have feared for their jobs. Elliot Minor, the Cramm sales director, who would be made expendable by a merger. Cheryl, who could envision Robert moving to a new life at Vector's Florida headquarters that might not include her. Or was all this fancy? Was George right that he was grasping at straws? Perhaps the loss of *Siren* involved nothing more than the failure of his design. A failure he was unable to accept. And perhaps Cheryl *was* falling back into her dark illness.

Sean walked back to the design shed. He would try to put all the questions aside until he had seen Whaley's photos. Maybe they showed nothing. And if that were the case, then probably he should follow George's advice and encourage Cheryl to sign the documents.

45 WHIT HOBBS WAS NO SAILOR. HE STEPPED ABOARD the *Solomon Cramm* in his black wing tips, leaving heel marks across the old yacht's wooden decks. When he had to cross the deck to the aft cockpit, where lunch had been set under an awning, he tried to reach for one railing without letting go of another, and dropped his briefcase in the process. George shook his head as he retrieved the case.

"How in hell did you grow up in this town without developing sea legs?"

The lawyer accepted a helping hand until he was safely within the confines of the cockpit. "My grandfather made a fortune in shipping without ever leaving the dock. It turns out that seasickness runs in the family."

George looked at the bar and the brightly set table for two. "Is this going to be okay?"

"I'll tell you after a dry martini," Hobbs said.

While they were having their cocktail, George laid out the problem that was the reason for their meeting. The Vector deal was dying, and Cheryl was becoming more and more unreachable. He was, he told Whit Hobbs, beginning to be concerned about his own legal liability.

"I'm the company's senior officer, and the other shareholders are pressing me to complete the sale. If I don't do something, they could sue me."

Hobbs shook his head. "It's a board decision and Cheryl controls the board. She's the only one who can put through the sale."

"Whit, for God's sake, Cheryl can't put through anything. She's hearing voices."

The lawyer set down his drink, his face saddening. "I heard she was . . . distressed."

"Distressed?" George leaned forward confidentially, even though there was no one else aboard. "She thinks Robert is calling her on the telephone and singing songs to her daughter."

"Dear God . . ."

"She also thinks Robert was screwing all the women in town, including the little college girl who takes care of Rachael. I wish there were a better word for it, Whit, but the fact is that Cheryl is crazy. It's gone well past 'disturbed.' "

Hobbs drained his glass and handed it to George for a refill. "You can't persuade her to sign?" he asked.

"She thinks that she and Sean Patton can save the company."

"Sean Patton. The one with the ponytail?"

George nodded as he handed back the freshened drink. "Hard to believe, isn't it. A screwball woman and an airhead boat designer ruining a deal that could make a lot of people very rich. And all I can do is stand around and watch the whole thing go down the toilet."

"No, that's not really true. There are steps that we could take."

George set down his drink, his interest obvious in his narrowing eyes.

"First, we could have her declared incompetent, and have you appointed to act in her best interest. The courts are generally skeptical of beneficiaries who claim that their benefactor is crazy, but when the evidence is overwhelming—"

"Jesus, Whit, she was climbing the boatyard gate in her nightgown."

Hobbs nodded. "I heard. Which is why I mentioned the possibility of going to court. The evidence of mental incapacity is certainly substantial. But the problem is time. With the psychiatric reviews that would be required, we're probably talking several months."

Williamson shook his head. "Vector is already having second thoughts. If I can't get us signed in a few weeks, the deal will never happen."

"In that case," the lawyer decided, "I would concentrate on getting her to sign. And I would put an end to all talk about her being . . . disturbed."

George didn't seem to understand.

"If she's not of sound mind, she *can't* sign a legal document."

Williamson's shoulders sagged in defeat. "Catch twenty-two," he mumbled. "She's too crazy to sign, but if she should come to her senses, then her signature would be worthless because she's too crazy to sign."

Hobbs looked around suspiciously, making absolutely certain that they were alone. "Never repeat this, George, because I'll swear I never said it. . . ."

They leaned close together. "We could stage a scene that might scare some sense into her. Hand her a document that tells her it's either approve the sale or risk the sanitarium. What we want to do is get her signature on the damn thing. The signed contract will speak for itself and, if she later objects, the burden of proof will be on her."

George recoiled in shock. "Christ, that's fraud—"

"It's in Cheryl's best interest," Hobbs interrupted. "You'd be helping her do what you know she would want to do if she had it all together."

Williamson shook his head slowly. "I don't think I could do it," he whispered.

The lawyer watched him carefully. Then he confided, "I'd hate to tell you how many times I've helped children to get an incompetent parent to sign a paper. And I've never seen a court get suspicious if it was obvious that the arrangement was in the parent's interest."

George rose slowly and took the covers off the cold luncheon that was waiting on the table.

"Think about it," Hobbs said. "And, in the meantime, I'll begin drawing up the petition for an incompetency ruling."

46 SHE AWOKE WITH A SHOCK, SUDDENLY ENVELOPED in icy seawater. There was no light to orient her, so she was unable to tell which way she was moving. And there was no air in her lungs to lift her back to the surface. She was lost, at the bottom of an ocean, and growing desperate for her next breath.

A dream! Gretchen would be shaking her back to consciousness. It was all a dream. But still, she was drowning. Even in a dream, she had to try to get back to the surface.

She sensed her head beginning to rise slowly while her feet continued to sink, the natural buoyancy of her body righting her and lifting her back to the surface. She followed her instincts and began kicking in the direction that the sea was moving her. She had to get back to the air.

But there was a weight dragging her down. She was wearing her bathrobe, and the quilted material was soaking up weight like a sponge. Cheryl struggled with the belt and then pushed the robe off her shoulders. Now she was swimming in her nightgown.

A dream. She had been here before, swimming under *Siren*, and then screaming after Robert as he sailed away. At any moment she would feel Gretchen shaking her and the housekeeper calling her name. But, somehow, this was different. The pain in her lungs was spreading like a fire, and the cold of the water was numbing her limbs. It seemed too real.

Her face exploded through the surface and her mouth sucked in the fresh air. But she could see nothing except impenetrable darkness, nor hear anything but her own gasping.

She began to slip under again, and as the tiny waves washed across her face she knew she was awake. This wasn't a dream. She was in water. Salt water. And she had no idea which way she should be swimming. Cheryl coiled, and then sprang back to the surface, leaping out of the water. She saw lights, close to the water and only a few yards away. And then she could make out other lights, higher up and at a greater distance. As she sank back down, she recognized the backdrop. She was in the water, somewhere off the company pier. The lights close aboard were on the *Solomon Cramm*, moored to her dock. The distant lights were coming from her house, high up on the hill.

Cheryl fought back the panic. She breathed regularly, treading water. Then she took her bearings and saw that she was drifting with the outgoing tide. The lights on the dock were moving farther away. She kicked off and tried to swim back toward them.

But something was wrong with her. Her coordination was gone, so that her smooth, strong stroke was more like flailing. She couldn't keep the rhythm in her breathing. And the lights were moving farther away. Cheryl realized that she wasn't going to make it.

She settled back to treading water, concentrating on just her breathing. Then she took a deep breath and screamed out for help. She felt her body sink as the air rushed out of her lungs. She sucked in more air and then screamed again.

Suddenly there were images. Lights seemed to be flashing on and off. They were floating by her as she was carried down a long, endless flight of stairs. And then she was lying on her back, watching lights float past over her head.

She heard a voice scream back to her. Sean's voice, she thought. She looked in the direction of the sound and saw that the pier lights had been turned on. She could make out the graceful old steam yacht, bobbing at her permanent mooring. The big cruiser. And then she could see someone rushing out on the pier. Cheryl screamed again. But now the lights seemed too far away. No one could hear her.

The voice answered. It was Sean. She could see him on the pier, fully illuminated, staring out into the darkness. "Sean!" she yelled, and then felt herself sinking again. His voice answered back, screaming her name. Then the surface washed across her eyes and she could see nothing. Just the memory of lights floating by as she drifted down an endless staircase. And the black sea, which no longer seemed as cold.

But she couldn't surrender. This was real. There would be no one shaking her out of a nightmare. If she was going to survive, she would have to save herself. Cheryl fought back to the surface. She was able to breathe, but she had come up into total darkness. She leaned her head back, trying to float easily, and saw stars through the night. Perhaps they were the lights that had floated past. Had she been falling through space?

"Cherrrryl!" Sean's voice came from behind her. She turned carefully, keeping her head up. There was the dock, still illuminated, with the yacht tied in its berth. But there was no one there. Sean was gone, his voice calling to her from somewhere in the darkness.

She began to sink, too exhausted to keep treading and fighting for air. The rising edge of the water blocked out the light from the dock, then the lights on the hill, and finally the stars. All she could hear was a distant rumble, like a drumroll leading up to the finale. She was sinking gently toward the bottom.

But something was holding her. A fist had closed like a vise around her arm, and she was being dragged back up. She could see a powerful light even before she erupted through the surface. And there was Sean's face, close enough to her own so that she could taste his breath.

"Hold on!" He pushed a line into her hand. "Grab it. Hold tight!" Then his arm was around her waist, lifting her up out of the water. She was in a boat. She was safe. But Cheryl was too tired to care.

NEWPORT

47

SEAN PACED THE COLORFUL CORRIDOR THAT HAD BEEN cheerfully decorated to belie the grim proceedings behind the emergency room doors. He watched the constant flow of doctors and nurses, and the sheeted forms that rolled by on the gurneys, looking for some clue to Cheryl's condition. All they had told him was that she had swallowed a bit of water, was completely exhausted, and was having difficulty remembering. But it had been nearly an hour since he had carried her in, and more than twenty minutes since the emergency room resident had assured him she was out of danger. She should be alert by now and ready to talk with him. Unless there was a problem the doctors weren't sharing.

George rushed in through the emergency room door, wearing a light sweater over his pajama top. An inch of the matching pajama pattern was visible under the cuffs of his trousers. "How is she?" he demanded as soon as he saw Sean.

"Okay, from what they've told me, but I haven't been able to see her."

"Thank God," George whispered, shaking his head in despair. Then he asked, "Any reporters here?"

Sean hadn't even considered the possibility. He shrugged. "Not that I know of."

"Did she use her own name when she checked in?"

Sean grimaced. "She didn't use any name. She wasn't talking when I carried her in. I gave them her name."

George glanced through the admittance window. The overweight clerk behind the desk seemed bored, completely uninvolved in the life-and-death struggles that were the business of his surroundings. More than likely, he didn't even notice the name, much less connect it to a prominent family. "Maybe I can get it off the record," he thought aloud. Then he turned to Sean. "I hope we can keep this quiet."

Sean couldn't believe George's priorities. "You haven't even asked what happened to her."

"I already know. I stopped at the house, thinking that she might be on the way home. Gretchen told me that you pulled her out of the bay. Damn good thing you were still awake."

"Do you think . . . ?" Sean tried to ask.

"Yeah, I think she tried to kill herself," George answered. "I suppose I should have seen it coming. Her condition . . . her fantasies . . ."

"I'm not sure everything that's happened to her is a fantasy," Sean snapped.

"Well, there's not much doubt about what happened tonight. She was in bed, asleep, when Gretchen looked in on her. Half an hour later, you're pulling her out of the water. She must have walked down to the yard, let herself in the gate, and then gone straight out to the pier."

"The gate was wide open," Sean remembered.

George reached into his pocket and took out an ornate key ring. "She left it open," he said. "These are her keys. I found them in the lock."

"Christ . . ." Now it was Sean who slumped in despair. If Cheryl had thought to bring her keys, and had opened the gate herself, there was little doubt about what she intended.

The doctor pushed through the swinging door and nodded to Sean. "She's doing better, but we've checked her in for the night. If you go around front, they'll let you up to visit her."

Cheryl's was the only room with its lights still burning. She was sitting up in the raised bed, dressed in a green hospital gown. Her eyes were wide with fear.

"What happened to me?" she asked anxiously. "How did I get into the water?"

Sean was stunned. He had expected that Cheryl would be able to answer those questions for herself.

"Let's not talk about it now," George consoled. "You get some rest—"

Cheryl's anger flashed. "Damn it, I want to talk about it now. I was just pulled out of the water, and I don't know how I got there. Tell me, for God's sake!"

George stole a glance at Sean and waited for him to answer.

"I don't know," Sean told Cheryl. "I was working late and heard a splash. I thought someone was down on the dock, so I looked out the window. I heard a scream and I ran down."

"It was you, then . . . who rescued me."

He nodded.

Cheryl turned her face away, almost in shame. "I don't remember, damn it. I went upstairs. Kissed Rachael. And the next thing I knew I was in the water."

"You don't remember *anything?*" George sounded suspicious.

"Some lights floating past. Almost as if I were being carried," she said with difficulty. Then her expression brightened. "I must have been carried. Someone must have brought me down to the dock."

George patted her hand. "I'm sure you'll remember," he promised. Then he tugged at Sean's still-damp shirt, indicating that they ought to leave. They spent a minute telling Cheryl that her color was returning and that everything would be all right. But she was still sitting upright as they backed out the door. The determination in her face told them that she would spend the night searching her mind for answers.

As they rode down in the elevator together, Sean asked, "What do you think?"

"Sad. Very sad," the older man intoned.

"I mean about her being carried. Do you think someone could have carried her down to the pier?"

George shook his head. "If there had been someone, you would have seen them. There's no way out of the yard without going past you and back through the gate. If anyone carried her down there, they would have had to have left her long before you heard the splash."

They walked in silence around to the emergency entrance, where George's Mercedes was parked beside Sean's pickup. The bright lights over the doorway reflected across the mist-covered driveway. As they stepped into the pool of light, Sean asked, "Do you suppose she was right about Robert and Gretchen?"

George rolled his eyes. "You don't think, for one minute . . ."

"It's the only explanation I can think of. How the hell could she walk out without Gretchen noticing?"

"You think that little girl could carry Cheryl all the way from the house to the boat dock?" Williamson smirked at the absurdity of the idea.

"She's a strong girl," Sean fired back. "She works out all the time. And she could have put her in a car, or in that stroller she uses when she takes Rachael for a run."

"And then vanished into thin air . . . along with the stroller . . . after she tossed Cheryl off the dock. For God's sake, Sean, face facts."

Sean was nodding. "I know it's far-fetched, but if Robert were involved with Gretchen . . ."

"Sergeant Grattan told me—confidentially of course—that Beth was the other woman in Robert's life," George said. "Apparently several of the officers had come upon them together, and had the good sense to look the other way."

"Grattan told me, too. Do you believe him?"

"There was a long time when Robert had no wife," George answered as he slipped into his car.

Sean asked, "How did Philip McKnight know that he was going to own *Siren*?"

George didn't seem to understand the question.

"You said McKnight wouldn't have sunk *Siren* because he was going to own her in a few days. How did he know? Had Robert already agreed to sell the company?"

"Robert wouldn't have had any choice," George answered.

"Why? Because he had been dipping into the till?"

George nodded.

"But McKnight wouldn't have known about that. As far as he knew *Siren*'s victory would have brought business to the company."

"I see your point," George agreed. For the moment, his confidence seemed to have deserted him. He seemed troubled and confused by Sean's analysis.

"If *Siren* blew up," Sean went on, "there are really only two people who could have done it. McKnight, because he wanted the company, or Robert, because he wanted to vanish."

"Or Beth," George added, "because Robert had broken off with her. Or Cheryl, because Robert hadn't broken off with Beth. There are any number of suspects, probably including you and me."

He slipped back behind the wheel. "But that's only *if* she blew up. And I don't think that she did."

48 "IT'S A GODDAMNED PIPE BOMB," SEAN INSISTED, AS George bent over the photo prints. They were in the design shed the next morning, examining Whaley's photos under the bright magnifying light that swung out over the drafting table.

"It could be anything," George mumbled, without lifting his eyes from the prints.

"It's attached to the hull right at the head of the keel. It would have blown the boat in half. For certain, it would have blown the keel off, and that alone would have sunk her."

George raised his head. "If it's a bomb. I can see some sort of object up against the top of the keel. But it could be anything. Even something floating in the water that just happened to be drifting past when the picture was taken."

"George, *Siren* sank without explanation. There's the explanation."

"It could even be retouching," Williamson speculated. "Didn't you say the prints were computer enhanced?"

"Why the fuck would Whaley touch in a bomb?" Sean demanded, his impatience with his friend close to exploding.

"To swindle us out of five thousand dollars. He could probably guess that we weren't going to pay that kind of money for a photo that showed nothing."

"George, it's the best lead we've got. Someone attached something to *Siren* an hour before she sailed. And then she blew to pieces and sank."

George glanced back through the magnifying lens at the prints. After a few seconds he agreed, "Okay. I'll show them to Grattan and let him decide whether they should go to the police or to the Coast Guard. And I'll go so far as to say that the shots were taken by a Vector photographer. But we're not charging Vector, or Philip McKnight, with anything. I'm hoping we'll all be one company within a few days."

Sean looked up from the photos he was gathering. "You're still going to push the sale?"

George went on, "I'll be stating my case in a very difficult meeting I have coming up with Cheryl. I hope I can count on your support."

Sean looked back curiously, but said nothing. George settled on the edge of the straight-backed chair that was in front of the drafting table. "I'm going to insist that Cheryl agree to the sale. If she refuses, I'm going to raise the issue of her competence. All this has gone on far too long. I have a duty to act in the interest of the shareholders."

Sean looked stunned. "How can you sell to Vector when they may have murdered Robert?" And then he was pleading. "At least let the police look into these photos before you decide."

"Of course. And if there's hard evidence, we'll change course," George agreed. "But in all probability, the photos will settle nothing. There will always be questions about the circumstances of Robert's death. Questions that are aggravated by Cheryl's condition. But the bottom line is that the deal is in the best interest of all the owners, Cheryl included. And I'd be clearly guilty of malfeasance if I let the opportunity pass."

"Just wait until they have a chance to investigate. . . ."

"I'll have Grattan pursue the photos," George promised.

Sean thanked him, and then added, "I'll try and find out why there's no record of the phone calls."

49 CHERYL HAD RETURNED HOME DURING THE morning, wearing clothes that the housekeeper had sent to the hospital. Gretchen had been waiting with Rachael in the driveway when the company car got to the top of the hill and Cheryl had rushed out to scoop her up. But Rachael had begun to cry, and had reached back for Gretchen. There was fear in the little girl's eyes that told Cheryl she had once again become a stranger.

She still hadn't remembered anything. She had no recollection of taking the key to the yard gate and leaving the house. She was certain that she had never walked down the hill, and still had no idea how she had gotten into the water. It was all lost . . . everything from the moment she kissed her sleeping daughter and left the nursery until she was sitting upright in the hospital bed.

There were glimpses. The recollection of being carried downstairs and past several lights. The sensation of floating on her back while lights passed overhead. The icy reality of being in the water, struggling for each breath. Crying out, and hearing Sean's voice answer. The feel of his arm around her as he lifted her into a boat. But they were all unconnected, just as events had been unconnected during her illness. She could only conclude that once again she had lost her fragile grip on reality.

"What happened to me?" she asked Gretchen.

The au pair responded with a look that was frightened and confused. "I feel so guilty," she finally managed. "I should have kept an eye on you. . . ."

"No," Cheryl snapped. "Your job is to watch Rachael. I'm supposed to be able to take care of myself." And then Cheryl had begun trembling with grief until she was crying uncontrollably.

Sean came by, and took her for a ride in his truck down the coastline to the open sea. He told her about the photographs that George was investigating, and his own call to the telephone company to have one of their technical experts come out to the house and go over the phone system. But she didn't respond, instead sitting quietly, close to the door, and staring out the window.

"I don't remember," she finally said, as if Sean had been pressing her for information. "I don't remember any of it." Then she turned to him. "It's just like last time. People tell me what I've done, and I think they're talking about someone else."

"You've been through a lot," he answered. "You just need time."

He pulled the truck into a public parking lot and helped her down onto the sand. They carried their shoes as they walked in silence, side by side, along a nearly deserted beach.

"It was Robert's baby," Cheryl suddenly said.

"Don't be silly—" Sean started to argue, but he stopped when she turned on him abruptly.

"I knew when I found them working together on *Siren*. They were so involved, so together, until I walked in. And then they were suddenly awkward, trying to pretend that there was nothing between them. Even when he made me his crew, I knew he would rather be sailing with her. And I think I understood. I understood what it must have been like for him when I was sick, and how important she probably was to him."

Just as abruptly as Cheryl had stopped and turned to him, she suddenly turned away and resumed her walk along the water's edge. Sean scampered to catch up with her.

"Robert loved you," he told her.

Cheryl showed no reaction. Then, without warning, she asked, "Could I have killed them?"

Sean grabbed her shoulders and spun her toward him. "Don't say that!"

"I might not even remember," she argued.

"You had nothing to do with it. If it wasn't my design, it was a bomb fixed to the keel. And there's no way you suddenly learned how to make bombs."

"I might have found someone. Paid them . . ."

"You could never do that."

She broke away from him and screamed. "I could never kill myself! But I'd be dead right now if you hadn't pulled me out of the water."

They were back in the truck, driving home, when she asked, "What should I do, Sean?"

"Forget Cramm Yachts," he answered with a certainty that he found surprising. "Try to forget Robert. Sell the company. Take your daughter. Find a new home, and a new life."

"Can I do that? Or am I a danger to my daughter?"

The answer to that question was obvious in the Cramm house. Once again, Cheryl found them all hovering around her. The housekeeper peeked around doorways to follow her movements through the rooms. Gretchen seemed always to find a reason to be nearby whenever Cheryl was with Rachael. It even seemed as if the little girl were looking around uneasily when she was with her mother, as if needing assurance that someone else was watching over them.

It will never change, Cheryl thought. And why should it? She had spent a year in her own colorless world, remembering nothing of her life. Now she was lapsing back into the darkness, unable to remember how she had gotten to the boatyard gate, or how she had found herself in the water. It was easy to understand why everyone would be concerned. What was to stop her from taking Rachael with her the next time she tried to kill herself? Or simply taking her daughter for a nighttime walk down a dark, winding road? It was clear that she didn't know what she was doing, so it followed that even her most innocent intentions could turn out to be dangerous to the child.

Except that this time it was different. When she was sick, Cheryl had been completely unaware, totally detached from her surroundings. Now she felt involved. She had a clear image of the people around her and a live sense of their presence. She could feel the pain of Robert's loss, understand his needs, and forgive his unfaithfulness. She was up to the minute on the issues that his death had created, and completely able to analyze all her choices. Most important of all, she could recognize her moments of darkness, pinpointing the moment when her mind went blank, and then the moment when reality returned. When she was sick, she hadn't cared that she was alone in a world of her own making. Now she was frightened sick by the thought that she had gone blank, and determined that it should never happen again. But first, she had to know why it had happened at all.

Cheryl had no doubt that Robert had defrauded the company. She had read his financial work sheets. She was sure that Gretchen had been in love with her husband. The letters were in his desk drawer. Nor did she have any doubt that the private phone in his office had rung on two occasions during the past two weeks, nor that the person on the other end knew things that only Robert could know. What she couldn't do was assemble these random facts into hard evidence of what had happened to her husband, or what was about to happen to her. But that didn't mean she was insane. All it meant was that someone was manipulating her life. She had to find out who and why.

50 "SHE HEARD THE DAMN THING RING," SEAN insisted.

"Well then, let's see how," the telephone company serviceman said pleasantly as he followed Sean into the Cramm house. Cheryl met them at the foot of the stairs, and they marched in a procession to the second floor.

"You're the first person from your company who didn't act like I was crazy," Sean told him.

"Well, it is disconnected. And it drew a blank when we tried to test it."

"It rang," Cheryl added over her shoulder. "Twice."

They stood to one side while the serviceman lifted the phone, listened, and then tapped the button on the cradle. His expression told them that he wasn't hearing anything that he hadn't expected. Then he followed the wire from the desk unit, over the back of the desk, and down to the jack box on the baseboard. He pulled a tester off his belt and connected it into the jack box. Then he keyed in some digits. After a few seconds, he unplugged the instrument and folded his wires like a doctor who is finished with his stethoscope. "I can't tell you that it didn't ring," he explained sympathetically. "But it wasn't a telephone call. There's no power on that line, and no connection to our central office. What you've got is a phone and a wire, with nothing on the other end."

Cheryl turned away in despair and started for the door. "I *must* be going mad," she said. There was no sarcasm in her voice.

"No," Sean said, as he grabbed her arm to stop her from leaving.

"You heard it. There has to be an explanation. He wheeled on the serviceman. "We're missing something. Let's start from the beginning. Tell me all the ways that you could make that phone ring."

The man glanced from Sean to Cheryl. They both seemed desperate. "Two ways," he said. "Neither of them very likely. First, you reconnect the line that the phone is plugged into. That would mean cutting it at the pole, and connecting it to another line that *is* connected to the central office. We wouldn't have any record of delivering the call here, because we would have sent it to another exchange number. But this phone would be connected to the other number's line. So you'd get the call, and we'd have no record."

"Can that be done?" Sean demanded.

"Sure. By someone who can climb a pole, find an active line, and splice into it. Like I said, it's not very likely."

Sean nodded his agreement. "What's the second way?"

"Plug this phone onto another line. This house has service. Are there any extension jacks in the room?"

"Yes!" Cheryl was already moving past Sean to the other side of the room. "There was a phone over here when this was another bedroom. She pulled the sofa back from the wall and dropped down behind it on her hands and knees. "Here it is."

Sean and the serviceman lifted the sofa away. There was a phone jack in the wall, just above the baseboard. He and Cheryl stood back while the telephone man connected his instrument. "Yeah, this is live." He stood up, went back to the desk, and returned with the phone. He plugged it into the empty jack and then held the handset up to Cheryl. She listened for a second, and then smiled as she handed the instrument to Sean.

"Hang it up," the repairman said. He moved quickly to the door and disappeared, leaving the two of them waiting. A few seconds later, the telephone rang. Sean picked it up.

"It's me," the repairman's voice announced. Sean handed the phone to Cheryl, who listened as the repairman counted from one to ten. Then they rushed to the door to meet him as he came back to Robert's office.

There was a simple code that anyone in the house could use to make the phones in the house ring. The desk phone could have been connected with an extension cord to the unused jack, and then the ringers turned down on all the other phones. Dial the code, and the desk phone would ring. And any of the other phones could be used to talk.

"So the call had to come from within the house?" Sean reasoned.

"No. Actually, it could come from anywhere. Once the phone was switched to the extension jack, all someone would have to do was call the house."

Cheryl began re-creating events. "Someone would have to switch the connection on this phone, turn down the other ringers, and then either call or signal someone outside that it was set up for a call." Sean and the repairman both nodded. "Then," she continued, "after the call, they would have to turn up the other ringers, and then switch this connection back to the original jack."

"Yeah, if they wanted you to think that it had been connected to the private line all along."

Cheryl looked at Sean. "That means someone who has the run of the house. Who can walk past me in the hallway and in and out of rooms without me even noticing."

"There would be no record of the call?" Sean asked.

"Not if it came from inside the house," the repairman said. "And if it came from outside, it would be logged to the house number. Nobody asked us to check that one."

"It doesn't matter," Cheryl said. "Wherever the call came from, someone in the house either called, or knew the caller."

"Is there any way we can trace it?" Sean wondered.

"Check your phone bill," the serviceman advised. You know the time and date of the calls. Maybe you'll see a call at that time, and be able to trace the number. I know the police have been asking, so the company will certainly cooperate."

Sean walked the phone man to the front door, thanking him several times on the way. "I don't *know* that's how it was done," the man kept repeating. "I'm just saying those are ways it might have been done." At the doorway he added, "I'm going to check the line records when I get back to the office. Maybe there was another line in here that we've all forgotten about."

Cheryl was standing at the foot of the stairs when Sean turned back into the house.

"Gretchen," she said calmly.

"Damn it, get rid of her!" he answered. "You should have sent her packing as soon as you found her letters."

Cheryl shook her head slowly. "Not until I give her a chance to lead me to Robert."

51 WHEN CHERYL ARRIVED AT THE OFFICES OF WHIT Hobbs's law firm, George was already waiting in the reception area. He kissed her on the cheek, exchanged a few pleasantries, and then steered her into Whit's private office, which had obviously been left available for their use. It was a dark wood enclosure, with great volumes of the federal and state code lining the walls.

The large desk was in front of a credenza, with two rich leather chairs on the other side. Across the room, there was an arrangement of sofa and chairs that appeared to be only slightly more comfortable. Hobbs's office was designed to humble visitors rather than comfort them.

"What's going on?" Cheryl asked.

George got her seated on the sofa and sat nervously in a soft chair directly across from her. His smile vanished. "This is very difficult," he told her. And then lowering his eyes, "I really don't know how to begin."

"George!" He looked up at her. "What's very difficult?" Cheryl asked.

He cleared his throat. "I'm asking you, for your own peace of mind . . . and for Rachael's welfare . . . to sign the sale agreement with Vector Yachts. I know you're hoping to save the company . . . and I admire you for it," he hastened to add. "But the delay is causing . . . insurmountable problems. . . ."

"You had to bring me here to ask me? Why?"

He squared his shoulders. "Because Whit has a very distressing duty to perform, and I'd like to spare you . . . and him—"

"George, for God's sake, will you speak English. What the hell is going on?"

"Please, sign the papers, and then all Whit will have to do is notarize them. Believe me, it will solve all your problems."

Cheryl shook her head. "No. I'm not ready to throw in the towel. Now what's this 'very distressing duty' that Whit has to perform?"

George rose slowly, suddenly older and more burdened. "He'll tell you." He went to the door and gestured to Hobbs's secretary. Then he turned and crossed slowly back to his chair, his eyes never looking up toward Cheryl.

Hobbs entered carrying a legal folder, wearing a particularly conservative suit with a tie that would have dressed down a pallbearer. He gave Cheryl a hair-trigger smile as he sat across from her. "Cheryl," was his only word of greeting, and then he put on his glasses and opened the folder on his lap.

"The other members of the Cramm family," he began, "have directed me to petition the court for a declaration of your mental incompetence. Specifically, they want you removed from the board of Cramm Yachts, and your shares placed into a voting trust."

Her face registered shock, but then her open mouth closed into a smile. "*They* think *I'm* crazy," she said incredulously.

"Ill," Whit corrected. "Mentally ill."

"That's truly funny," Cheryl answered. "One of them has spent his inheritance attempting to raise the dry martini to an art form, and the other has blown her fortune on face-lifts. And they think I'm crazy."

"The petition cites recent behavior and illusionary episodes—"

"They're minority shareholders," Cheryl interrupted. "If they don't like the management, they can always sell." She turned to George. "I have half the shares. You have another . . . what? . . . fifteen percent. We'll file our own petition to have theirs dismissed as frivolous."

Through his hands, George mumbled, "I can't . . ."

"George is also being sued for dereliction of duty," Hobbs said. "Considering your . . . condition . . . I have advised him to join in the petition."

Cheryl was beginning to understand. "You advised," she said to Whit. Then she asked George, "and what did you respond to Mr. Hobbs's advice?"

Williamson seemed a broken man when he looked up. "That I would do everything in my power to get you to sell. Then you can take your fortune . . . and your daughter, and close the book on this whole episode." He forced a bit of enthusiasm back into his voice. "I've arranged for Vector to create an office anyplace you want to live. They'll sell boats in the middle of the desert, if that's what suits you. And they've agreed to pay you a consulting fee. . . ."

"George . . ." Cheryl's stare silenced him. "Thank you for trying to make it easy for me. Robert would be grateful, and I'm grateful. But I'd rather you help me keep the company in the family."

She patted his hand, then stood and crossed the spacious room to its heavy door. She stopped in the doorway.

"By the way, Whit. You're fired!"

52 AS SHE DROVE BACK UP TO THE HOUSE, CHERYL SAW Gretchen playing with Rachael on the colorful plastic slide that had been set up on the side lawn. She kicked off her high heels and stepped easily into the game, which consisted of pretending to chase the little girl to the top of the slide, and then running around to catch her as she slid to the bottom.

"How do you keep up with her?" Cheryl asked after a few minutes. "She has more energy every day."

"I've grown up with her," the au pair answered easily. And then her expression froze in the realization of what she had said.

"It's all right," Cheryl told her, looking at Rachael so as not to seem accusing. "I know I missed a year. I'll just have to keep trying to catch up."

Rachael screamed her delight as she flashed down the small slide. Cheryl scooped her up at the bottom and set her on her feet so she could run back to the steps and start again to the top. Cheryl stood waiting at the bottom, but Gretchen was still nursing her embarrassment, and didn't follow close to the child. Rachael was already up two steps when they both realized that no one was holding her. Before either could move, the little girl lost her footing and fell back down the steps, crying more out of fright than pain. As the two women raced around both sides of the slide they found themselves reaching down for her together. Rachael's arms stretched out for Gretchen.

It was Gretchen who rocked her and comforted her, and finally carried her into the house for a promised cookie. Cheryl found herself alone, leaning against the slide as she stepped back into her shoes. Great morning, she thought to herself. The lawyers are taking my company, and the au pair is walking off with my daughter.

Back in her room, while she was changing into jeans, Cheryl weighed the choices that confronted her. It would be a long, hard fight to hold on to the company, especially now that there were enemies inside the walls. While she was battling, Rachael would turn more and more to Gretchen. She would be risking her own relationship with her daughter. But if she focused her energies on raising her child, then the work of saving Cramm Yachts would fall entirely on George Williamson. The man she had met with in the morning had seemed anxious to surrender, hardly the combative figure that the task would demand. The company wouldn't survive.

And that was precisely what George had been telling her: "Take the money. Take your daughter. I don't even want to tell you what the fight will be like if you stay."

Except she couldn't walk away from the possibility that her husband was still alive. And, if he were dead, she couldn't abandon the cause he had died for.

Gretchen tapped lightly on the door and pushed it open a crack. "She's asleep," the young girl whispered.

Cheryl smiled. "I'll be out for a while." When she saw the apprehension on Gretchen's face, she added, "I'm just going over to the office."

Gretchen nodded. She went directly to Cheryl's bedside phone, turned it on its side, and pushed a thumb screw that turned off the ringer. Cheryl froze in the doorway. She had often seen Gretchen turn off the upstairs telephones when Rachael was napping. Now the simple adjustment seemed sinister.

53 As soon as she stepped into Robert's office, she phoned down to the design shed. When there was no answer, she asked a secretary and learned that Sean had left for the day. "Something about a dealer in Marlborough, who didn't know what inventory Sean was talking about. Does that make any sense?" It did, and the message was frightening. Sean had found discrepancies between the records of finished boats carried on the company books, and the boats that were actually delivered to dealers. The secretary's report indicated that the problem had cropped up again. Maybe the inventory she was counting on didn't actually exist.

She wasn't surprised to find George's office empty. She could imagine the discussion he had had with Whit Hobbs after she left. Undoubtedly, he had been counting on Hobbs to defend him against the family's action. By firing Hobbs, she had deprived George of his counsel. They were probably still at Whit's desk, each trying to persuade the other to change sides.

She unlocked Robert's desk and searched through until she found the folder of the accounting work sheets. The formats looked familiar. Robert had little interest in the flow of figures through the accounts, caring only to track the final postings. It was one of the tasks he had turned happily over to Cheryl when he introduced her into the business. She was able to establish the time frame and begin to trace the inventory turns, putting quantities on Sean's theory that some of the boats supposedly already in the hands of dealers didn't actually exist.

The cost figures she had on the *Siren* project were much higher than the numbers that George had indicated. And there were increases in the general production ledgers that ran counter to the lower production rates.

She turned through the details. There were dozens of entries circled in red, and no matter how she tried, she was unable to trace them through the books. After working for over two hours, she threw down her pencil in despair. When she looked up, George Williamson was standing in the doorway.

He looked at the files she had spread on the desk, and then into her eyes.

"You know about this?" Cheryl asked.

He nodded.

"It doesn't add."

"I know," George answered. He came into the room unsteadily, and seemed to hold the chair for balance before he sat in it.

"You said Robert had taken out funds while I was sick. I found those records in his drawer. But this . . ." Her hands raised hopelessly over the papers.

"He charged Cramm Yachts for boats that were never built," George said mournfully. "There's almost five million siphoned out of the company."

"But you . . . you ran the business. You must have known."

"I knew," he admitted. His eyes rose slowly. "But what was I supposed to do? I mean, it was *his* company. He was only taking what was his. And he was my friend."

Williamson got up and walked to the window. "Oh sure," he continued, "there were tax considerations. And I kept warning him that he could get into serious trouble. But he was sure he was going to be able to put it back."

Cheryl's eyes were wide with amazement. "Dear God," was the best she could manage.

George turned back to her. "For God's sake, Cheryl, you've got to sign the papers. The sale is the only way out of this mess."

She looked down at the work sheets. "I found this in a couple of afternoons. How long do you think you can keep it from Vector? Once they buy the company and try to consolidate the accounts . . ." It was obvious to her that Vector would know they had been cheated within a few weeks.

"My stock will be worth fifteen million," George answered. "I'll put whatever it takes back into the company. I think I can have everything back in balance before Vector has time to find anything."

Cheryl studied his face. His eyes were darting and his color was ashen. "You were going to use all your money to cover up Robert's theft?"

He slumped back into the chair. "I owe everything to Robert."

"So I've been trying to save a company that is already lost."

He nodded. "That's why I've been pressing you to sell. That's why I don't want the relatives, or the courts, near those books."

George watched anxiously as Cheryl folded the work sheets and replaced the evidence of fraud back in her husband's desk. He waited for her answer, never thinking of the question that was churning in her mind.

"Is Robert alive?" she asked when she looked up from her work.

"Alive? No!" Their eyes were locked on one another. "Cheryl, don't torture yourself. If her were alive, he'd be here with you."

"Unless he's running away from everything. The company . . . his crimes . . . me . . ."

"Jesus!" George jumped to his feet. "You think Robert and I are in some kind of conspiracy. You think I could sit here, watching you drive yourself mad, to help Robert get away with a robbery?"

"You just said you owed him everything," she recalled.

"Not my integrity. But all this is nonsense. *Siren* is gone. So is her crew. We all have to move on."

"Then who's calling me?"

He turned to her, his head shaking sadly. "No one is calling you. The police have investigated. That phone isn't even connected. It's your imagination . . . your grief."

"No, George, it's Gretchen. I know how she connects that phone. And I know how she fixes the other phones so that when calls come in, that's the only phone that rings."

George sagged back into the chair, looking at her in despair. He listened patiently while Cheryl explained the phone man's visit, and his demonstration of connecting Robert's phone to the house extension. "She's working with someone on the outside," Cheryl concluded. "The only question is whether it's Robert, or someone who wants me to believe it's Robert. And if it's Robert, who is he calling: me"—her eyes suddenly flooded with tears—"or Gretchen?"

He rose slowly and made his way carefully around the desk until he was standing beside her. "Robert is dead," George whispered. "And Gretchen has done nothing except take care of your daughter."

"The letters," Cheryl reminded him.

"There are no letters. And when you talk this way, you're making it easy for them to get their petition and have you declared incompetent. Please, Cheryl. Let me take you home. Get some rest. And then sign the papers. Take your fortune and your daughter. Save yourself."

She thanked George at the doorway to her house. "I'll have your car sent up," he promised. He kissed her on the cheek, and watched her through the doorway until she disappeared at the turn in the staircase.

Cheryl went straight to the office. She checked the phone cord to be sure that it hadn't been extended into the live jack. She went to her own room, reset the ringer on her telephone, and then took the key to Robert's desk out of her jewelry box. She went back into the office, sat at the desk, and opened the file drawer.

The files were just as she had left them, and Cheryl pushed them back on their hangers to get to Gretchen's letters. But the space under the files was empty.

There were no letters.

54 "THERE ARE FIFTEEN BOATS THAT WERE NEVER delivered," Sean told Cheryl, spreading his inventory records across the sundeck table of the *Solomon Cramm*. It was almost sunset, and the fire in the western sky was growing more intense by the second.

He noticed that Cheryl seemed distracted, scarcely glancing at the evidence he was setting before her.

"That's about what the figures would indicate," she said.

Her tone was unenthusiastic, just as it had been when he had phoned the house. He had told her that someone had inflated the inventory figures, and that some of the boats didn't exist. "Thank you," she had answered calmly, as if the news held no significance. Then she had suggested that they meet aboard the old family yacht instead of in her office.

"You know about the inventory?" he asked, disappointed that the information he was bringing was already stale.

"Not the number of boats, but the cost of the fake boats. It's a little more than six million dollars."

He looked bewildered.

"Robert was pulling out a great deal of money, apparently to meet my medical bills as well as *Siren*'s overruns."

"That's nonsense," Sean fired back. "We hit the number on the head, and that was money that had come out of his personal account."

Cheryl dismissed his argument. "Well, my costs then. It doesn't matter why. He had taken over seven million dollars. I traced it through the accounting work sheets."

"Robert wouldn't do that," Sean said.

"He did, and George knew about it. He told me Robert intended to replace it, but they both knew it had gone too far. The only chance was the insurance on *Siren*. And on himself. And even that wouldn't be enough."

"He wouldn't have killed himself," Sean argued. "And he sure as hell wouldn't have killed anyone else."

"He never intended to kill himself," she said, "but I think he intended right from the beginning to kill someone else."

"Beth?" There was anger rising in Sean's voice.

"Not Beth," Cheryl answered matter-of-factly. "Me."

The color drained out of Sean's face. "You can't mean it. . . ."

"We both know there were phone calls. And we both know how they were set up. I watched Gretchen turn my telephone down so as not to wake Rachael. She has to be the one who set them up."

"Maybe," he allowed. "I'm still checking on the outside line—"

Cheryl interrupted him. "Forget the outside line. Gretchen's letters are missing."

Sean remembered the love letters she had described, where Gretchen had hinted that she was a better mother than Cheryl, and could be a better wife.

"Except for you and George, Gretchen and Robert are the only ones who know about those letters. And I never told you or George where they were."

Her thinking was clear. It had to be Gretchen who took the letters. Unless, as George kept hinting, the letters existed only in Cheryl's unstable mind.

"It all adds up if you remember that I was the one who was supposed to be crewing with Robert. He escapes his losses and gets rid of his crazy wife with one faked disaster at sea. The insurance covers his debts, so no one in the family has any reason to question the company's resources. And then Gretchen joins him, probably bringing Rachael along."

It was all too fantastic. Sean couldn't believe Robert capable of anything so cold-blooded, nor could he believe that Cheryl would ever suspect him of such a plan. For the first time, he found himself wondering if Cheryl really was having delusions.

"There's just one link missing from the chain," Cheryl went on. "That was how Robert hoped to get his hands on the money. After all, if he were going to play dead, he couldn't show up at the reading of his own will and claim a share."

Sean protested, "There wouldn't be any reason for Robert—"

"So I reread the will," Cheryl went on, just as if Sean had never spoken. "In the event of my death, everything goes into a trust fund for Rachael. And George is the administrator of the trust fund."

When she turned to Sean, there was a wildness in her eyes that he had never seen before, not even during the months she was a ghostly figure rocking on the porch. "Don't you see," Cheryl said, raising her voice. "George is in on it. He and Robert set this up together."

"George?" Sean couldn't believe it. She was imagining a conspiracy that was spreading out to include everyone she knew. It wasn't possible, was it?

"What they never counted on was my staying ashore. George probably would have had to figure out a way to get rid of me. Except Vector fouled everything up by making an offer for the company that was worth twice as much as the company itself. So now, to get top dollar, I needed to sell to Vector. That's why George is pushing for a quick sale. It will cover the fraud, and give him and Robert access to a fortune."

He was looking at her open-mouthed. Her plot was getting ever more elaborate, and ever more fantastic. She was involving everyone close to her in a murderous scheme that simply didn't make sense. If George had planned to kill her, there was nothing to stop him from killing her now. The trust could sell to Vector as easily as Cheryl could.

Sean reached out and took her hand. "Cheryl . . . Robert is dead. He's not calling you. And George isn't plotting against you. He's trying to make things easy for you and Rachael."

"No . . ." she argued.

"Listen to me." It was a command, and she was startled into silence. "If the calls came from inside the house, then they have to be coming from Gretchen. And letters or no letters, it's pretty obvious that she thinks Rachael is hers."

She was looking at him, but his words weren't registering.

"Get rid of her," Sean said. He wanted to add that she was in no condition to be fighting to save Cramm Yachts. Her grip on reality was faltering. See George. Sign the papers. Get another au pair. Take the money and leave. But he knew that none of that would register. She wouldn't begin thinking again until Gretchen was gone.

George knew that. He had been ready to fire the young Danish girl the instant he heard about the letters. Sean decided to talk with George. He wouldn't get into Cheryl's wild fancies, nor would he repeat her suspicion that George had joined Robert in a plot to get rid of her. All he would tell him was that Gretchen was the one placing the phone calls, and probably using a recording of Robert's voice. The only alternative was that it was Robert calling for Gretchen. Sean knew what George's reaction would be. It was unthinkable that Robert was still alive.

55 "YOU STILL BELIEVE THERE ARE PHONE CALLS?" George said the next morning, when Sean told him about his conversation with Cheryl. His tone was skeptical, nearly mocking Sean for being taken in. "Phone calls from dead men . . . disappearing letters . . . how can you take any of this seriously? Doesn't it sound a bit pathetic, especially coming from someone who keeps trying to throw herself into the sea?"

"I'm going to keep looking until I find some answers," Sean responded.

George threw up his hands in surrender. "Suit yourself, Sean. But the answers are there for anyone to see. *Siren* broke up because her design set up too many stresses in the hull."

Sean's eyes narrowed angrily, but George hastened to calm him. "I'm not faulting you. You gave Robert exactly what he wanted. What I am faulting is your willingness to believe anything but the obvious. Bombs! Plots between Robert and the au pair."

"I believe that she had the letters. And I believe that there were phone calls. That's why I've told her to send Gretchen home. The girl has to be in on it."

"Gretchen is not the problem," George countered. "Cheryl is the problem. And as for your bomb theory . . ."

He reached into his drawer, and then threw a thick envelope on the desk. The return address indicated that the package had come from the Broward County coroner's office. He pulled out a thick file of legal paper and saw the heading. It was Whaley's testimony before the coroner.

"They were curious about the photos, so they subpoenaed your photographer friend. As it turns out, he isn't much of a friend at all."

Sean looked up curiously, so George went on. "According to Whaley, you beat the hell out of him to make him show you his photos, and then you paid him five thousand to do some creative retouching. 'Computer enhancement,' he calls it."

"That's a lie! That's not what happened—"

"I know," George cut him off. "But the coroner was about to haul you in for interfering with his investigation. They're very impatient with fabricated evidence. I told him you had every reason to believe that the photos were genuine."

Sean dropped the envelope and stood, thoroughly chastened. "Thanks," he said, but then the anger returned to his face. "But I still think Vector had a diver under the boat. And I still think they're involved."

"I hope not," George said before Sean could get out the door. "I'm going to plead with Cheryl once more, and if she signs, I'm still going to do the deal with Vector."

"I told her to sign," Sean said. "Take her money and run. But I don't think she will."

"Then God help her," George said. "She'll never survive a suit on her competence. She'll lose everything. Maybe even her daughter."

56 THE TELEPHONE COMPANY SERVICEMAN CALLED late in the morning. He had checked through three years of line records and had been unable to find when Robert's private line had been connected to the house.

Absently, Sean had asked him what that meant. "Well, if it's not our line, the question is where in hell does it lead?" the man had explained. "Not much point in putting in a line that doesn't connect to anything."

Sean wasn't enthused. He had lost badly on his investigation of Whaley's photos. His faith in Cheryl had been shattered by her own wild suspicions. George, it seemed, was the only one making sense, and Sean was just beginning to accept that the calls could be coming from Cheryl's imagination. But the phone line was one mystery that had not yet been exposed as a fraud.

They met in front of the house and walked around all four sides. There were two lines that left the house together, and were wrapped around the same support cable that stretched over the grounds and down the hill. They walked underneath it, following it all the way to the pole.

"Well, we know one of them connects back to our office. That's the family line with all its extensions." He went to his truck and put on his tool belt and climbing spikes. "Let's see if we can find out where the other one goes."

Sean watched while he climbed the pole, and began connecting his telephone set to the different wires. He looked puzzled when he came down.

"What kind of phone system do you have down at the office building?" he asked.

Sean shrugged. "How many kinds are there?"

They climbed into the telephone truck and drove down to the Cramm offices. The serviceman looked up as they entered, tracing the line from the pole to the side of the building. Inside, he looked quickly at some of the desk phones, and then found the door to the equipment closet.

"Okay," he said, as soon as he opened the door. "That explains a lot of things."

"Like what?" Sean asked.

Cramm had a private telephone system, installed several years before by an interconnect company. It was an on-site switch that was connected to the individual instruments on each desk, and in each office throughout the yard. All the telephone company did was connect its lines to the outside of the switch. Everything inside was maintained by the interconnect company.

"I'm not supposed to look any further," the man told Sean as he unwrapped the connecting wires from his portable telephone. "Everything in here is your problem, not ours." But, without hesitating, he began to test out the lines. Sean watched, bewildered by the constantly changing expression on the serviceman's face. As he made one connection and listened, his brow wrinkled with confusion. At his next test, he smiled knowingly.

"Okay," he finally said. "We're done in here."

Sean followed him back outside the building and helped him carry a ladder from the truck to the building, where he climbed up to examine the phone line connections.

"Anyone going to bother me if I go back inside?"

"I'll go with you," Sean said.

The serviceman shook his head. "You go back up to the house. Make sure that phone is plugged into the dead jack. The one behind the desk."

"The phone is dead," Sean protested.

"Just make sure it's connected, and then wait next to it." He walked away and turned back into the Cramm Yachts building. Sean sighed his frustration, and then began jogging back up the hill.

Cheryl wasn't in, and Gretchen was playing with Rachael out on the front lawn, next to his parked truck. He ran up to Robert's private office, found the phone on the desk, and made sure that it was plugged into the dead line. He stood staring at it for a few minutes until he felt foolish. Then he turned away from the desk and glanced around the room.

It was a reflection of the Robert he remembered. Masculine, seafaring, venturesome. The desk, in the middle of its nautical surroundings, suggested that business was only a sideline for Robert. Boats and the sea came first, just as they did with Sean. It was no wonder that they had worked so well together, and had such respect for one another.

Robert, scheming with an au pair to murder his wife and take the company funds? Standing in this room, the idea seemed even more ridiculous than when Cheryl had explained it.

Carefully, he looked through the open door into the bedroom that Robert and Cheryl had shared. It was simple and comfortable. Traditional New England patterns on the wall decorations. Bold enameled moldings around the windows and doors. Strong oak furniture, a large dresser with three rows of drawers for Cheryl, and an enormous armoire for Robert's clothes. Everything was traditionally functional. There was no pretense. Sean could feel the presence of honest, level-headed people. There was nothing to suggest madness, nor anything that resembled uncontrolled greed.

The telephone in the office rang like a shot through the afternoon quiet. Sean spun and raced back to the desk. He lifted the phone, suddenly apprehensive at what he might hear. "Hello?"

"It's me," said the telephone man's voice. "So now we have another way that the calls could have been made."

"How? Where are you?"

The man chuckled. "I'm in the equipment closet. That phone was never connected to our central office. It's an extension from your company's private telephone switch. Once this line is connected you could call that phone from anywhere."

"I'll be right down," Sean said. He hung up the phone and took the steps down to the front door two at a time.

Cheryl had figured out that George had to be in on it. George, Robert, and Gretchen. He had ignored the idea, thinking that Cheryl was rambling pathetically. But George certainly had the run of the Cramm offices, and would probably be the only one who knew that Robert's private phone was an extension of the business telephone system. Robert could call the phone in his home office from anywhere in the world. All he needed was someone to reconnect the extension line in the equipment closet. And that could very easily be his best friend, George Williamson. Suddenly, Cheryl didn't seem crazy anymore.

57 CHERYL WATCHED CAREFULLY UNTIL GRETCHEN jogged down the front driveway with Rachael in her three-wheeled stroller. It was the perfect time. The housekeeper was off, and the cook was busy in the kitchen. George and Sean were involved at the boatyard. And Gretchen wouldn't be coming back up the driveway for at least forty-five minutes. Cheryl left her room, slipped quietly down the hallway, and turned the handle on Gretchen's door. Like all the other rooms in the Cramm house, it was unlocked.

She had thought carefully about what she was doing, and had analyzed all the mistakes she might make. Notice how things are before you touch them, she reminded herself. People who want to know if their things are being searched leave their cabinets and closets in a specific way. When she was in school, the girls were constantly guarding against room searches by parents looking for alcohol or drugs. They would leave a dresser drawer slightly ajar, knowing that after opening it and looking through it, their parents would close it tight. In their closets, they would hang clothes in alternating groups of three and four. Parents wouldn't notice the arrangement, and after tossing through the pockets would inevitably leave all the hangers equally spaced.

Some of her friends had been even more devious. A thread stretched from the leg of a bed to the leg of a dresser was invisible against the floor. Someone going through the room would generally break it without noticing. Or a matchstick closed into the jamb of a door would fall unnoticed to the floor if the door were opened.

Cheryl had to believe that young women in Denmark were just as suspicious as their American counterparts. She moved into Gretchen's room with great care, examining the floor in front of her before taking each footstep, and examining every door before opening it.

She began at the dresser, and moved carefully through each drawer. When she hit on an envelope of photographs folded into lingerie, she flipped through the shots without taking them out of the package. They were family shots, and photos of groups of young people that had been

taken during school trips throughout Europe. She went through the
night tables, lifting each item and carefully setting it back. As she
finished, she checked her watch. Twenty minutes had gone by. She had
to hurry.

She examined the closet door and found a small fold of paper pinched
into the jamb. She replaced it carefully after she had run her hand
between the layers of sweaters and slacks, and checked the pockets of
the hanging coats. Thirty minutes gone.

She couldn't count on Rachael tipping her off when they returned.
On the evening run, the little girl often fell asleep. Then Gretchen would
be careful not to make any noise that might wake the child.

The bookshelf was a logical hiding place, but also a very dangerous
one to search. There were too many things that could be arranged—the
order of titles, the distance of one of the books from the front edge of
the shelf. She had to notice everything, and be particularly careful about
replacing each piece. When she flipped through the pages she had to be
certain that nothing was placed between the folios.

Her time was up, and she had found nothing. Gretchen should already
be at the front door. But there was still the drawer of Gretchen's desk.
She checked for anything caught in the front, and then ducked under
the desk to see if a paper had been wedged next to the back of the drawer.
She opened it slowly. There wasn't time to look item by item, but it was
a flat drawer. It would be easy to see even a small packet of letters. She
bent down, satisfied herself that the letters weren't there, and was
beginning to push the drawer shut when her heart stopped. There was
a photograph in the front of the drawer. It showed Gretchen and Robert
together. The cottage at Buzzard Island was in the background.

She stood in shock, staring into the drawer, not touching the photo
or lifting it for a closer look. Then she heard the front door slam shut.

She tried to compose herself. She had to move quickly, but she
couldn't afford to make a mistake. Quietly, she slid the drawer closed.
She pushed the chair back, exactly as it had been. Then she tiptoed to
the door and listened through it. She could hear footsteps on the stairs.

Cheryl could rush out, but she would have to pass across the top of
the stairs. She might be seen. Or she could stay put, hoping that
Gretchen would turn the other way and carry Rachael directly to the
nursery. She reached for the door handle. The au pair might see her,

but she wouldn't be certain that she was coming from her room. It was risky, but it seemed better than taking a chance on being caught in the room with no excuse.

She stopped. It was Gretchen's voice at the top of the stairs, only a few feet from the door. The girl was humming softly to Rachael. The voice paused. She was deciding which way to turn. Cheryl held her breath.

And then the footsteps moved away. She listened as the nursery door cracked open, and then heard the click of the light switch. Cheryl opened the door quickly, stepped out into the empty hallway, and closed the door behind her. When she stepped into the nursery, Gretchen had her back turned to her.

"Is she asleep?" Cheryl whispered.

Gretchen smiled as she turned. She nodded that the little girl was gone for the night.

58 IT WAS A CLEAR NIGHT, WITH THE SUMMER TRIANGLE bright in the center of a field of crisp stars. An easy northwesterly was keeping the air clear, and bringing a bit of relief from the summer heat.

Sean had the windows open as he packed his drawings into file folders, and then slipped the folders into cardboard boxes. He had few personal things. The cartons of his plans and engineering data would take up much more room than his clothes.

He had decided that it was time for him to leave. Not that he had given up on pursuing Whaley's photos further, or running down the person who was calling on the private office line. Nor had he been able to put to rest completely the lingering doubt that Robert might still be alive. But he knew for certain that Cheryl wasn't up to the long, drawn-out fight that was ahead of her. He agreed with George that the best thing she could do was take the money and run with her daughter. Sean knew for certain that his hopes for rebuilding *Siren*, his interest in the inventory, even just his presence, were encouraging her to fight on. He was her ally. When he told her that he was giving up, then maybe it would be easier for her to give up.

He was suddenly aware of a voice down by the dock. He clicked off the light in the design shed and peered out the open window. At first there was nothing. No sound. No movement. But then he saw an edge of light, cut off almost the instant it appeared. It was aboard the *Solomon Cramm*. Someone was moving below with a flashlight, searching the old steam yacht. The glow was reflecting on the bulkheads and showing through the portholes. Sean reached for his own flashlight and slipped out through the darkened door.

He stepped carefully, to minimize the crunch of the gravel as he crossed the yard. He eased down the gangway that connected to the floating docks, and moved even more slowly as he walked across the planking. When he reached the yacht, he saw that its companionway was down, the gate in the lifeline left open.

From the dock, he stared down through the portholes. The boat was dark, seemingly deserted. But he had seen the light sweeping below her decks. Someone had been aboard and he would have seen the person if he or she had come out on the pier. He moved aft, and then stepped across the open space to the gunwale. Silently, he slipped over the lifeline, and let himself down into the cockpit.

Sean went first to the outboard side, to make sure that there wasn't a small boat alongside. That would be the only way someone could get aboard without coming through the gate, or through the office building. All he could see was the open water lapping up against the side.

He moved forward, under the overhead, and pressed his face against the glass window in the heavy wooden door. Light from the yard came through the side ports and crossed through the yacht's saloon. He could see the comfortable lounge and the gracious dining table with its twelve captain's chairs. The space was empty. Sean lifted the latch and stepped inside.

He used his flashlight to find the switch at the base of the turn-of-the-century gas lamp. The boat had been outfitted with low-voltage electric lighting for use at sea, and with shore power. But when he turned the switch, nothing happened. Someone had opened the breakers and killed the power. He followed the beam of the flashlight through the dining room, to the carpeted steps that led below.

At the bottom, he panned his light aft. He was in a paneled passageway, with doors on each side that opened into guest staterooms, and the door to the owner's stateroom at the end. On the port side, there was a pull-up hatch, with a ladder down to the diesel engine. Forward, there were steps down to the galley, and then farther forward, to the crew's quarters in the bow. He moved aft.

Each of the staterooms was made up as if guests would be boarding at any moment. The beds were made, dresser cloths in place, and towels hanging in the heads. He had seen the house staff come aboard to prepare the yacht for meetings and luncheons, but he had no idea that they also freshened up the rooms. Now he realized that the *Solomon Cramm* was fitted out for extended cruising. It was a small hotel sitting unnoticed at the water's edge. Perfect living quarters for someone who wanted to disappear.

He went forward, down the steps, and pushed open the door to the galley. His light found the heavy metal ice chests that had been equipped with refrigeration, and the stove, hung on gimbals, so that it could be used when the yacht was underway. He started around the small island counter that was used for the preparation of food.

Sean sensed the movement behind him before he glimpsed something arcing down toward the back of his head. He had just begun to move when he heard the crack inside his skull and felt a rush of nausea in his gut. There were colors, and brilliant wild shapes suddenly moving out of focus. And then there was darkness.

It didn't seem like a long time. Perhaps just a few seconds. But he was aware that he was lying on the deck, between the island and the gimbaled stove. His head hurt, and there was a sick, sweet smell that filled his nose and mouth. He tried to lift his head, but found that his body wasn't responding to his will. It was easier to close his eyes and go back to sleep.

The odor was getting stronger, and he was gagging on its sweet taste. His eyes opened quickly. He heard a steady hissing sound that he recognized but couldn't place. Painfully, he pushed his chest up from the deck, and then turned so that he was leaning against the side of the island. He was staring straight at the stove, and at the tank of propane gas that was fitted under the stove. He followed the hissing sound to the top of the tank, and then he recognized the smell. In a flash, Sean knew exactly how he was going to die.

He rolled forward on his knees and reached for the valve. The handle was broken cleanly off the stem, and the wet gas was escaping right into his face. He pulled back, rolled away, and crawled back to the door. When he reached up and twisted the handle he found that the door was locked from the other side.

Sean dragged himself to his feet and staggered forward toward the door to the crew's quarters. It too was locked tight. He looked up at the vent over the stove. Without power, it was useless. He was locked into an airless chamber below the decks of a heavy wooden yacht. And the space was filling with lethal gas.

The bomb. He had been looking for a bomb attached somewhere to the keel. And now he was inside a bomb. The gas would build until it bubbled through his blood and filled the channels of his brain. And then, when it was dense enough, it would explode under the slightest spark, even the static electricity that his body would create as it slid down the bulkhead.

He ducked low as he drove himself back to the after door. The hinges were on the inside, which meant that the door swung in. To get out, he would have to split the heavy wood down the center and reach around for the lock. As he looked around feverishly for a tool, he tried to remember whether there was a key. If there were no key, he would have to cut a hole big enough for his escape.

As he tore through the drawers and cabinets, he was aware that he was losing focus, perhaps the lingering result of the blow to his head. More likely the first effects of the poisonous gas. He had to work quickly and, God help him, be careful not to do anything that might cause an electric arc.

There were knives that might serve as screwdrivers. And a meat mallet that he could use as a hammer. It should be simple to pop the hinges. But the metal against metal would act like a flint. One mistake and he probably would never even hear the explosion. He took the wooden mallet and wobbled back to the door. He swung with all his strength and saw the varnish shatter like glass across the door panel. But the heavy wood held fast. Sean pounded again and again.

Was this how Beth had died? Was she locked below in a cabin filling with gas, struggling to get out? And then what? Friction between her rubber-soled shoes and some part of the deck? Or a knife blade scraping against a lock? A spark. A blinding flash of light. And then a concussion that had shattered her body and scorched her skin as it was blasting the hull of *Siren* to little pieces.

The paneling cracked. And then the next blow of the mallet sent shreds of wood flying as it punched through the door. He slammed at the edges of the hole. More wood flew away. He could see through, out into the darkened passageway. Sean pushed his face into the hole and breathed deeply. His leaden arms suddenly seemed lighter. The sick fog blew clear of his brain.

He pulled back and pounded again. The hole quickly widened as huge splinters broke free. Then he reached his arm through and found the handle on the other side.

There was no key.

And then the fog returned. The hole was too small to vent the enormous amount of gas that was hissing out of the tank. Sean lost his balance as he swung back with the mallet, and his blow missed the door entirely.

Dear God, it was too late. He wasn't going to make it. He struck again and again, but now the wooden chips were smaller. His strength was vanishing as quickly as his mind was shutting down. He dropped the mallet and fell against the door, his face staring though the hole out into the darkness.

He thought he saw a light swinging somewhere above. But perhaps it was only his last glimmer of consciousness.

59 HE HEARD POUNDING ON THE DOOR, AND THEN IT was being forced open from the other side, pushing him back onto the deck. He tried to get back to his feet, but his body was limp. Sean looked up and saw an enormous figure behind the half-open door.

Hands wrapped under his arms, and then he was being dragged up the steps and into the passageway. There was light above him, and the sweet smell of the gas seemed to be disappearing.

"Come on! Try to walk. That's it! Up the steps. Take it slow. One step at a time."

He tried to follow the instructions. His arm was over someone's shoulder, supporting most of his weight. But it took all of Sean's effort to lift his foot onto the first step. Only when he was standing did it begin to make sense, and then he lifted his foot to the next step.

"That's it. You're going to make it. Another step now. That's it. You're doing fine."

It was George's voice. George was holding Sean's arm over his shoulder, nearly dragging him up the steps to the saloon. A large flashlight glowed on the saloon table, and the air seemed fresh. They stumbled through the room and out onto the open afterdeck. George eased Sean into one of the deck chairs.

"The propane," Sean managed.

"It's okay," George said. "Just sit here. I'm going forward to open the bow hatch."

Sean sat by himself, sucking in air. The confusion began to vanish, and he was gradually aware of the stinging pain at the back of his head. When he put up his hand, he could feel a sticky ooze. He remembered the blow flashing through the darkness and knew that the stain on his hand was blood.

He stood unsteadily and worked his way to the stern. He could smell the salt being blown off the water by the northerly wind. When he looked up, he could see the explosion of stars. "Jesus," he whispered. "I'm alive."

George came back around the dockside deck. "The crew's compartment is open. It's venting from both ends."

"Can you shut off the gas?" Sean asked.

"There's no gas left," George told him. "The tank is empty." He helped Sean back into a chair. "What the hell were you doing fooling with the propane tank?"

Slowly, Sean found the words to explain what had happened. He showed George the blood from his head to support his story.

"Someone tried to kill you? Jesus!" George seemed amazed. "I thought you must have hit it when you fell." Then he added, "Thank God you tried to bust through that door. I was getting into my car when I heard the banging. Why the hell didn't you call the police?"

Sean didn't understand the question. He had been locked in the galley, inhaling a deadly gas. How was he supposed to call the police?

"Instead of going aboard," George clarified. "When you heard a prowler you should have phoned Security. Why in hell would you try to corner a burglar?"

"It wasn't a burglar," Sean said, listening to his own words to make sure they were coherent. "I think it was Robert. I think he's been hiding out aboard the yacht."

"Robert?" George looked down at Sean with a look of skepticism. "Let's get you up and walking."

Sean brushed away his arm. "No, I'm not delirious. Listen to me. I figured it out. It all makes sense." Reluctantly, George sat on the gunwale, his knees nearly touching Sean's chair.

"First, the explosion. That's how *Siren* was sunk." Sean pointed down into the cabin where the smell of gas was still apparent. "Robert waited until Beth was sleeping and then broke the valve on the propane tank. He had probably set it up with someone to take him off on another boat. Then they probably fired a flare into *Siren*. When the boat blew, he was rid of Beth, and free of his financial problems."

"Jesus," George whispered. Then he snapped at Sean, "Who do you figure took him off and helped him kill Beth?"

"I don't know," Sean said. "I guess I was figuring it was you . . . until you just saved my life."

"I came home," George reminded him. "And then I went to Bermuda."

"I know," Sean agreed. "But we really didn't know when *Siren* sank. We figured it was when Robert didn't file a position or answer our radio calls. But he could have been sitting out there, waiting for you to arrive on a powerboat from Bermuda."

"That's absurd," George said, seeming not to take any offense at the accusation of murder.

"I know that now," Sean said. "But someone must have picked up Robert and brought him here to Newport. And he's been hiding out here on the yacht."

George stood in exasperation. "For God's sake, Sean. Listen to yourself. You're beginning to sound like Cheryl—"

"I checked the telephone line," Sean cut in. "The one in Robert's office at the house. It's connected to the switch in the business office, upstairs."

George suddenly seemed interested.

"All someone had to do was take that wire and reattach it to the switch. Then Robert's extension was live. You could direct-dial that phone from anywhere in the world."

"Then why was there no record of the call?"

"Because the call didn't come from outside," Sean said. "There's another extension in the saloon." He pointed into the yacht's dining area. "You could call the house from in there, and it would just be an intercom call. Nothing that went through the phone company. Nothing that would leave a record."

George stared at Sean for a moment, then walked into the saloon and lifted the phone. He realized he was holding a live extension. The intercom button would let him call any phone in the building, or the extension in Robert's office at the Cramm home. When he returned he told Sean, "Go on. . . ."

"We wondered how Cheryl got into the water. It had to be suicide, because no one came past me and went out through the gate. But they didn't have to come past me. When he threw Cheryl over the side, he simply went below and hid down in one of the staterooms. I was so busy helping Cheryl and getting her to the hospital that I never thought to look for anyone."

"Why would Cheryl come down to the yard during the night?" George wondered aloud. "Unless . . ."

Now it was Sean who looked bewildered.

"That would certainly explain why she was trying to break into the yard," George continued, "if she knew that Robert was hiding here on the yacht."

"No . . . no!" Sean was shaking his head. "If Cheryl were part of a plan to pretend that her husband was dead, why would she be the one claiming to be getting phone calls from him?"

George's expression darkened, but then suddenly brightened. "Gretchen," he said. He was suddenly enthusiastic, as if he had solved the riddle. "Cheryl was right. The calls were for Gretchen. And maybe Cheryl followed Gretchen down here."

Sean was thinking.

"The night you had to take her down off the fence," George reminded him, "Gretchen was already there with Cheryl, wasn't she?"

Sean nodded.

"And it was Gretchen who never heard the calls . . ."

"Even though she was right outside Robert's office," Sean added.

They stared at each other for a moment. Then George turned away. "I just can't believe that Robert is alive," he said.

Sean stood up. "There's one way we can find out."

George looked interested.

"Let's put a tap on that phone line. If there's a call, we'll record the conversation."

George blinked in dismay. "Do you know how to do that?"

"No," Sean admitted. "But I think the guy from the telephone company is as curious as we are. I think I can get him to set it up for us."

60 SEAN DECIDED NOT TO TELL CHERYL ABOUT HIS narrow escape aboard the *Solomon Cramm*. Nor did he mention the wire tap. Cheryl, he reasoned, had been through enough. Instead, he repeated his conviction that Robert was dead. And when Cheryl told him about the photograph she had found in Gretchen's room, he fell back on his earlier advice that the au pair should be paid off and sent away. "It doesn't matter whether she was setting up the calls for someone or making them herself. It doesn't even matter if she had nothing to do with them. The fact is that she's too close to your daughter, and you have good reason not to trust her. You'll never be sure of yourself while she's around." He could only shake his head dejectedly when she repeated her hope that Gretchen would eventually lead her to Robert.

When Cheryl restated her determination to fight Whit Hobbs's incompetency petition, Sean argued that it was unnecessary. "Sign the papers," he advised her once more. "Take your money and get on with your life."

But she still had some vague plan about saving Cramm Yachts and bringing the company back to its former glory. Sean reminded her that with the fraudulent inventory figures, she probably didn't have enough money to keep running for more than a few months. And when she mentioned the offer from the French syndicate, he brought up George's view that Baron Murot was an unstable partner.

He wasn't abandoning her, but he was determined not to offer her any encouragement. He could delay his departure for a few more days. If there were phone calls, if Robert was involved in an enormous con game, he would find out. Involving Cheryl any further was risking her emotional stability, and maybe even her life. He would continue to search the old yacht for any sign of someone living aboard. He would continue to talk to his industry contacts. He would continue to monitor the phone lines, from his office where a blinking light had been rigged to tell him that the extension had gone live. Somewhere, there had to be an answer.

But Cheryl would not be put off. She joined George in interviewing attorneys who might defend her against Whit Hobbs's action. She had the company's accounting firm make survival projections on exactly how long she could hold out. And most of all, she watched Gretchen. She wanted to give the au pair the complete freedom she had always enjoyed to come and go, roam through the house, and make all the daily arrangements for Rachael. But at the same time, she wanted to be certain that the girl was never out of her sight.

When she was home, she worked in Robert's old office, so that she could be close to Gretchen's room, and close to the nursery. She found reasons to change Rachael's schedule abruptly, which threw off Gretchen's plans and made it difficult for her to set aside time for herself. When she was working at the office, she would ask the au pair to bring the little girl down to the boatyard, or to be available so that she could call her daughter on the phone. If Gretchen and Robert had any scheduled time and place for meetings, it would be nearly impossible for Gretchen to make the rendezvous. And that increased the chances that one of them would make a mistake and give the other away.

George told Sean that they were all wasting their time. He repeated over and over again that there was no mystery, and certainly no sinister plot. There had been no bomb fastened to *Siren*'s keel, nor had her cabin filled with propane. The boat had broken up and sunk, carrying both Robert and Beth to their graves. The phone calls had never occurred, but were an unmistakable symptom of Cheryl's illness. And Gretchen? She was simply an overly protective schoolgirl with a crush on her handsome boss. George was frustrated that Cheryl was still refusing to conclude the agreement with Vector, and kept muttering that it would be tragic if the deal slipped away from them.

But he couldn't explain who had tried to kill Sean aboard the *Solomon Cramm*, speculating when the two men were together that it might have been Gretchen, or even Cheryl. Either of the women could have hit him from behind and knocked the valve off the propane tank. Nor would he totally dismiss the possibility that one of the yard workers might be working with someone outside the family, although he resisted Sean's suggestion that the "someone" might be Philip McKnight, or one of his people at Vector.

George also joined Sean during the day in checking the recorder that had been attached to the telephone extension. It was nonsense, he kept insisting. But each time Sean went to the equipment closet, George was right at his heels. He seemed vindicated when the recorder showed that the line hadn't been used.

Sean came down from the office building and was heading for the design shed when he saw Cheryl standing out on the dock. She was in a skirt and blouse, and wearing heels, an outfit far too formal for the normal workday attire at Cramm. And she was staring vacantly out into the bay. Sean found the scene bizarre, and then as he watched her, even frightening. She seemed to be looking longingly at the water, as if it were the answer to all her problems. He walked out to join her, trying to appear casual even though he wanted to rush to her side.

"You okay?" he asked, after he had stood behind her unnoticed.

When she turned, her eyes were red from crying. "No," she answered, and then she explained, "It seems that I'm incompetent to manage my own affairs."

He looked puzzled.

"Our new attorneys," she went on. "They've been trying to prepare my response to the stockholders' petition. I think they agree with Whit Hobbs that I ought to be put away."

He took her arm. "Come on. Let's sit down." Then he led her aboard the old yacht and got her seated on the afterdeck. "What happened?" Sean asked.

"Do I remember running out of the house during the board meeting?" Cheryl asked herself in a forced voice. And then she answered in her own voice. "Not really. I just found myself walking down by the yard."

"Do I remember running out in the middle of the night and trying to break into the yard?" She shook her head and answered her own question, "No, again."

"How about jumping off the dock in the middle of the night? Sorry, I have no idea how I got into the water."

"And these phone calls that you say you keep getting . . ."

Her voice broke and she had to struggle to hold back the sobs.

"Don't do this to yourself," Sean begged.

Cheryl sneered. "That's not me. That's the attorney who's on my side. Can you imagine what Whit Hobbs is going to do to me?"

Sean took her hands. "What did George say?"

"What George always says. Don't put myself through this. Sign the damn papers and make myself a millionaire."

"Not bad advice," Sean said.

She pulled her hands free, and started away from him. Sean caught her at the gangway. "Listen—" he started.

Cheryl was almost screaming. "No, you listen. Someone is trying to get rid of me. Someone blew up the boat I was supposed to sail on. Someone tried to drown me off the dock. And someone has been calling on Robert's private line. And the best you and George can do is tell me to take the money and run."

"That's not what I mean," Sean said.

"Don't you understand? Someone is either going to kill me or have me sent off to an asylum."

He shook her gently. "That's not going to happen. I won't let anything happen to you."

But Cheryl wouldn't be consoled. She twisted free and stormed down the gangway. Sean let her walk away.

He went into the office building, where George was still working at his desk. "What happened to Cheryl?" he asked.

George heaved a sigh. "Awful scene," he whispered. "She accused the new lawyers of working against her. She started crying and ran out of the building. They looked at one another and then they all looked at me. They were polite . . . professional. But their meaning was clear. How are they supposed to defend her when she's so obviously"—he hesitated for an instant, and then whispered—"mad."

"She thinks someone is trying to kill her," Sean said.

George nodded. "I know." He stood, his frame sagging in a posture of despair. Then he added, "I don't suppose there's much sense in listening to the recorder."

61 SEAN PAUSED AT THE FOOT OF THE CRAMM DRIVEWAY as he drove his truck out of the yard and thought of turning up the hill. He remembered Cheryl's rage as she had run away from him, and knew that she needed someone to talk with. He could make a drink for her, and they could sit in the library until she vented her rage. He might even persuade her to go out to dinner with him. Someplace casual and quiet, just to get her out of the house. But he knew she wouldn't leave Rachael alone with Gretchen. She probably wouldn't even take her eyes off the au pair girl long enough to have a drink. He slipped the truck back into gear and headed for the town.

Newport was enjoying its tourist season, with hundreds of visiting yachts at the moorings and the docks, and the waterfront alive with vacationers. He found himself in a line of cars that could scarcely move through the pedestrians who were spilling off the sidewalks. He swung onto a side street, parked, and joined the flow that was window-shopping all the bars and restaurants.

I should have asked her, Sean thought. This was exactly what Cheryl needed. A night on the town and a chance to unwind.

He found a pub that was just the right blend of merrymaking and sanity, slid onto a bar stool, and drained the first bottle of beer in one long swig. He was sipping the second when he noticed two women at one of the side bars, attractive and available. Their heads were together, one whispering and the other smiling with her eyes darting back and forth toward Sean. He could almost hear them deciding which one would leave if he made a move on them.

It's been a long time, he realized. He smiled, wondering if he still knew how to play the game. He'd have to think back several years, probably back to when he was involved in the baron's Cup campaign. Since then, he had thrown everything into *Siren*. There hadn't been time for cruising the bars.

The girl who had been stealing glances at him put her cigarettes in her pocketbook, stood through a few more words with her friend, and then left. The whisperer, now with an empty chair beside her, turned her shoulders so that she was looking directly at Sean. She seemed to enjoy being obvious and was so fixed on him that Sean saw other men at the bar follow her glance directly to him.

He pushed the change toward the bartender and stood slowly. But even before he started toward her table, he realized that he wasn't even slightly interested. He'd be playing games, and wasting her time, because all he would be thinking about was Cheryl. Sean turned abruptly and walked out the door.

OF COURSE HE was thinking about Cheryl. She was a fine person and a strong woman. Life had given her a bad hand, and she was trying to play it as best she could. He admired her, and cared what happened to her.

Or was it more than that? Had he stayed around to try to save the company, or had it been just to stay around her? Did he want to prove his yacht design? Or did he need to prove to Cheryl that he hadn't killed her husband?

Why hadn't he told her the truth about Robert, and his involvement with Beth Hardaway? Sure, he wanted to protect Robert's name. But more than that, he didn't want to cause Cheryl any pain. She needed to know that Robert loved her, so that's what he would tell her, in words and in actions. He had respected her as a woman who was still in love with another man.

And why couldn't he leave now? He had packed his things. He had no more work to do. Cramm Yachts was about to come crashing down, and he should be touring the industry looking for another job. It wouldn't be hard to find one if he were bringing the Frenchman's new yacht with him, and all the money it would earn. Yet he was still living in the Cramm design shed, and still looking up at the house on the hill.

There was no point in lying to himself. He was staying so that when it did come crashing down, he would be there to protect Cheryl.

"Jesus," he whispered, beginning to understand himself. He was in love with her. He had always felt sorry for her, the lovely, vibrant woman who had fallen into darkness. But all he knew about her was what other people remembered. She had no mind. There was nobody to know.

Then she had recovered, and come out of her shell. She blinked at the light, and seemed to find the world exciting all over again, as if she were enjoying a second childhood. He found that he liked her, but only from a distance. He was focused on his boat. So much so that when Robert had named her as his crew, he had been unable to appreciate what it would mean to Cheryl. All he could think of was the extra seconds her inexperience and even instability would probably add to *Siren*'s time.

So when had he begun to care for her? Probably when he had first driven her back from the boatyard on the day of Robert's memorial service. That had been the lowest moment in his life, filled with thoughts of his own failure, and the price that others were paying. She had lifted him up. First, by her strength, when she wanted to save her husband's company. It was loyalty that Robert didn't deserve. And then by her kindness. She had told Sean she needed him, when he was desperate to be needed.

But that was admiration. He had gone from indifference, to civility, and then to admiration. When had he crossed the line making her more important to him than he was himself? When had her well-being become more important than his own? When had he reached the point when he had no interest in an attractive, available woman because all his interest was focused on a beaten, unavailable woman?

He worked his way through the flow of people until he was back in his truck. Then he eased the truck into the trickle of traffic, prepared for the hour it would probably take him just to get out of the downtown area.

Tourists were nearly touching the cars. He stopped abruptly when a thoroughly soused young woman walked right into his side-view mirror. Had he been moving, he would have cracked her skull. A moment later, a line of party goers dashed directly in front of him. An unsteady young man had to be lifted off the front bumper by his friends.

And then suddenly there was a familiar face. A group of men, outfitted for yachting, were moving along the sidewalk in the opposite direction. Leading the party, wearing a white captain's hat set at a jaunty angle, was Philip McKnight.

At first Sean didn't believe it. McKnight had enough party strips surrounding his south Florida base. What in hell was he doing in Newport? Sean thought of the sale, which was supposed to have been signed weeks ago. Had George signaled that the deal was ready to go down? Maybe Cheryl's scene with the lawyers was the final episode in her resistance. Perhaps now it was obvious even to Cheryl that she had no hope of keeping the company.

In that case, George would certainly have informed Philip, and Philip might have decided to use the Newport social season as a backdrop for his takeover of Cramm Yachts.

Sean wanted to follow the group, but he was stuck in the middle of the street, cars in front and behind, and traffic streaming down both sides. It took him ten minutes just to reach an intersection where a policeman let him turn onto a side street. And then it was another ten minutes locating a place to park.

Once again, he was touring the waterfront bars and restaurants, stepping into doorways and glancing through windows. Who was McKnight with? That might give some clue as to his purpose. At a minimum, Sean wanted to find where he was staying so that he could pick up the trail in the morning. He still remembered the cylinder-shaped object attached to *Siren*'s keel in Whaley's photos. Whaley had told the coroner that the whole thing was a fake. But he was a man who sold truth to the highest bidder. Sean still believed that, if Robert Cramm had been murdered, Philip McKnight was the prime suspect.

But the party had vanished. Sean spent nearly and hour patrolling the waterfront bars, and then more time at the docks and landings where some of the boat parties were taking place. It was after ten when he gave up his search and walked back to his truck.

He let his headlights linger on the dock and the two moored boats when he turned into the yard. He was sorry when there was no sign of Cheryl. He wanted a chance to talk to her again, and explain more sympathetically why he wanted her to cut her ties with Cramm. Maybe he would put his thoughts into plain words, and tell her that he couldn't bear the thought of her being hurt anymore. He unlocked the door to the design shed and was reaching for the light switch when he noticed a red blinking light on his desk. It was the signal that the telephone engineer had rigged to the recorder in the telephone equipment room. Someone had called the phone in Robert's private office.

BUZZARDS BAY

62

SEAN LEFT THE DOOR WIDE OPEN AS HE TURNED AND rushed around the office building and up the front steps. Inside, he moved unerringly through the dark secretarial area and flipped on the light in the equipment closet. The recorder was blinking, indicating that a call had been copied. He hesitated for a moment, examining the keys to make sure that he wouldn't erase the message. Then he bent close and pushed the play button.

There were clicks and motor sounds as the small cassette was rewound back to its beginning. A short hiss of electronic air. Then a voice.

"Hello, is this you?" It was a man's voice, a deep baritone like Robert's with the hint of laughter that made Robert's voice pleasant. But it was coming through static, as if the words had been recorded over and over again, or were being spoken into a child's toy radio telephone.

"Yes . . ." A woman's voice. Clear, even though the word was whispered. He couldn't recognize it.

The man. "Tonight's the night. You know how to get here." It could be Robert, but Sean wasn't sure. A better telephone. Maybe a few more words. He understood exactly what Cheryl meant when she said she thought it was her husband, but couldn't be positive.

"Yes, I've checked her. She's full of petrol."

Gretchen! He recognized the distinctive accent that she had brought with her from Europe. And she was the only one he knew who called gasoline "petrol."

"I'm dying to see you again."

The voice. Damn it, he couldn't lock on to it. Like Robert's in many ways. But yet different. Was it the phone? Was he calling through a radio link? Was it someone else?

"And your daughter will be thrilled to see you."

Sean winced. Oh, Jesus . . . oh, sweet Jesus . . . how could they do this to Cheryl?

"It will all be behind us tomorrow. . . ."

Who else could it be, Sean thought? It had to be Robert.

"I'm coming. . . ."

Gretchen's voice, filled with almost childish delight.

"I'll be waiting."

There was a click, a rush of electronic noise, and then another click. The line had gone dead. And then, a second later, the recorder shut itself off. The silence inside the equipment closet was total.

He remembered the words.

"You know how to get here."

"Your daughter will be thrilled to see you."

Gretchen was running away to join Robert. And she was taking Rachael with her. Sean flew through the dark office, falling flat-out on his chest as he tripped over a waste can. He half crawled, half ran toward the door until he was back on his feet and down the steps. A second later, and he was pumping the accelerator in his truck to keep the engine running while he shifted into gear.

The house was dark, seemingly undisturbed by the telephone call. As he raced up the hill, he could make out the faint glow of the night-light in the nursery window. All the other rooms were dark. The tires squealed as he braked at the front door, and the cab was still rocking as he ran up the steps. He pulled to a sudden halt. The front door was wide open.

Cautiously, he eased himself through the front door. Looking up the stairs, he could see only darkness. But at the end of the ground-floor hallway, there was a light coming from under the kitchen door. He walked slowly down the hall, past the playroom and the library, and pushed open the kitchen door.

Mrs. Callen, the cook, was sitting at the small dining table, her chair pushed back so that she was facing the door he had just entered. Her eyes widened when she saw him.

"Sean . . . oh, Sean, thank God, thank God."

Rachael was cuddled in her lap, wrapped in a blanket, her pajama-clad feet hanging out.

"What happened?" he demanded.

The woman was near hysteria. "She's gone," she said. "She just ran out."

He looked at the baby. "Without Rachael?" She had told Robert she was bringing his daughter with him.

"Where's Cheryl?"

"I told you," the woman wailed. "She's gone. She woke me, handed me the baby, and then ran out. There was blood down the front of her. She looked crazy. I was so frightened."

"Cheryl?" he repeated dumbly. Cheryl had run out. Covered with blood. Jesus, what had happened? Where was Gretchen?

"Oh my God!" The words came with his revelation. He turned slowly, went back down the corridor, and began climbing the stairs. She couldn't have, he told himself with each step. But she had been grossly betrayed, and the girl she had befriended was taking her daughter.

He turned the corridor and pushed open the door to Gretchen's room. The window was open, and the breeze was rustling the curtain. He touched the light switch. The bed was empty, and still neatly made. Gretchen had not slept in it. He opened the closet door. Her clothes were all still there, hanging neatly from their wooden hangers.

Sean doused the light, and then crossed the hall to the nursery. In the glow of the night-light he could see the bare sheets in the youth bed. Rachael had been lifted, still wrapped in her blanket, and carried down to the cook's room. Someone wanted to keep her safe.

He pushed open the door to Cheryl's room. There was a pale glow coming from the open door to Robert's office. It gave him enough light to see that the bed had been slept in. On the ottoman next to the soft chair, her office clothes were laid out neatly for the morning. She had roused suddenly and grabbed other clothes from her closet. Sean was fearful as he walked around the bed to the office. This was where the telephone had rung. It had apparently awakened Cheryl, and summoned her to Robert's private space. Whatever she had found might still be there.

He moved through the door and turned toward the desk, dimly lighted by its small lamp. Gretchen was in the chair, facedown on the desk, her right arm dangling loosely over one side. Blood was dripping from her fingertip into the center of a spreading stain on the carpet. The elaborate handle of an ornamental letter opener stood up from her back.

He eased closer, careful to step around the bloodstain. He saw the telephone handset hanging by its cord. Apparently she had still been on the phone when she was attacked. But there was no sound. The phone line was dead.

Gretchen's eyes were still half open. Blood had matted her blouse against her back, so that he could see the shape of her spine. It had pasted her hair against her shoulders. Sean touched her neck. There was no movement, no pulse.

He backed up until he was in the doorway, and then ran across Cheryl's room, pulling up short at the bloodstained nightgown that had been thrown into the bathroom doorway. At the bottom of the stairs, he pushed open the kitchen door and saw the cook still sitting in a trance, Rachael stretched comfortably across her knees.

"Call nine-one-one Mrs. Callen. Tell them Gretchen has been stabbed. And for God's sake, don't go up there."

He didn't wait for her reaction, but ran out the front door and bolted up into his truck. "She's full of petrol," he had remembered Gretchen saying in the telephone conversation. She had to be a boat. And traveling to meet Robert by boat had to mean that he was waiting on Buzzard Island.

The truck raced through the yard gate. In the swinging headlights, Sean could clearly see someone aboard the launch, taking in the lines as the launch drifted slowly back from the pier. Without turning off the engine he was on the ground and running toward the launch.

As his feet hit the wood planking of the catwalk, Sean heard the launch's big engines begin cranking, and then explode with energy. He could see that the boat had already drifted several feet away from the dock, and was almost outboard of the moored *Solomon Cramm*. When he reached the dock, he cut sharply to his left and headed for the old steam yacht. Sean took off from the edge of the pier and landed on the gunwale, forward of the wheelhouse. He clutched at the lifeline to keep from falling backwards, and then stepped onto the foredeck. As he raced across to the outboard side, he saw the launch pulling abreast, picking up speed as its engines roared. Cheryl was at the wheel, looking straight ahead toward the channel marker.

There was no time to stop her. Sean doubted that she would even hear him over the roar of her engine. Without weighing the risk, he went over the *Solomon Cramm*'s outboard lifeline like a hurdler, and flew through the air over the launch's churning bow wake. He crashed down on the overhead of the after stateroom, snatching at the line cleats to keep from sliding off.

63 CHERYL HAD BEEN AWARE OF THE HEADLIGHTS shining out on her, and then of someone running down the pier. She knew they were coming to stop her. But the boat had already drifted ten feet from the dock, and the engines had caught on the first try. When she pushed the shift lever forward and the boat responded with a sudden leap, she exhaled a sigh of relief. She had made it. In less than an hour she would have her answer.

The launch had been gathering speed as it slid by the moored steam yacht, when she suddenly picked up movement out of the corner of her eye. Someone was hurtling through the air. She heard the crash landing on the deck behind her. Cheryl snatched up the old antique pistol that she had placed on the pilot seat and whirled toward her attacker.

Sean, had toppled off the cabin, and landed on the deck on all fours. As he sprang to his feet he heard Cheryl scream.

"No! Keep away from me!"

He was staggering forward, trying to regain his balance, when he saw the gun flash. The pain hit his shoulder just as he heard the explosion. The sound began to fade, leaving him staring in disbelief at Cheryl.

Cheryl looked wide-eyed at Sean, and then at the gun in her hand. "Sean?" she gasped. It was a question. Then she scarcely breathed, "Oh my God. It was you. . . ."

He fell backwards, crashing through the after hatchway and tumbling down the ladder to the lower level.

Cheryl took a step aft to help Sean, but lost her balance as the unattended helm began turning the boat toward shore. She sprung back to the wheel, centering the boat back into the channel. Then she took a deep breath, trying desperately to get a grip on herself.

There were lights all around her. The outdoor lights of the mansions up on the hill to her left were illuminated. On the far shore, there were lights in the windows of the houses, and then another pattern of glowing streetlights. Channel markers blinked on the water nearby, setting off reflections on the wave tips. Waterborne phosphors twinkled in her wake. She felt her world spinning, as if she were inside a kaleidoscope of constantly changing images. The weeks of uncertainty. The hours of self-doubt. The black holes in her memory. The constantly shifting alliances. All her foundations and supports had been torn away. And then, in the flash of recognition as she listened to Robert's message, her mind had begun to churn like a whirlwind.

She had been awakened by the phone conversation in the office, and had heard Robert talking to Gretchen as she slipped into her robe. The next thing she remembered was the letter opener in the young girl's back, and the blood running down her finger. She had seen the stains down the front of her robe.

She remembered stripping out of her nightgown, and pulling on the slacks and windbreaker she would need for a trip out into the bay. In her frenzy, she never even noticed the blood from her hands that smeared on the front of the slacks.

There was only one certainty: She had to keep Gretchen's rendezvous with Robert. That was her point of focus. And dead ahead was the point of focus that would get her through the confusing patterns of the channel. Brenton Light was blinking its distinctive code at the entrance to the open sea.

She took another glance aft, thinking that she should go back to help Sean. But then she remembered that there was only one reason why he would have tried to stop her. He was the one who had been trying to stop her right from the beginning.

When she had found the photo of Robert with Gretchen, it was obvious that someone was with them. Little Rachael certainly hadn't taken the picture. So there had to be someone, close to Robert, who knew about his fling with the au pair. Someone Robert trusted. And that same person had to be in the Cramm office, where the phone line terminated. She had narrowed her suspects down to George and Sean. But only the one who was listening in on her phone line would know about the rendezvous with Robert. And that person would be the one who tried to stop her.

She had reasoned that it must be George, until Sean had begun urging her to sell, and to leave Cramm behind her. And then she was uncertain, especially since it was George who had rescued Sean from the deadly gas aboard the yacht. She had begun wondering if they could be working together even while she was hoping that neither of them was involved.

Could it really be Sean? Who had he really meant to kill when he lifted *Siren* out of the water and fastened the bomb to her keel? Was it her? Or was it Beth? Or Robert? How had Robert escaped? Or was he working together with Sean?

If he had wanted to kill Robert, then how could he have believed her story about the phone calls? Had he been listening in on Robert's private line? Had he heard all the calls, or had he just pretended to believe her in order to invent an excuse for tapping the line?

If Sean knew about Robert and Gretchen, why wouldn't he have warned Beth? Could he have stood by idly while Robert murdered his friend, and then helped Robert plan his escape with Gretchen? Or had he assumed that Robert was dead, and been dumbfounded to learn that Robert was alive and calling his private line?

There were questions everywhere, and it seemed she could regain her sanity only if she could find the answers. Sean knew, but she had shot him in her panic. If the rest of her life were to make any sense, she had to get the answers from Robert.

64 SERGEANT GRATTAN WATCHED AS HIS FORENSIC people carefully lifted Gretchen's face from the desktop and wrapped her hands in plastic bags. He put on a cellophane glove and then lifted the receiver back to the desktop.

"It's live," he said to the uniformed policeman who was standing next to him. The police officer's return glance told the sergeant that he sounded like a fool. Why wouldn't a desk telephone in a business office be live?

"We were here before. The lady was getting threatening calls. Only the telephone wasn't connected."

The policeman's eyes grew more clouded. How was she getting calls over a dead line?

Grattan hung up the phone. He watched as his men struggled to get Gretchen's form into the body bag. She was already beginning to show rigidity, which was surprising since the lady downstairs said everything had happened only an hour ago. No, that wasn't exactly true. She had called an hour ago. She had said that something had happened to the au pair girl, and that Mrs. Cramm had run off and left her with the baby. Mrs.—he glanced at his notes—Callen hadn't been specific as to when Mrs. Cramm had left.

The sergeant went back down the stairs. Mrs. Callen was sitting in the living room. The housekeeper was at the other end of the sofa. The little girl, covered by a blanket, was sleeping between them.

"Mrs. Callen," he whispered. And then he hooked his finger to tell her to follow him. When they were out on the porch he explained, "I didn't want to disturb the little girl."

He sat her in one of the rockers and then slipped into the chair beside her. For the next few minutes, he simply joined her in looking down the hill and out over the harbor. "A terrible shock," he allowed a few times, and she nodded in agreement. Then, casually, the sergeant began to reconstruct the events of the evening.

Mrs. Callen was asleep, in her room near the kitchen. She jumped up when she heard a knock on the door. Mrs. Cramm was standing in the doorway with Rachael in her arms. There was blood down the front of her clothes. No, she wasn't sure it was blood. There were big red stains. She had handed the baby to the cook and asked her to mind the little girl. Mrs. Callen was thrilled to see that little Rachael was happily asleep. They had all been afraid that Mrs. Cramm might do something that would harm her.

Mrs. Cramm had told her not to go upstairs. Just to keep Rachael in her room. She had watched Cheryl run out the back door, and then had carried the little girl into the kitchen. Mrs. Callen knew she couldn't get back to sleep, so she had decided to make herself a cup of tea.

"How long was it between the time Mrs. Cramm knocked on your door and the time you called nine-one-one?" Grattan asked.

The old woman thought. "About five minutes until Sean Patton came in. And then he was upstairs for a few minutes—"

"Sean Patton?" the sergeant interrupted. He clearly remembered the big ponytailed guy who had visited him at the police station. He had seemed so out of place in the Cramm household.

Mrs. Callen told him how Sean had rushed in, gone looking upstairs, and then come down and told her to call the police.

"Counting the time you spent with Mr. Patton, how long was it between Mrs. Cramm knocking on your door and the time you called us?"

She guessed ten minutes. Certainly no more than fifteen. Then he tried to figure how long it would have taken Mrs. Cramm to pick up her daughter and bring her downstairs. A few minutes, tops. So the young woman upstairs would seem to have died less than an hour and a half earlier. Two hours at the outside. And yet there were already signs of rigidity. Something wasn't quite right. Mrs. Cramm must have stood over the body for at least an hour trying to decide what to do. Or maybe she did something else with her daughter before she woke the cook. But whatever, Grattan was fairly certain that the au pair had been dead for at least an hour, and probably longer, before Mrs. Cramm had left the house.

He went back upstairs to the murder scene. The body bag was waiting on a dolly for its trip to the medical examiner's office. The forensic team had already cut the stain out of the rug and wrapped the desk and the chair in plastic. The telephone had been dusted, printed, and packaged.

"Check the bedroom," Grattan ordered, indicating Cheryl's room next door, "and the corridor outside this room." He turned to his partner, who was leaning in the doorway with his arms folded. "Why don't you take Mrs. Cramm's picture and get a description of the outfit she was wearing. We'll get all our guys looking for her."

The detective nodded.

"And find out what you can about a drifter named Sean Patton. He works for Cramm. Put out an all-points. Bring him in for questioning."

65 SEAN WAS AWARE OF THE SOUND. HE BLINKED HIS eyes open, and found only a small square of starlight. Then he felt the pain through his chest.

The scattered sensations began to pull together. The roar was the sound of the boat's engines, humming along at a slow cruise. The patch of sky was what he could see through the opening in the hatch at the top of the ladder. And the pain was from the bullet that had hit him like a fist and driven him backward.

She was up there, with a gun. And if she even guessed that he might be alive, she would come to the open hatch and finish him off. Sean looked back over his head and saw that he was in the entrance to the after stateroom. Carefully, quietly, he pushed on his heels and slid across the polished deck, farther into the cabin. He didn't try to sit up until he was completely clear of the open hatch. Then he hoisted himself until his back was leaning against the side of one of the bunks.

He looked down at his sweatshirt, saw the hole just under the collar hem, and the pattern of blood that was soaking into the left sleeve. His skin burned as he pulled the shirt away and tried to look inside at the wound. But the light coming through the portholes was pale and flickering. It doesn't make any difference, Sean thought. However large the wound, he had to stop the bleeding. He eased one of the pillows off the bed behind him and slipped off the pillowcase. Folded, it made a huge bandage that he slipped down inside his sweatshirt. He pulled the shirt tight to hold the bandage in place.

The engines suddenly picked up speed, the dull roar turning into a steely whine. He felt the boat lurch forward and begin pounding instead of pitching. They had turned Brenton Light, he figured, and Cheryl had opened up the throttles. A few seconds later, the pounding became a steady tapping as the big boat lifted up on the hull step and began planing over the wave tops. They were moving quickly out into Rhode Island Sound. Sean guessed that Buzzard Island would be less than an hour away.

He had no thought of stopping Cheryl. She had a gun and, despite what he wanted to believe, she was ready to use it. He was in pain, probably weak, and with limited mobility. It would be no contest. What he had to concentrate on was staying alive.

Cheryl was racing at full throttle, so there was little chance that she would come down below before they reached the island. And if she did, she would have to idle the engines, which would give him a few seconds of warning. So there was a good chance that he would make the island alive. Then what?

Robert was expecting Gretchen and his daughter. So he would be right at the shore in case Gretchen had trouble maneuvering in the dangerously small cove. He would see that it was Cheryl, probably before she had even put over a line. What would Robert's reaction be?

If he truly intended to disappear, then what? Kill Cheryl? Could Robert do that, he wondered. It seemed absurd, but if he had planned his own disappearance, then he had also planned to get rid of Beth. So killing wasn't beyond him.

If Cheryl were doomed, then he was, too. A man who had killed two women, both of whom he loved, would have little difficulty adding a wastrel boat bum to his list.

Suppose Robert turned Cheryl away. He might explain his fraud, and tell her to go back to their daughter. He had created a fortune for them, and while he had chosen to vanish, he wanted them to have a fine life. If he turned her around and sent her back to Newport, Cheryl would have to decide whether she would be safe returning. She had left her au pair girl brutally murdered, and had the girl's blood down the front of her. Going back would certainly mean medical confinement, perhaps even prison. But she had also left her daughter, so running away might be impossible. Sean didn't know what she would decide, or what she would do with him.

But what if Robert recognized that Cheryl was mad? What if he learned that she had murdered Gretchen? Then he might regard Sean as an ally. Sean could take her back, and deny that Robert had been waiting on the island. He could leave Robert free to disappear, and at the same time make sure that Cheryl received medical care and that his daughter was taken care of.

That seemed to be his best chance. To go topside a few moments after he heard Robert come aboard, and then to tell Robert what had happened back in Newport. But first he should make sure he could make it up the ladder to the cockpit. He put his hands on the floor and tried to push himself up. A mistake! He had to bite his lip to keep from screaming out with the pain. Wherever the wound was, the bullet had damaged his left shoulder. He couldn't put any pressure on it at all.

Sean rolled onto his knees, using his good hand to hold the edge of the bunk for balance. He stood, without any noticeable problem. He felt reasonably strong, and he seemed to have perfect balance even though the deck beneath his feet was bouncing lightly and pitching a bit from side to side.

He looked for something he could use as a weapon. There was a small fire extinguisher behind the ladder he had tumbled from, at the hatchway entrance to the engine spaces. It would mean stepping out under the open hatch. But the engines were still roaring, so Cheryl had to be forward, at the controls. He stepped out, pulled the extinguisher out of its mounting, and ducked back into the cabin. Then he sat on the end of the bed and pulled a pillow under his elbow to take the weight off his wounded shoulder. If the engine slowed, he was only one quick step to a hiding place behind the stateroom door.

Now he had to wait, and pray that Robert had some use for him.

66 CHERYL PUNCHED THE BUTTONS ON THE SATELLITE navigation system. Months earlier, Robert had pulled the boat up to the dock at Buzzard Island, and hit memory button "one," which gave the dock a satellite location. By pushing that button, Cheryl instantly got a course and distance to the dock, accurate to within a yard. It told her 105 degrees, 12.32 miles. She eased the bow to 105.

She glanced back to the after hatch. The door had shattered under Sean's weight and now hung in splinters from its hinges. She looked down at the pistol on the seat beside her. For a moment, she thought about throwing it over the side. It was a vivid reminder of the horror she had been through, and she wouldn't need it when she met Robert, no matter what his reaction to her arrival. She would tell him that Gretchen was dead, and that his daughter was alive. The choice would be his.

She was horrified that she had used the pistol on Sean. For a while, he had been her only ally. She didn't have to fire. She could have circled back close to the dock and ordered him over the side. But he had come to stop her. He had started toward her. She had fired instinctively, preserving her only chance of finding out why her husband had left her to madness.

She lifted the gun over the side, but then thought better of it. She had no idea what might be waiting for her on the island.

She checked her heading. Buzzard Island was dead ahead, according to the satellite navigation system, and less than six miles away. In the daylight, she would already be making out the bluffs of Martha's Vineyard to the southeast, and then the hazy point of the family island. At night, she would probably be up to the island before she began to pick up Gay Head's lights.

Cheryl suddenly realized that she had never slipped past the rocks and into the narrow cove at night. There was a shoal ledge running to the northwest with a buoy on the end of it. But she would never see the buoy. Best to adjust her course to the south until the satellite told her that the dock was dead east. That way she would be sure of coming in well below the danger line. When she got within a few hundred yards, she could use her searchlight to find the rocks that broke the surface right at the entrance. After that it was easy. Cheryl turned to the south, keeping her throttles wide open. When her heading to the island was 090, she turned to the east. The distance was down to three miles.

She picked up the running lights of an approaching boat that seemed to be angling toward her from her starboard bow. For a moment, she felt panic. Was it just another cruiser, making for Newport, or one of the fishermen from Point Judith? Or was it the Coast Guard, sent out to head her off? Should she stop, douse her lights, and let the boat pass? Not much point, because if it were the Coast Guard, they would already hold her on their radar.

The boat turned north, and then the lights suddenly disappeared. It must have turned away from her, she realized, toward Buzzard Island. And then she remembered the high-speed cigarette boat that she and Sean had seen running from the cove. Had it returned? Was this Robert, coming from the sea to a rendezvous at the family cottage?

She checked the satellite monitor. The dock was dead east, one mile. She looked at the clock. In two minutes, she would cut her speed and turn on the light.

Cheryl suddenly saw the island, a dark bump against the pale light of the horizon. She pulled back on the throttles, and the boat dropped down from its step and began pounding against the sea. When she turned on the searchlight, she saw the rock at the cove entrance dead ahead.

Her hand gripped the throttle as she eased back to idle. She could see the waves exploding into vapor as they hit the rocky shore. She turned into the entrance and added a bit of speed to keep the boat from drifting as she moved past the rock. And then the searchlight picked up the dock, with the sleek cigarette boat tied to the far side. When Cheryl glanced up the hill, she saw a pale light beginning to glow in the cottage. Robert had arrived and was waiting inside.

Skillfully, she turned the boat parallel to the seaward side of the dock, and moved the levers into neutral. She watched as the wind and the current pushed her steadily toward the pier. A quick hit on the throttle adjusted for her drift. And then she took the spring line in her hand and jumped out onto the dock. It didn't take much strength with the wind pushing the cruiser into its berth. Within a minute, she had tied a bow line and stern line, and doubled up the spring.

She stepped back into the cockpit and retrieved the pistol from the seat. Then she started back to the after hatch. She had to find out about Sean.

67 SEAN HAD FELT THE BOAT HEEL WHEN CHERYL HAD adjusted her course to the south, and then he had heard the engine slow. He had moved close to the compartment doorway, just a few feet from the base of the ladder. When the boat maneuvered and the engines idled, he knew that they were in the cove. Then he had felt the bump against the dock.

But he didn't hear Robert's voice. There seemed to be no one on the island waiting to greet her. Then there were Cheryl's footsteps on deck, and on the dock, along with the squeak of docking lines being levered tightly around wooden cleats. They were secure to the pier, and Cheryl thought she was alone with a dead body aboard. If she looked down the hatch and no one was there, she would have to come below to find out what had happened to him. He had to let her find his body.

He heard Cheryl come back aboard, and followed the sound of her feet on the deck as she walked forward. Quickly, he moved out of the cabin and dropped down on his back. He splayed out his legs, and positioned himself so that the bloodstained shirt would be visible from above. His face and arms were back in the passageway, out of sight from the open hatch.

Her footsteps started aft. Sean breathed in, and then held his breath to stop the rise and fall of his chest. He waited. The footsteps came to the hatch. A flashlight suddenly illuminated the steps.

Sean tried to remain motionless, even though every instinct told him to scramble for cover. He watched the round beam of the light find his feet, and then pan up his legs. He heard Cheryl's foot land on the top step of the ladder. With each step she came down, the light beam reached higher on his body. When it got to his face, she would know that he was still alive.

Another footstep. The light jerked up to his belt line. Sean could feel the tremors in his legs. Did it show? Or was it masked by his trousers? He should have brought the fire extinguisher instead of leaving it on the bunk. He could wait one more step and then fire it into Cheryl's face. It would be a mismatch—a chemical spray against a bullet. But it was better than the odds he had right now.

Another step. The light bounced up to his chin, illuminating the dark red gore that had oozed through his shirt.

"Oh my God!"

It was Cheryl's voice from only a few feet away. "Oh, Jesus . . ."

Sean heard a gagging sound as Cheryl choked on the sight before her. The footsteps raced back up the steps.

Sean gasped as he ran out of breath and sucked in air. But Cheryl didn't hear it. She was vomiting over the side.

He lay perfectly still until he heard her cross the deck and step out on the pier. He endured another few seconds of silence. Then he rolled to his knees, stood up, and moved slowly up the ladder.

Sean hesitated at the hatch. He could see forward and knew that Cheryl was no longer aboard. Carefully, he eased his head into the opening, gradually seeing more and more of the dock. There was no one there, but he was startled to see the long cigarette boat tied up on the other side. Robert hadn't been waiting at the dock, but he had certainly come out to the island.

And then he saw the flashlight. Cheryl was walking carefully up the rugged path toward the cottage, shining the light ahead of her. He could make out part of the cottage outline, because there was a dim light in one of the windows. He pulled himself up onto the deck and then struggled forward, suddenly realizing that he had a better chance to escape.

68 CHERYL HAD BEEN SURPRISED WHEN SHE STEPPED TO the open hatch and looked down the steps. From what she could see, Sean was uninjured. At that instant, she had prayed silently that she hadn't killed him. If only he hadn't tried to stop her! No matter what he had done to Gretchen, she still hadn't wanted to be his executioner.

As the light had panned up his motionless body, her hopes had risen. He had fallen, he was unconscious, but her panicky gunshot must have missed him. He didn't seem to have been shot.

But then the flashlight had shown her the wound. There was a ragged hole in the shirt, pouring out a circle of crimson blood. Through the hole she thought she could see the white of bloodstained bones and sinew. It was like something hanging from a meat hook. Her stomach had turned over, and she had suddenly been dizzy and sick.

It had dawned on her that she was a murderer, just as her husband was probably a murderer. They had both killed people who had tried to help them. And at that point all Cheryl could think of was Rachael. She no longer cared what happened to her and Robert.

But she had to know. Even if she turned the pistol on herself, she had to know why Robert had abandoned her. And even if he had good reason, she needed to know why he had tried to destroy her. She had taken her pistol and started up toward the dimly lighted cottage.

She saw that the door was ajar, as if someone had not wanted to make a sound by forcing it shut. She moved silently up the stone steps. Carefully, she pushed the door open and looked inside.

The oil lamp over the fireplace was burning on a low flame. The room seemed empty, but the weak, flickering light didn't reach into all the corners.

"Robert?" Cheryl whispered his name as if she were afraid someone might overhear.

The room was deathly still.

"Robert?" Her voice was a little louder, but the response was still just silence. All she could hear was the sound of her own breathing.

Cheryl lifted the flashlight and pointed it into the corners. Furniture appeared, and a large striped bass that was mounted on a wall. To the other side, she saw the small dining set, a heavy wooden table and four chairs. Straight ahead, faintly lighted by the oil lamp, was the stone hearth, where she and Robert had talked for hours. In front of the hearth was the thick shag rug where they had first made love.

She looked to her right, to the door of the kitchen, which had a pump handle, an ice chest, and a small propane stove.

"Is anyone here?" she called in a full voice.

The old frame windows rattled in a sudden gust of wind. Then there was more of the deafening silence.

There was the boat at the dock, and the burning lamp. Someone had arrived only a few minutes ahead of her. They certainly knew she had come ashore.

"I know you're here," Cheryl called.

She eased toward the doorway to the lightless kitchen. Her light found the odd shapes of the crude appliances, and the table that served the function of a countertop. She recognized the stains on the table, fish blood soaked in from years of cleaning the catch. She lifted the light to the knife rack that was above the table. The handles of two large knives protruded. The space for the third knife was empty.

"Robert?" she pleaded.

She listened to the absolute silence.

"*Robert is dead!*"

Cheryl jumped and wheeled, trying to aim the light and the revolver.

A hand grabbed the pistol and wrenched it out of her fingers. The stinging tip of a knife jabbed into the side of her neck. A strong, heavy physique leaned against her, pushing her back against the ice chest.

She raised the flashlight as a weapon, and instantly stopped her struggle. The white light made George Williamson look like a bloodless ghost.

"George . . ." It was a gasp of relief. She was safe with George.

"He died with *Siren*," George said. Then he turned Cheryl around so that she was facing the wall, and set the serrated edge of the knife blade against her throat. He pushed the revolver into the pocket of his windbreaker, and twisted the flashlight away from her. He forced her, with the knife ready to cut off any sudden move, into the main room and pushed her down onto the rug.

She looked back to him, her expression more amazed than frightened. "George? Why? We're your friends."

He was taken back by her apparent calmness. And she was right. They were his friends. "Why in God's name didn't you sell? I had everything set up. Everything. You could have gone anywhere . . . been anyone." And then he screamed, "Why didn't you sign the stupid papers?"

"I couldn't betray Robert," Cheryl answered.

His eyes widened, and then his face began to laugh. "Betray Robert? You stupid bitch, Robert was betraying you. He had knocked up Beth, and was fucking your mother's helper. And he was betraying me. The arrogant bastard was going to turn me over to the police."

"He was your friend," she yelled back, unafraid of the ugly knife he held in his hand, and the gun that was bulging in his pocket.

"He used me," George said. "Just as he used you to give the finger to his society friends. Just as he used Beth when he needed a lay, and Gretchen when he needed a mother."

She was stung by insults to her husband. But at the same time, she knew that they were probably true. And she suddenly understood why Robert was going to send George to jail.

"The phony inventory," Cheryl said, "the embezzled funds. That was you, not Robert—"

"I was entitled," George snapped, no longer amused by Cheryl's naive defense of her husband. "I kept that leaking company afloat while he did his playboy act. I ran the factory, sucked up to dealers, begged loans. And then, when Rachael was born, the bastard told me I better begin looking around, because his company was failing and he was going to close it down." George looked up at the oil lamp, his eyes glistening with tears that he was fighting hard to hold back. "Look around!" he wailed. "Like I was his office boy." He looked back at Cheryl. "Believe me. What I took was only a fraction of what your precious Robert was wasting."

"So you murdered him."

George sank to his knees so that he was looking directly into Cheryl's face. "You don't understand, do you? He would have destroyed us all."

"You were going to murder me. . . ." Cheryl realized. "I was supposed to be aboard *Siren.*"

"He was going to kill you," George shouted. "Robert would have killed you during the race." He was begging to be believed. "Don't you see? He was getting rid of everything. You . . . me . . . the company. He was going to take the money and start over again with Beth. . . ."

Cheryl's hands went up to her face. "I don't believe you," she lied, because she knew that what George was telling her was true.

He labored back to his feet. "You should have gone along with the sale. It would have made you rich. And you never would have had to know. It would have solved all your problems." Then George nodded in admission of his own interest. "And all of mine." He took the revolver from his pocket as he said, "Everyone would have been better off."

He was backing toward the kitchen as he spoke. For an instant, he disappeared from her view as he put the knife back into the holder. When he stepped back through the doorway, he ordered, "Get up. We have to get going."

"Going where?" Cheryl asked uneasily as she got to her feet.

"To a shipwreck," George answered. He took her shoulder and turned her around so that he was standing behind her. Cheryl felt the muzzle of the revolver against the back of her neck. "You should have signed," he repeated, his voice sounding almost sad.

69 SEAN'S FIRST THOUGHT HAD BEEN TO CUT THE lines, start the engines, and run back toward Castle Hill. He could probably clear the harbor before the noise of the engine brought Cheryl and Robert racing from the cottage. And even though the cigarette boat could easily overtake him, he didn't have much to fear from Cheryl's antique revolver being aimed from a bouncing speedboat.

When there was no key in the ignition, he had glanced over at the cigarette. But he was afraid to step out into the open and cross the pier, especially since Robert probably hadn't left his key in the ignition either.

Sean had begun searching the cabin for an extra key. When it wasn't in the most likely small drawers, he had to decide whether to keep looking for the needle in the haystack or whether to use his precious seconds to trace the wires and hot-wire the ignition. It would take longer, but it was a better bet than looking for a key that might not be there.

Sean had fumbled through the darkened cabin until he found a tool kit. He studied the key slot on the instrument panel, cursing when he found it was cleanly molded, with no screws that would let him remove the faceplate to get at the wires. He thought of smashing one of the instruments next to the key, but he had no idea how the wires were run. He might have to bash the panel to pieces. And the noise would bring them back from the cottage.

Instead, he took the tool kit aft, keeping low to the deck, and made his way painfully down the ladder to the after stateroom. The engine room door was next to the ladder, right where he had found the fire extinguisher. Sean opened the door and let himself into the narrow space between the two gasoline engines.

There were two starters, one on the forward end of each engine. "Christ!" He would have to strip both sets of wires, and have them ready to connect, before he started either engine. If he started them one at a time, the roar would alert Robert and Cheryl before he could start the second engine.

He found the ignition connection to the port engine starter, and was able to identify the wires from the bridge and those from the batteries. But they were all in armored cables, screwed into the body of the starter motor. Not a problem if you had time, and if you had the use of both hands. But a problem Sean hadn't anticipated. He would have to back off the metal wire guards, run topside and throw over the lines, come back down below and connect the circuit to power the starter, and then get back to the pilot seat in order to advance the throttle and steer out of the cove. It seemed impossible, but he had little choice. He lay on his back and slid under the starboard starter motor. Then, balancing the flashlight on his chest, he began to unscrew the cable bolts with his good hand.

70

"NICE AND SLOW!" GEORGE ORDERED. HE DIDN'T want her getting ahead of him where she might be able to dive into the black trees. He wanted her moving slowly, knowing that the pistol was only inches from her back.

"What are you going to do with me?" she demanded with more authority than she felt.

"You should have sold. . . . You think I want to do this?"

"What are you going to do?"

But George was more interested in his own peace of mind than in Cheryl's. "We were both victims. Robert was destroying us both. We should have been working together." And then he added with anguish in his voice, "If you had just signed the goddamned papers. We could have both had the last laugh on Robert."

"George. What's going to happen to me?"

She could hear his footsteps crunching behind her. "You're going to have a boating accident."

They reached the dock. George ordered her to stand out in the middle of the cockpit, so he could watch her as he slipped the lines. Then he untied the lines to the cigarette and held its bow line while he stepped aboard the cruiser. He tied the bow line to the cruiser's stern cleat. "Start her up," he told Cheryl, waving the point of the revolver toward the pilot seat. "And then take us out."

She took the key from her pocket, put it in the ignition, and then held down the two starter buttons. Both engines growled, and then roared with power.

George was standing directly behind Cheryl. "Let's go," he ordered. "Nice and easy."

Cheryl put the engines in gear and tapped the throttles. The boat began easing out, towing the cigarette boat behind.

Cheryl suddenly asked, "You killed Gretchen, didn't you?"

"I had to," he answered.

"Why? She didn't do anything except fall in love with Robert. . . ."

But even as she was saying it, Cheryl knew it wasn't true. Gretchen must have been working with George. He had just told her that he used Gretchen to get her off the boat.

"She wanted Robert, and wanted his child. She hated Beth. And then, when Robert died, you were the one who would keep her from taking Rachael, and becoming the woman in the Cramm household."

The boat eased past the rock that guarded the entrance. Cheryl reached for the throttles, but was cut off by George's command. "Leave them where they are. Keep it slow."

"Gretchen helped me," George went on. "When I wasn't there to drug your Scotch, she was putting the drugs in your tea."

Cheryl felt suddenly relieved, as if what had happened in the past could do her any good now. "Then I wasn't crazy. I wasn't having blackouts."

"When you wouldn't sign, I tried to frighten you. Then I tried to fake your suicide. Gretchen helped me get you down to the car."

"Then, why—" Cheryl started.

"Because she began to feel sorry for you. When I told her you had found the letters, she expected you to send her away. Instead, you forgave her. Or, at least, that's the way she saw it. She told me we had to stop. And then when I told her to get you to Robert's office, because I was going to make another phone call from Robert, she refused. She decided that we both had to sit down with you and confess our sins."

"So you killed her, and then rang the phone so that I would find her and hear the recording.

"I'm sorry," George said. "But you left me no choice. You and Sean, when he figured out how the phone calls were being made. But he became my partner . . ."

Both of them, Cheryl thought. She remembered thinking that it had to be one or the other.

"I left the recorded message where he would certainly find it. He's probably turned it over to the police already, setting up your motive for killing Gretchen and racing out to the island."

Oh, Jesus, she had shot the wrong man. She had killed the one person who was trying to help her.

"Turn to three-five-five," George suddenly ordered.

"That will put us on—"

"The rock ledge," he said, completing her thought. He started aft. "Now keep that heading and keep it nice and slow." He grabbed the bow line of the cigarette boat and began to pull her close aboard.

Cheryl tried to figure out what he was doing. He intended to run the launch up on the ledge, tearing out her bottom. And he planned that Cheryl would be aboard the wreck. But that probably wouldn't work. The big launch could hang up on the rocks for days before sinking. And if he were planning to leave the launch by stepping aboard the cigarette, then he would have to pull his escape boat up on the rock ledge as well.

"I'm sorry, Cheryl," his voice said behind her. "Truly sorry."

She felt the pistol crash across the top of her head. Her knees buckled, and she fell away from the controls. She was dazed and unfocused. But she could still feel the pain. She wasn't unconscious.

His hands were under her arms, dragging her across the deck. He lifted her against the lifeline. "You should have sold," he said, almost in despair. Then he pushed her over the side.

71 THE COLD WATER SHOCKED HER TO HER SENSES, AND Cheryl quickly struggled to the surface. She could see the stern of the launch, still moving slowly on its course toward the ledge. It was like her dream, being in the water, and watching Robert and Beth sail away. But this wasn't a dream, and she wasn't in her scuba gear, wearing her wet suit. It was more like her suicide, when the weight of her clothes was pulling her under.

George stepped out of the cruiser into the cigarette boat, bringing the line with him. The two boats moved apart, the cruiser still powering onto the ledge, while George's boat drifted free. Then the huge engines of the high-speed boat exploded into life, settling to a roar that thundered across the open water. The boat began moving, turning away from the lethal rocks.

Cheryl understood. George had left her to drown. Her boat would impale itself on the ledge, probably hanging at a precarious angle. To an investigator, the scenario would be clear. A madwoman had murdered her au pair, and then rushed to an imagined rendezvous with her husband. She had run straight across the ledge, the boat crashing and the impact throwing her out into the water. In the accident, she had smashed her head, explaining the wound from the pistol blow. She was dead as her body drifted away, to be found days, perhaps weeks later, bloated and white like Beth's.

But she might be stronger than he had given her credit for. Let George speed away. The tide was carrying her toward the same rocks that the cruiser would soon crash against. And, to make everything realistic, he had left the cruiser's running lights burning. She could swim toward it. And she could probably make it. Unlike her last struggle in the sea, she wasn't drugged to near helplessness by the chemicals that George and Gretchen had been feeding her. If she made it, she could stay aboard the boat as long as it kept afloat, which would probably be for hours. And if it sank, there was a life raft and life preservers aboard. As the speedboat rumbled away from the doomed cruiser, Cheryl slipped out of her windbreaker and pushed out of her slacks. She kicked off and, with a steady stroke, began swimming after the big cruiser.

She had gone only a dozen strokes when she was aware that the sound of the cigarette boat had changed. She lifted her head out of the water, in time to see the boat's searchlight turn on. George had turned around and increased speed. He was panning the searchlight, trying to find her.

And then she knew. He was leaving nothing to chance. When he ran her over with the cigarette boat, her body would be battered and hacked just as if she had been thrown under her own boat. He had set the stage. But he intended to make certain how the drama played out.

The light beam panned back and forth in front of her, moving in a search pattern that was coming ever closer. She glanced back at the cruiser. There was no chance that she could reach it before the speedboat reached her. And then she was bathed in light. When Cheryl turned back to George's boat, she was blinded by the white-hot glare.

She couldn't see the boat, but she heard the outrageous howl of its engines. And then the light was bearing down on her more quickly than seemed possible. The cigarette boat was pouncing on her like a cheetah, with quick, darting speed. The roar was suddenly deafening. Cheryl dove under.

The noise pounded louder as she struggled to swim down. The shock wave from the hull drove her sideways, and then the churning propellers sliced inches above her head. She was caught in a backwash that sent her tumbling as if she were caught in the surf and was being tossed about by the breakers. She was battered and disoriented, and realized that she was swallowing water. It took all her strength to fight out of the white-water wake and swim up to the surface.

The boat, like the bull in a ring, was turning in a tight circle. A second later, the glowing eye of the floodlight was searching down the wake. The next second, Cheryl was blinded by the glare. The engines crackled with more energy, and the angry animal came charging back for another pass. She waited until she saw the bow cutting the waves. Then she drew a breath and dove under again.

There was the shock wave, and then the sudden blow of the boat's sharp chine glancing off her back. She could feel the propellers sucking her in.

72 SEAN HAD FREED THE ARMOR AROUND THE IGNITION wires, and pulled himself out from under the starter motor. He had crawled out of the engine space and was at the bottom of the ladder when he had heard them come aboard.

"Stay out there, in the middle of the cockpit," he had heard a voice order. But it wasn't Robert's voice. It was George's.

He had his foot on the ladder, ready to dash up the instant George stepped aboard. But then he realized what he once suspected and then dismissed. It was George. It had been George all along. He had stolen the money and bombed *Siren*, probably planning to kill Robert and Cheryl together, leaving him in control of the company. Then, when Cheryl lived and took control for herself, he had found a way to make good his plan of murder. The message on the recorder had been created by George, and used to lure Cheryl out to the ocean grave she had barely escaped. It had been George who had trapped him aboard the *Solomon Cramm*. And George who had saved him to end his suspicions.

He had listened as George came aboard, heard him order Cheryl to start the engines, and then heard the boat as it ghosted away from the dock and headed out of the cove.

The pieces had come together. Carefully, Sean had edged up the ladder until his eyes were level with the top step. He could see the wisps of windblown clouds that were rushing past the cover of stars. He could feel the sea in the air. And he could hear George explaining, with a self-justifying tone, how he had been forced to deal with Gretchen. He knew what he was planning for Cheryl.

Sean had found a new weapon, a spanner wrench he had taken from the toolbox. But George had a gun, so Sean had to wait for an opportunity. He had ducked down when George came aft, and waited patiently while the cigarette boat was pulled up alongside. Like Cheryl, he had figured George was going to abandon the cruiser to its destruction on the rocky ledge. The smart thing was to wait for the killer to leave, and then help Cheryl save the boat, or at least save themselves. Sean had been confused by the sound of something heavy falling overboard. When he had raised his head up over the lip of the hatch, George was stepping off the cruiser into the speedboat. There was no sign of Cheryl.

Now he was up on deck, watching the boat charge across the water. In the eye of its blazing light, he saw Cheryl in the water. While he watched in horror, the growling boat plowed over her.

His first thought was to rescue her. Sean was running forward to the pilot seat when the deck under his feet shuddered and heaved. He struggled for balance, and then the deck pitched abruptly, throwing him on his face. He heard the awful wrenching noise of the hull ricocheting off the rocks, and saw a spray of white water leap up over the side. He was seconds late. The big boat was already caught in the waves that were breaking over the rocky ledge.

Sean used the cockpit edge to pull himself to his knees. Next, he was able to grasp the edge of the pilot seat. He was almost to his feet when the deck shuddered again under the impact of the next white-capped crest. He was thrown forward against the forward bulkhead, his left shoulder smashing in a flash of agony. Then the bow screamed against another rock, and he fell back onto the deck.

He rolled into the space between the seat and the console, and then pulled himself up on the steering wheel. The stern of the boat was rising on the next wave, and the bow was moving forward, about to slam again into the rocks. Sean closed the two throttles, and then snapped them past neutral, into reverse. He pulled back and set the two engines roaring. But before the propellers could pull back, the bow crunched again, and cracked with the sound of a rifle shot. In the next instant, the boat began to back away.

Sean held the rudder centered as the next wave began to lift the stern. The cruiser hesitated, the wave coaxing it toward its death on the ledge, the propellers trying to pull it to freedom. He felt the wave roll under the keel, and then the boat backed out of the white water.

He looked back as he turned the wheel, and snapped the throttles back into forward. Cheryl was in the water, frozen in the spot of the searchlight like a deer on a highway. Then the stiletto of the bow cut right over her.

73 THE HULL WAS RACING OVER HER HEAD, AND THE propellers were coming right at her. Cheryl was trying to swim down deeper, but she was trapped in the boat's wash, caught between the shock wave that was being thrown out and up, to form the wake, and the faster-moving stream directly under the keel that was being pulled through the screws. She felt herself suddenly firing upward. The hull hit her across the back of her head and the churning water went black.

George felt the boat strike something, and immediately cut back on the throttles. He turned slowly, and then stood as he aimed the searchlight back over his wake. He couldn't see her, so he began panning slowly, widening the area that the light was illuminating. He knew he had hit her. More than likely he had broken her so that she had gone straight to the bottom. And even if she were still alive, there was little chance of her swimming to safety. But he wanted to be sure. He had waded so deep in blood he had to be certain that she was finished. He eased the throttle forward, heading back over his course, examining the water for the evidence he needed.

Sean reached for the switch to his searchlight, but he stopped with his finger on the button. George's boat was much faster, and far more maneuverable than the cruiser. If he were going to get even close, it would have to be under the cover of darkness. Instead, he switched off the running lights, hoping that the boat would disappear into the murky night. With his engines running slowly, he began turning the cruiser, pointing it at the light that was carefully searching the surface of the sea.

Cheryl found herself riding the curl of a wave, rolling over and over in a black tunnel. And then the churning wave passed under her, and she was bobbing in a flat sea. She wanted to swim, but her arms wouldn't move. She tried to kick up higher in the water, but her legs seemed paralyzed. Slowly her body turned, moved easily by the flow of the sea. And then she saw the light, pale, distant, almost unreal.

The boat's angry roar had stopped, its engines gurgling as it ghosted back at her, the light aimed down into the water close aboard. This was her chance. She could duck under and swim away from the area. The light would never find her. But even the thought sent sick pain through her body. She was struggling for breath, barely able to stay afloat. The will to fight had been beaten out of her. When the light beam finally reached out to her and became blindingly bright, all Cheryl could manage was to close her eyes.

George spotted her floating in the water, only twenty yards ahead. Her face was looking up, the water closed around her shoulders. Her hair was matted straight back. Was she dead? He thought so, because there was no movement in the water around her. She wasn't swimming. She didn't even seem to be struggling to stay up. But as he got closer, he found that he couldn't look. The thought of Cheryl's dead eyes staring at him was too much to handle. Better just to make sure, and leave her to the sea.

He kept the light aimed as he backed the boat, opening up some running distance between himself and his victim. Thirty yards. Forty yards. He guessed it would take him about seventy-five yards to get the cigarette boat up to full speed.

Sean couldn't be sure that George had found her. But as he watched the cigarette boat backing away, he could make out Cheryl's face floating in the water. Was he leaving her? Had he already determined that she was dead? Sean didn't understand what was happening until the speedboat's big engines began to crackle, setting themselves for a great surge of power. Then it was obvious. The victim had been bled and exhausted. George was lining himself up for the kill.

Sean pushed his throttles to the fire wall. The big cruiser struggled to lift her bow, which was flooding with seawater. Then she pitched up out of the water, and charged toward George's target, which was brightly lit in the circle of the searchlight.

Cheryl heard George's idling engines suddenly burst into life. She was blinded by the light and couldn't see her tormentor. But she could feel the boat's fury as it began accelerating directly at her. She was helpless, scarcely able to keep herself afloat. She stopped struggling, hoping that she would sink before the propellers reached her.

George was focused on the target in the water. His senses were emerged in the roar of his own engines. He didn't have any idea that the cruiser he had left headed for the rocks had come around, and was rushing toward him on an intercept course.

Fifty yards. The cigarette lifted up on her step, the long bow settling as she began to build up speed. Twenty-five knots, the speedometer signaled, then the needle moved up quickly past thirty. He had lost her for a second when his boat leveled off. But now George held her dead ahead. Not Cheryl. Not a person. But just a target that had to be destroyed and sunk. That was the only way he could think about it.

Sean saw that he had picked the right angle, racing straight at Cheryl. He could intercept George's boat there. If he had headed toward the cigarette, he never would have caught up with it.

Cheryl felt the water lapping up on her face. She turned her eyes away from the glare. And suddenly she saw it. A high white bow, breaking out of the darkness, spraying out a wake as it came bearing down on her.

George saw it a second later. An apparition. A giant cruiser bow, already high above his head, bearing down on his starboard side. He threw his wheel to the left, skidding into a desperate turn as he tried to avoid the collision.

Sean knew that there was nothing else George could do. He swung his wheel left, away from Cheryl, and directly at the cigarette boat that had slowed in its skid but had not yet changed direction. He could see the sudden terror in George's face as he realized he had turned too late.

Then the stiletto shape and George's sudden scream disappeared under his foredeck.

Cheryl watched the cruiser draw its bearing on the speedboat. The light turned wildly away from her. The side of the boat threw up an enormous spray. Over the roar of engines, she heard a piercing scream. The cruiser hit the cigarette broadside, and rode right up on top of her as the sleek cigarette broke in half.

George realized there was no escape. He was screaming when the cruiser hit him, just forward of the cockpit. He was crushed by the bow as it slid up across the windshield. Then he was in the water, the stern of the boat with its massive engines rising high above his head.

There was an explosion above him. A wall of burning gasoline began to run down on top of him. Mutilated and burning, he was caught under the weight of the engines, and dragged under.

George knew what was happening. In his nightmares, he had seen Robert die in exactly the same way.

Sean reversed the propellers and backed out of the flaming wreckage. Then he shut down the engines, grabbed the life ring in his good hand, and jumped over the side. He began kicking and reaching, keeping the ring under his chest for flotation. The water was illuminated by the curling flames. He could see the light flickering against Cheryl's face.

His hand was out, and he felt her hand clasp his. He pulled her close and pushed her arm through the ring.

"Hold on! Hold on!" he tried to tell her, but his words were garbled in the water. He put his arm around her, reached out and began hauling in on the line. Cheryl's hand came up and she began pulling in with him. Painfully, they were able to haul themselves to the swimming platform. It was Cheryl who freed the ladder and swung it down into the water. Sean got a foot on the step and used the leverage to push Cheryl up onto the platform. Then she took the collar of his shirt and helped pull him up.

"Get aboard, quick!" he told her. He moved forward, staggered to the wheel and started the engines.

"We're sinking," Cheryl said as she came aboard behind him.

"Can you get the raft?" he asked as he pushed the throttle forward. The cruiser began to move slowly. The rocks, and then the crash with the speedboat, had destroyed the bow and left it open to the sea. The boat was moving back toward Buzzard Island, but its forward speed forced more water into the hull. It was a race to see if they could reach the island before the big cruiser sunk.

He had to leave the wheel, using his right arm to help Cheryl haul the heavy raft out of its container. "Don't inflate it till I tell you!" He knew it was best to wait until the last moment so that the raft didn't get fouled in the wreckage. Then he was back on the wheel, the searchlight turned on and looking ahead for the cove.

The island's edge came into view just as the bow wash came up on the foredeck.

"To hell with the harbor," he said to Cheryl, and aimed the boat at the rocky beach. She held enough speed to catch a wave, and then rode up on the shore with a sickening screech. Sean raced the engine, holding her on the beach while the wave receded. The next wave left them resting securely on dry land.

They stood side by side at the console. Then Cheryl dropped exhausted onto the pilot bench. Sean lifted the radio microphone and called the Coast Guard. Then he went aft to the owner's stateroom, which was still floating above the water level, and returned with dry blankets from the bed. He wrapped one around Cheryl and pulled the other around his shoulders.

"Can you make the cottage?" he asked.

"I think so." She rose slowly, and then got her first good look at Sean since she had seen his blood-spattered body at the bottom of the ladder. "Can *you* make it?"

He put his good arm around her and helped her up onto the foredeck, where they could step off onto the rocky shore. They reached the shelter of the cottage, and then fell down together on the carpet in front of the fireplace.

74 CHERYL COULDN'T BELIEVE THE AMOUNT OF BLOOD that was soaked into the makeshift bandage under Sean's shirt. The entire pillowcase had turned crimson, and the seawater had spread the stain across his body.

"I'll be okay," Sean kept protesting. His hand reached up to the oozing bruise on the side of her head. "Take care of yourself."

But she could tell the difference. The cut on her head wasn't bleeding much. If she had suffered a concussion, it had been mild. She was sore from being grazed by the speedboat and thrown around in its wake. But she wasn't in critical danger.

Sean was close to shock. The bullet had entered under the shoulder joint and exited under his arm. The exit wound was like a knife slash, a ragged tear that had never been bandaged. She was pressing the pillowcase under his arm to stop the flow, but the cloth was soaked so thoroughly that it couldn't absorb any more.

She got up from the carpet and went into the kitchen. There was a first-aid kit, Cheryl remembered, in one of the cabinets. But when she found it, it seemed like a toy. A tube of antiseptic salve, a few rolls of gauze, some cotton, and a few Band-Aids. Great for a finger cut on a fish hook, but almost insignificant next to the damage of the gunshot. She flattened out the roll of gauze to make a thick pad and taped it into the gaping exit wound.

"I'm freezing," Sean said. He felt cold and clammy. Cheryl dragged heavy blankets out of the bunks and piled them on top of him, but he began shaking so violently that she had to hold them over him. She added some split wood to the charcoal from an earlier visit, and started a fire. But it seemed to take forever for the new wood to catch and begin pumping out heat.

By then, Sean had lost even more color. His breathing was shallow and quick. "I'll be all right," he kept insisting. But she could see fear in his eyes. He was beginning to realize that he wasn't invincible. The cold weakness in his body was a new and frightening feeling, and it had suddenly dawned on him that he needed help, and needed it now.

"Hang in there," Cheryl encouraged. "They should be here any minute." But they both knew she was lying. There was no way they were going to set a helicopter on the island, especially at night. And the cutter out of Woods Hole was still more than an hour away.

"Listen to me," Sean managed. Then he swallowed hard, and had to pant for air before he could go on. "Robert loved you . . . things got crazy . . . but he loved you. Do you understand?"

She nodded. "I know. I don't believe he would have hurt me."

Sean nodded. His eyes rolled momentarily to white, and Cheryl gasped before she could stop herself.

"Hang in there," she said again. "They're on their way."

His eyes struggled to focus on her. Then he smiled as his eyes closed.

"Sean! Sean!" She was yelling at him. "Stay with me. Keep talking to me."

He swallowed hard, trying to find his voice.

"Do you know why I stayed?"

"I think so," Cheryl said.

"I was going to try to hold you together if you started to break."

"Why?" she asked. "You had a better deal."

He shook his head. "No . . . you're the best deal I ever had. Even if you loved someone else."

"Sean, I never knew you. When you came to help Robert, I wasn't there. But I know you now, and I don't want to lose you."

He forced a smile. "I love you, Cheryl."

His eyes began to roll, but he forced them back into focus. "I've never said that before," he managed. "It sounds nice." His lids fluttered as he struggled to hang on to his consciousness. But slowly they closed.

"Sean!" There was no response. "Oh God, Sean, don't leave me now."

The fire sparked, and a crumbling log threw off a flash of heat. But as Cheryl lifted his head into her lap, his face felt ice cold.

"Please, Sean, please! Hang on. They're coming. Don't leave me now."

RACHAEL

"LAND, HO!" CHERYL YELLED. "DEAD AHEAD."

She had been watching intently for over an hour, ever since the satellite fix had put them just ten miles southwest of Somerset. The island should have been visible to them, but it was still shrouded in the morning haze. Now it had broken through, right on the bow. She reached back into the map case and slipped out the chart for Hamilton Harbor.

It had been a long and uncertain journey, beginning when the Coast Guard had come ashore on Buzzard Island. They had landed in a rubber dinghy because the cove was too small for the cutter. The pharmacist mate had decided that Sean would never make it back, and called for a helicopter. He worked over Sean for half an hour with medication and plasma that he had brought in with him, and then used a litter to get him out on the dock where the chopper could hoist him aboard.

"How's he doing?" she kept asking, refusing to leave Sean's side.

"He's lost a lot of blood," the medic told her, avoiding any hint of a commitment. His work was skillful, but his manner was infuriating. Anyone could see that Sean had bled terribly. She had watched the helicopter lift him away.

When the cutter brought her into Newport, she had been shocked to find herself in a different hospital from where Sean had been brought. The only information they could get for her was that he was critical, and then two days later, that he was out of danger. While she waited, Mrs. Callen brought Rachael to visit, and Cheryl had been thrilled to find her daughter playful and happy. When she returned home after she was released, the little girl had flown into her arms. From time to time, she asked for Gretchen. But she accepted the answer that "Gretchen has gone away." She seemed thrilled with all the time that Cheryl lavished on her.

She had been terribly apprehensive when Sergeant Grattan called and asked if he might stop by. Cheryl had been so glad to find answers that satisfied her that she hadn't thought at all about the police investigation that was obviously necessary.

But Grattan didn't have much to ask her. He had been able to put together most of the details of her weeks of terror on his own, and was actually able to answer some of the questions that had been bothering her.

The police had been able to solve the mystery of telephone calls very quickly, as soon as the phone company service manager led them to the recorder that he had installed in the equipment closet at Cramm headquarters. The cassette had recorded the conversation between Robert and Gretchen. In George Williamson's home, they found the tape player that had created the telephone message, and numerous tapes of George's conversations with Robert, and Gretchen. George had been splicing together words and phrases. He simply reconnected the extension to the house each time he called, and then disconnected it the second he was finished.

The search of George's things had turned up several bank accounts, with deposits that ran up to eight million dollars. An auditor had matched the deposits up with the forged entries in the company's books. George had begun stealing months before Cheryl had recovered. Robert's decision to build *Siren* had simply given him an additional source of income.

Gretchen had apparently been George's accomplice, manipulating events within the household in the hope of being needed to stay on longer, perhaps even permanently. The police had found the missing letters hidden in her room. There was an additional letter that Cheryl had never seen because Gretchen had not yet finished it. It was to Cheryl, confessing that she had done a terrible thing in trying to alienate her husband and daughter from her. It begged for forgiveness. Apparently, it was Gretchen's decision to bear all that had forced George to act quickly. He had killed her, and then tried to make the murder look like another example of Cheryl's madness. The medical examiner had fixed the time of Gretchen's death early in the evening, several hours before Cheryl was drawn into the private office by the staged telephone call.

But two of her most painful questions remained unanswered. The police had no way of knowing whether there was anything between Robert and the au pair. George had told her that there was, but that affair may have been the product of his own sick mind.

George had also told her that Robert intended to kill her, and that he had saved her by having her called home before *Siren* sailed. If he had actually been responsible for Gretchen's phone call, there would never be any way to prove it. Both parties to that arrangement were dead. But it seemed more likely that George would have wanted Cheryl to vanish with her husband. Only with both of them gone would the trust that owned Cramm Yachts have fallen under his complete control.

Philip McKnight had phoned her several times, always expressing condolences at the tragedies that had befallen the Cramm family. "I had several meetings with George Williamson regarding buying the company, and not once did I suspect his loyalty to Robert and you." Cheryl had admitted that she never suspected it herself, at least until the very last moments. McKnight had renewed his offer to buy Cramm Yachts, and promised Cheryl any position she wanted in the new company.

But she had other ideas. She still thought she might save the company, particularly since George's bank accounts, and Robert's key-man insurance, gave her funding she hadn't counted on. She was hoping that she could persuade Sean Patton that the company was worth saving.

First, however, she needed to analyze her own feelings. Sean had told her that he loved her. It had been only moments since they had been able to rescue their lives from the sea, and he had been close to delirious. His words were far from a proposal. But as she had accumulated the evidence, she had realized that Sean had always had everything to gain from the sale to Vector, or even from an association with the French syndicate. He had nothing to gain by sticking with her. Yet he had done just that, leaping aboard her boat to save her from her rendezvous on

Buzzard Island, and then leaping into the water for her after she had shot him.

So what exactly would she be offering him? A place in her company? Or a place in her life? Cheryl wanted to be very clear about the difference. She wanted Sean to have no misgivings about the contract she was offering.

A week after she was home, the Boston hospital where Sean had been transferred decided that he was well enough to take calls. Cheryl had fumbled the first conversation badly, asking him about his condition almost as if she were a student nurse. She realized after she had hung up that she had not acknowledged her debt to him, nor even admitted that she had heard him tell her that he loved her.

On her second conversation, she hadn't done much better. She had ventured into the state of the company, and been bubbly optimistic about rebuilding it back to its former stature. "We're exactly where we were a year ago, where a great performance in the Bermuda race could kick-start the whole operation." Later she realized that Sean wouldn't have been encouraged by her words. A year ago, they hardly knew one another. All she had told him was that she still had faith in his design for *Siren*.

Cheryl had still been rehearsing words as she drove to Boston. It would be the first time he had seen her since he lapsed into unconsciousness on the cottage floor, and the first time she had seen him since the helicopter lifted him away. But she still didn't know her own feelings. Was she still in love with Robert? Or was she just afraid of another relationship? Did she love Sean? Or was it just that she needed him? Even as she walked into the hospital lobby, she hadn't been sure of what she was going to say.

She had been stunned when they told her that Sean had checked out that morning. And then shocked when she had finally traced down his doctor.

"I don't think he's ready," the doctor had said, "but I can't hold him. He's healthy enough, and if he wants to go somewhere else for his restorative surgery and physical therapy, that's his decision. But if he wants to recover, he better take it easy. And if he ever wants to use that arm again, he better get to a good orthopedic doctor."

And then Cheryl had understood her feelings. The loss of him going away tore a hole in her. She realized that she had been talking about saving a company when what she really meant was saving one another. It would be easier to sell the company to Philip McKnight and leave with Sean, than to hold on to the company and watch Sean leave alone.

"Do you have any idea where he went?" she had begged the doctor.

"No," he had told her. "He didn't say much. Sean seems to be pretty much of a loner."

Cheryl had started with Baron Murot, who could tell her only that he too was looking for Sean. He wanted Sean to design his Cup entry, and he was still prepared to have the boat built by Cramm Yachts. He had promised Cheryl that he would call around. Nor did Philip McKnight have any leads on where Sean might have gone. He found it difficult to believe that Patton would have walked away from a chance to rebuild *Siren*, and seemed positive that Cheryl would be hearing from him shortly. Next she had called Professor Bladesdale at the Hoboken Institute. Sean had stopped by to pick up the engineering data he had left for analysis, but hadn't given any forwarding address. "That's the way he is," the professor sympathized. "You don't hear from him for years, and then he walks in and begins talking as if you had started the conversation yesterday."

Cheryl had begun calling everyone in the business. Designers, builders, outfitters and sail cutters. She recognized that Sean had made a choice when he decided to walk out of the hospital before her arrival. He had decided that he didn't want to go wherever her visit might have led them. But she needed to know why. He had risked everything for her, and told her that he loved her with what could have been his last words on earth. What was he telling her now by running away?

And then the Baron had called. Sean had opened a small studio and had contracted to design the French America's Cup challenger. "I shouldn't be sharing him with you," he said. "But when you called, I sensed that it was more than business. And I thought . . . well, as we say in France—"

"I know what you say in France," Cheryl had laughed. And then she had thanked him for breaking the confidence.

She had walked in on Sean in a rented section of a sail loft near the San Diego Yacht Club, and had been shocked by his appearance. He was gaunt and pale, his hair cut short and his eyes watery. As soon as they had finished their awkward greeting, he had rushed into a description of the baron's boat, and thrown pounds of drawings and plans in front of her. And, for half an hour, she had played his game, talking about the boat instead of about their relationship.

"Sean, you left the hospital an hour before I arrived," Cheryl said at her first opportunity. "Why didn't you want to see me?"

He had shrugged. "Probably because it would have been tough for both of us. Things had sort of worked themselves out. Your problems were over." He started stuffing plans back into the file drawers. "I'm really not much at saying good-bye."

"I had come to tell you I loved you," she said.

He looked at her skeptically.

"No," Cheryl had continued. "That's not true. I didn't know what I was going to tell you. It was only after I realized that you were gone—"

"You don't owe me anything," Sean had cut her off.

"I owe you my life," she had reminded him.

"That doesn't matter."

She had suddenly become angry. "It matters a hell of a lot to me!"

Sean had started to roll up the blueprints. "I pulled a guy out of the water once. He went over the side, and I went in after him. But that didn't give us a claim on one another. I don't even know where he is."

She had pulled the prints out of his hand. "Did you love him?" she asked seriously.

His eyes widened.

"Because you said you loved me. And I'm hoping that makes a difference."

"You've been obligated to Robert . . . obligated to his company. I think you ought to have a chance to decide what's best for you."

"You're best for me," Cheryl had said. "We can stay here, or we can go back to Newport. I don't care which, as long as we do it together."

"What will I tell the baron?" Sean asked as he took back the roll of prints.

"Tell him he's invited to the wedding."

.   .   .

SHE COULD NOW make out details of Bermuda's west end. She needed her crew to line up their approach and set the sails for their course change. "All hands topside!" she yelled.

Sean came up through the hatch, his skin bronzed and his hair once again in the ponytail that hung between his shoulder blades. "How much longer to the Hamilton marker?" he asked.

She looked at the chart. "An hour, tops."

He consulted the pad where he had worked out the figures. "That will put us in nearly nine hours under the old race record."

Cheryl laughed. "What do you want to do until the rest of the fleet makes it to port?"

He stepped up next to her at the helm. "Let's find a hotel with a bigger bed."

An hour later, Cramm Yachts' revolutionary new design flashed across the Bermuda finish line and tied up to a pier in Hamilton.

She looked like *Siren*.

But the name painted across her stern was *Rachael*. Her port of registry was Newport.